MORE PRAISE FOR THE CONFESSIONS OF GABRIEL ASH

"Lee Polevoi's novel, *The Confessions of Gabriel Ash*, is the relentlessly truthful story of a person giving his direct testimony of a masked existence. In the Kafkaesque unbearable then and the now of his life as an ambassador, Gabriel Ash cannot claim convictions or loyalties that have meaning, that can ever fully redeem him. Every part of his journey into hell and into lesser hells is extraordinarily compelling because even the most deeply hidden chambers are exposed by his harsh gaze. This excellent novel of conscience places your heart and soul on trial."

— KEVIN MCILVOY, AUTHOR OF *ONE KIND FAVOR*

"In *The Confessions of Gabriel Ash*, Lee Polevoi has deftly crafted a tale of international intrigue – a page-turner that leaves you wondering what will happen next. Clearly an accomplished and masterful writer, Polevoi has a particular knack for writing gripping dialogue and bringing his characters to life."

— TARA TAGHIZADEH, FOUNDING EDITOR & PUBLISHER, HIGHBROW MAGAZINE

"Ambassador Gabriel Ash—confined to a castle-prison somewhere in a mythical Soviet-bloc nation—records his crazy-like-a-fox views of Cold War diplomacy during war in the Falklands and before the fall of the Berlin Wall. It feels like *The Confessions of Gabriel Ash* is speaking to us from the front lines of conflicts unfolding on our screens every day."

— MICHAEL PRITCHETT, AUTHOR OF *TANIA THE REVOLUTIONARY*

"*The Confessions of Gabriel Ash* is so much more than just the usual Cold War thriller. Lee Polevoi has given us a dark tale, brilliantly told by the diplomat Gabriel Ash himself, of what happens when he finally confronts a lifetime based upon deception and lies."

— MARK C. JACKSON, AUTHOR OF THE SERIES, *THE TALES OF ZEBADIAH CREED*

THE CONFESSIONS OF GABRIEL ASH

LEE POLEVOI

For Maxine—
Now, then, and always

"A sincere diplomat is like dry water or wooden iron."

— STALIN

"Assume a virtue, if you have it not."

— *HAMLET*

CONTENTS

PART THREE
SEVERED RELATIONS

PART ONE
TOUR D'HORIZON

1

EASTERN EUROPE

SEPTEMBER 1982

The voice echoing down the mountainside—a sweet voice, tender and soothing—belongs to the only other prisoner here.

Today, I see him up close for the first time, as a guard leads him into the exercise yard and another guard ushers me out. Gaunt, middle-aged, wearing a faded canary-yellow shirt. His ashen complexion and the scars on his neck belie the smile he offers in passing.

In the courtyard, the guard hurries me past the barn and stables. Cows moan in their enclosure, geese squabble and honk. Above this pastoral hum rises the voice of the prisoner— call him Caruso—singing as he treads along the well-worn path of the exercise yard. He only sings outdoors, the circumstances behind his detention, whatever they are, certainly infusing the mournful tunes.

At the tower, the guard leads the way up a winding staircase. It's assumed I'll follow, as if there's any other choice.

Usually, on the top landing, he opens the door and invites me inside in a civilized manner. Today, there's a quick glance, a nod at someone or something unseen, and then I'm shoved through the doorway and into the kitchen. The guard, snorting disgust, slams the door shut behind him.

At the table sits a young man in a rumpled brown suit, not "sitting" so much as looking poured into the chair. Languid as a cat.

"The guards don't care for me," he says. "Maybe because I am not from around here."

Coming lazily to his feet, he nudges aside a briefcase at his feet and reaches out to shake hands. A firm grip, yet also sympathetic, as if reassuring me, *There's nothing to worry about.*

That's when I start to worry.

"Ambassador Ash, a pleasure to meet you! I am Comrade Pavel."

I recognize the lilt of stylized English, a non-native speaker's penchant for exactness in speech. Many years ago, I lived and worked among Czech citizens, but my memories of life in their Democratic Socialist Republic weren't happy ones.

"Sit, please."

I sit as instructed, confused and wary. Comrade Pavel looks me over in the food-stained shirt and burlap trousers I'm wearing—not *my* trousers, not *my* stains—old rubbery boots a half-size too large for my feet. Barnyard smells cling to these clothes.

"So," he says, gesturing at our surroundings, "how do you like your new home? *Ne jako* Manhattan, I think."

Home—a primitive kitchen, a sink and toilet in an adjacent water-closet. A second room with a lamp, nightstand, and stiff monastic cot—the cot room. Walls are clammy and cold, like touching the flesh of the newly deceased. Between bars in the window, there's a view of gray skies and a fog-shrouded mountaintop. No, not like Manhattan at all.

"I'm holding out for something better."

He smiles, his lips thin as slivered ice. "And your arm? Does it heal properly?"

A vibrant scar runs across my left forearm, where a knife-wielding ex-dictator attacked me in his dacha on the Black Sea coast. A nurse called to treat my wounds clucked indignantly at having to care for an enemy of the State; but in the end, her nursing skills trumped ideology, and a week has passed with no sign of infection.

"Just fine, thanks. *Dobře, díky.*"

Comrade Pavel's laugh sounds forced, a poor line-reading of a laugh. "Yes, I recall now. You were stationed in my country for some time. Embassy posting, am I correct? When was this again?"

I suspect he already knows. "Prague, 1968." Even fifteen years later, it's impossible to forget—standing with an angry crowd as Red Army tanks rolled into Wenceslas Square. "I'm guessing you were there, too."

He shrugs. Best not to talk about it.

A breeze sweeps the prisoner's voice up from the exercise yard below, chants and dirges in some Balkan dialect I don't understand. The words are unimportant. His rich, forlorn tenor brings a transcendent feeling to our distant mountain region, and brooks no interference from the guards, as entranced as I am by this open-air performance.

"Who is that singing?"

I lean towards the window, the voice fading away. "I call him Caruso ..."

"Yes, very beautiful."

On closer inspection I see my unannounced guest isn't as

young as I first thought. His gaze is hooded, his sand-colored hair gone thin and graying.

"Are you the one I talk to about getting out of here?"

"Out?" He sounds puzzled. "You only just arrived."

I sit up with something like the formidable vigor I once displayed in the Security Council chamber. "I am Keshnev's ambassador to the United Nations. Whatever charges there are against me, I deserve better than this."

Comrade Pavel produces a pack of Orbital cigarettes, the vintage Soviet brand with a tiny red Sputnik on the label. He shakes one free, seems to study it resting between his fingers. Thus engaged, he shares a little about himself, freely admitting he's here "on loan" from Czech security services, StB, among the worst of the worst secret police in the Warsaw Pact. He lifts the cigarette to his lips and then, with a visible tremor, reverses course and sets it on the table.

"A long flight to Keshnev aboard a jerry-rigged Tupelov," he says. "But when your Minister for State Security requests our assistance, who are we to refuse? Are we not all brothers under the skin in the Union of Soviet Socialist Republics?"

There's a damp odor of impending rain. Wind carries the grunts and groans of livestock being herded to shelter. Once, during my time in Prague, I had reason to visit StB headquarters on some bureaucratic matter; walking the halls, I felt certain I heard muted screams rising from underground interrogation chambers.

"Why you?" I ask him. "Why didn't Petrescu send his own goons?"

"It seems the Minister has lost faith in his inner circle and feels compelled to seek help beyond borders. It seems your actions have inspired a crisis of confidence at the highest levels."

I think back on my long acquaintance with Minister

Petrescu—*friendship* would be too strong a word—a history riddled with slights and offenses, some real, some imagined, nothing ever forgiven or forgotten. Anything that rattles his world is fine by me.

"I only wish I could have done more."

Another half-hearted laugh. "They warned me about your *ostrý jazy*, that sharp tongue of yours. But given your line of work, is that so bad? Isn't that just what Keshnev needs in the UN? A place where thugs posing as statesmen feast on the world's troubles."

"Yes," I also admit freely. "That would be me."

Comrade Pavel takes the stranded cigarette and places it between his bloodless lips. A brass lighter stands ready and waiting in his other hand; second pass, no flame is set to paper. He returns the cigarette to its place on the table, alongside the Sputnik-branded pack.

"My wife spent a summer in Oxford, England. Now she fancies herself a *continental*. This," he says, nodding at the orphan cigarette in his hand, "this she calls my 'perfectly beastly' habit."

Despite impending bad weather, Caruso's golden voice sings on, drawing our attention to the barred window and leaden sky beyond. What crime could he have committed, a man who sings like this? Even Comrade Pavel succumbs, his eyes half-closed, rocking gently in his chair—moved, I imagine, by memories of the screams of political prisoners on those heady Prague Spring nights.

For me, Caruso's melodies conjure up *La Boheme* at Lincoln Center, morning mist descending over the Woolworth building. Dim sum on Mott Street. Tugboats in New York Harbor, as seen from Windows on the World, North Tower. That magical morning in Central Park when John Lennon smiled at me and tipped his cap in passing.

I close my eyes, pinching off tears.

"A tribunal has been convened to review your situation," Comrade Pavel says. "Six gentlemen of impeccable Marxist-Leninist credentials will study the evidence and render the proper verdict. You will be able to offer testimony ..." He nodded obliquely at the briefcase at his feet. "But I hoped to ask a few questions first."

So, this inquisitor-for-hire wants to know what happened that night, and other details of my fall from grace. Are my interests best served answering his questions directly or does going over his head improve my odds of survival? With Minister Petrescu, there's no telling.

"Ach, *tin v oku*," he grumbles. "This whole business is a thorn in my eye."

This time, Comrade Pavel takes full possession of the cigarette, lighting it and inhaling deeply. A pungent smell fills the kitchen, something like goat cheese with a hint of excrement. He draws again on the cigarette, less frantic this time, emitting obscene sounds of pleasure.

"What do you want to know about?" I ask him. "Property values on the Upper West Side? The best place to find Korean food in the Village?"

My *ostrý jazyk* doesn't faze him. "A full account of your blunders in New York, how violence was provoked by your words alone—yes, there is interest in that. First, we must clarify your role in the attempt on Our Great Leader's life."

A storm breaks over the mountain, but Caruso keeps singing; his voice gathers strength, becoming an element, along with the wind and rain. Suddenly I have a vision of him as a freed man, walking out of the castle gates, greeting his long-lost wife and child, a family reunited and embarking on a new life. I point at the briefcase on the floor, stifling a giggle of terror.

"What've you got in there, Comrade? Thumbscrews? A rubber hose? Electrodes to tape to my genitals? Don't I at least get dinner first?"

Sighing, Comrade Pavel sets the briefcase on the table between us and opens the lid. Inside is a flat, square-shaped recording device and spools of cassette tapes.

"Answer the questions I put to you now, Ambassador, or talk into this thing and extend your confinement indefinitely."

I sit up, putting my fists on the table. "Want my testimony? First, release Caruso."

The StB agent's deadpan features twitch a little. "An oddly noble request, coming from one such as yourself."

"Think of it as a jailhouse conversion."

Beyond the window, the prisoner's voice has become too powerful to ignore. Comrade Pavel stands from the table and crosses the kitchen in his wrinkled suit—a loose-boned gait, almost jaunty. I can do this for Caruso, I tell myself. I can do this one good thing.

"Such beautiful singing," he says. "Such a distraction."

As if seized by a need for nicotine, he reaches into a coat pocket, but what emerges in his outstretched hand is no cigarette. He rests the barrel of the gun between the bars, aims and fires. A gunshot rings out, deafening in these tight quarters.

"What—what did you do—!"

I brush past Comrade Pavel, heedless of the weapon he places back inside his coat. Grabbing the bars, I strain on tiptoes for a view of the courtyard, just as a rain-soaked guard drags a lifeless figure in a canary-yellow shirt across the muddy ground. A *whoosh* roars through my head like a jumper's vertigo before leaping from a bridge. He guides me to the chair, enveloping me in a funk of Russian tobacco and traveled-in clothes. What sounds at first like words of compassion in my ear turns out to be barely contained rage.

"Do you imagine you are in a bargaining position? You have nothing to bargain with."

I sit, head in hands, dizzy and grief-stricken for someone I never knew.

"Look at you!" he says. "Once a man of influence in New York, now you stand accused of monstrous crimes against the State. It's time to decide where your loyalties lie, Ambassador. Out *there* in the steaming cesspool of the Western democracy? Or *here*, where you belong, in your adopted homeland."

Rain pummels the stone tower. Taking a deep breath, I let loose a high-decibel flood of invective at this Czech civil servant who, after all, is only doing his job; minutes go by before I make myself stop. Comrade Pavel closes the briefcase, sets it aside. On his face, the look of a troubled accountant who can't bring himself to disclose to his client just how bad the books are.

"Think of it this way," he tells me. "Now you have the place to yourself."

2

The castle in which I'm confined, built originally for a 12th-century nobleman, sits atop a peak of middling height in Keshnev's Lesser Alps. According to legend, it was here Keshnevite resistance fighters held off an armored Panzer division in the *blitzkrieg* of 1939. The fact that the siege ended in their bloody massacre is incidental to the legend.

Given the mountain region's harsh climate, I'm often deprived of life-sustaining sunshine. On rare occasions the sun breaks through the clouds and light gleams along the surface of things with uncanny precision. On those rare occasions, the castle where I reside against my will feels almost comfortable and warm, almost like—

No. This is not my home.

A cryptic label—TEK 3-RX—is printed in tiny letters on the recording device left behind by Comrade Pavel. There's a microphone, cassette-desk, three push-buttons, each with its own distinct function. To make things happen, I must press one of these:

—REC to get the cassette-tape spooling

—PAUSE when it's time to stop talking

—REW, if I should care to pause and hear myself talk, a thing of which I was once inordinately proud

A long cord attached to the microphone enables me to provide recorded evidence from up to twenty feet away. With the TEK-3RX set on the kitchen table, I can stroll from kitchen to cot-room and back again, yakking away. Everything captured on tape for the Gentlemen of the Tribunal, my unseen audience and ultimate arbiter of my fate. Today marks the start of my official testimony. I select a cassette-tape from a tall stack in the cupboard. The process is simple, even for me: Click open the transparent cassette-wall door, insert the tape-cassette, close the door again. Press REC, PAUSE, or REW, when you're ready to go.

The key to survival lies, I think, in being truthful about events at the Gray Wolf's dacha, telling the truth while casting myself in the best possible light. Find a way to explain how the aged, reclusive ex-dictator stood upright when I first entered his dacha and, a short time later, lay prone and unconscious on the hard-tiled patio. Best possible light? Not an easy task.

Press REC.

REC

For the record, I am Gabriel Ash, 56, chief delegate to the United Nations for the People's Democratic Republic. Born in Schenectady, New York, to Robert and Julia Ash, fierce adherents of the Church of the Nazarene. A younger sibling, Willy, whose early death from consumption spurred my parents' grief-stricken resolve to uproot the family and spread God's word in a remote part of Eastern Europe—with me, their sole surviving son, in tow. An adolescence spent chasing after village girls, in pursuit of one inadvertently saving the life of King Josef, our country's last monarch. I was rewarded with steerage to England and education at Cambridge, where I later learned of their deaths back in Keshnev during the first wave of Nazi invasion.

After the war, it was Petrescu—ten years older than me, already the Gray Wolf's trusted advisor—who tracked me down in London's East End, where I was busy wasting my life away among dissolute artists and criminals. It was Petrescu who talked me into coming back to the homeland, figuring an appeal to help "improve life for all mankind" might tickle my ego and induce me to join Our Great Leader's fledgling Communist regime. In fact, it did. After rigorous training, I worked in various backwater embassies, a dreary slog of post-ings in cities behind the Iron Curtain, before my transfer to New York to join Keshnev's UN delegation. Then a disastrous marriage to Eva Capshaw, a Kentucky whiskey heiress and undiagnosed manic-depressive, followed by the birth of Tess, our beautiful and neglected daughter. Then divorce, suicide, all the rest of it.

Gentleman of the Tribunal, if because I'm sitting here in confinement you have any doubts about my principles—no small question among those in the Turtle Bay diplomatic community—let me state this outright. Capitalism is and always will be the scourge of humanity and, like any good Marxist-Leninist, I'm committed to its inevitable downfall. But for the story I'm going to tell you, about when I lived and worked among capitalists—in Manhattan! Near the end of the 20th century!—certain ideological compromises had to be made. I could no more go about speechifying at the UN in these ragged prison trousers than walk on the moon. To live in the West, you must always look the part. What was I saying?

PAUSE

I wonder if anyone in the civilized world misses me. After my much-publicized formal recall and subsequent failure to return to New York, *some* fuss must have been made. Did my assistant press the Foreign Ministry for news of my whereabouts? Has my old friend Sergei Litvinov made inquiries to the Kremlin? In my gloomier moments, I picture a gaggle of East European delegates huddled in the shadows of the Dag Hammarskjöld Library and shedding crocodile tears over the fate of their missing colleague. The lesson of my misfortune is clear to this rogue's gallery of overfed brutes. Never forget who you work for, no matter how far away they are. Call it the Gabriel Ash Principle, for the idiot who did.

Damn it, begin again.

3

REC

The summons came early Sunday morning via diplomatic pouch, ensuring that in the not-improbable event the UN courier was struck by a bus, no one—not paramedics, beat cops, or innocent bystanders—could legally search its contents. Even if, as happened more often than you might think, the message inside the pouch concerned suggestions as to where some hungry UN delegates might meet for lunch. We diplomats like having our secrets.

Inside the pouch was a single folded page with OFFICE OF THE SECRETARY-GENERAL embossed on eggshell-blue letterhead. Curt, declarative sentences marched down the page with pomp and glory:

15 May 1982
Gabriel Ash, Permanent Representative
People's Democratic Republic of Keshnev
345 East Seventy-second Street, Apt 12
New York, NY

YOUR PRESENCE REQUESTED BY
SEC-GENL. MATTER OF URGENT
IMPORTANCE. ATTEMPTS TO REACH
YOU BY TELEPHONE UNSUCCESSFUL.
REPEAT. URGENT IMPORTANCE.

Yes, when seeking to preserve the sanctity of my personal residence, I sometimes left the phone unplugged. What was *this* about, coming on a lazy weekend morning when the whole world should be asleep?

I roamed my prewar Beaux Arts apartment, pacing the herringbone floor, switching Italian light fixtures on and off. In the dining room I stood before tall casement windows and a view of the East River and a goodly portion of Queens. In normal times, I enjoyed monitoring river traffic under the 59th Street Bridge, but today, the panorama seemed diminished and trivial, all because I was compelled to attend to my professional duties. I left the apartment and locked the door behind me.

At the elevator, something slithered against my leg—a tiger cat I'd seen a few days ago racing through the lobby. Built like a furred tank, one eye maimed and permanently shut, a Prussian arrogance to his whiskers and snout. It had decamped from life on the street and taken up residence inside the nooks and crannies of our no-pets apartment building. Surviving, no doubt, on the charity of tenants who furtively served him warm milk in Ming dynasty porcelain bowls. How the hell did he get up to the 12th floor?

Today, the tiger cat—I dubbed him Bismarck—sat on plush carpeting by the elevator as if he owned the place.

"Going down?" I asked.

The door to 12E opened just around the corner and a scruffy tenant emerged in a washed-out kimono and fur-lined slippers. Krasnoff by name, a known hater of cats. I nudged Bismarck with my shoe, boxing him against the wall behind me. A low Teutonic growl issued from his battled-scarred chest.

Krasnoff, on his way to the trash chute, stopped for a friendly chat.

"Good morning, Ambassador."

"Nice to see you, neighbor."

According to apartment lore, Krasnoff was heir to the immense fortune of the inventor of flip-flop sandals, apparel I never saw him wear. A bearded recluse obsessed with planetary catastrophes yet to come—global warming, nuclear winter, meteorites crashing out of the sky. This made small talk difficult at times.

Even with inch-thick glasses, Krasnoff's vision was weak; if Bismarck remained still, all would be well. But my fellow tenant happened to carry a plastic trash bag soaked through the juices of discarded tuna cans. I felt Bismarck tense behind me, every fiber of his carnivorous being ready to lunge at the trash bag. Krasnoff opened his mouth to describe extinction rates for land mammals, or something like that, but I spoke up first.

"Pestilence," I said. "*That's* the one that keeps me awake at night."

Krasnoff heard something in my tone he didn't like. I saw myself through this eccentric millionaire's eyes—a man in a gray pinstripe suit, six feet tall, full head of black hair lightly speckled with gray. Two hundred pounds on a good day. A man, as they say, in fighting trim.

He shuffled off with the trash bag, the front of his left slipper—why no flip-flops?—torn down the middle, exposing a swollen big toe. I took a delicate sidestep, releasing Bismarck to scurry down one of the old building's rabbit holes. At the trash chute, Krasnoff curled his upper lip, or what I could make of it in the beard.

"All a big joke," he said. "Until it isn't."

I smiled as the elevator doors opened. "Amen to that."

For years, the sovereign nation of Keshnev was little more than a joke in the halls of the UN. *Keshnev? Like Albania, but without a sense of humor.* Things changed last year upon our election to a rotating term on the Security Council. For the first time in UN history, a representative of the People's Democratic Republic occupied a seat at the same table as delegates of the Permanent Five—US, USSR, Great Britain, France, and China—alongside a small number of other member-states.

I took to my new role in the Security Council with a zeal I frankly didn't recognize in myself. When the time came to address the chamber, I rose to the occasion with great declamatory wrath. Against all odds, I had become a force to reckon with.

Why, then, this absurd summons on a Sunday morning?

I crossed the lobby at a moment when Javier, the doorman, was presumably on break. Outside on Seventy-second Street, I stood under a green canopy and surveyed my Upper East Side neighborhood. Gray sky, patches of dreary blue. Teenagers milling around the delicatessen, the Hungarian tailor on Third Avenue opening shop. All was in order. I turned to a gun-metal gray Bentley idling at the curb, opened the rear door and climbed in back. My driver, Emil Vaka, grinned as he eased the Bentley into downtown traffic.

"*Szera la tu?*" How is your day so far?

I frowned, growing ever more annoyed by the situation. "*Ples a situ,*" I said. Could be better.

Emil sat upright behind the wheel, gloved hands at ten and two, his stocky frame encased in a funereal black suit. Viewed from behind, his neck looked thick as a redwood. Gray hair sprouted out from under his gold-rimmed chauffeur's cap.

Though we'd known each other for years, Emil and I had little in common. I lived on the Upper East Side; he had a cold-water flat in the Bronx. I burned through large sums of Foreign Ministry funds with appalling ease, while most of his earnings went to a wife and ailing child back in Keshnev, whom he hadn't seen in years. Foreign Ministry rules strictly forbade the spouses and families of our UN support staff to travel abroad, and the cost to fly home was prohibitive. I'd offered financial assistance many times, but Emil always refused.

On the other hand, we liked conversing in a quaint patois of English and Keshnevite, his native—my adopted—tongue. We also shared a pointless nostalgia for the late Austro-Hungarian Empire.

"I get letter from wife," he announced. "It happens soon, you know? Tusk Festival! When they roast wild boar on spit and pour *vasu* on it. Do you remember, sir? In letter, wife tells this in a way I can smell *vasu* and taste on my tongue."

Vasu, a pungent, salty meat sauce my mother tried to make during our time in the village—not a success, though the good-hearted residents of Rogvald didn't hold it against her. No one expected the American missionary's wife to master this ancient folk recipe. Bless her for trying.

"Do you mind, sir, if radio is on?"

"Not at all."

"—demanding an immediate ceasefire to hostilities," a newscaster declared. "Uncertainty persists, regarding UN efforts to slow the race to war."

"Is this why Secretary-General asks for you today?" Emil asked. "Because of Falklands?"

Over the years, numerous incidents had placed me in my less-than-ideal standing with the Secretary-General. A messy indiscretion with a French envoy's daughter, fresh out of the Sorbonne. A public dispute with a New York City meter maid over the precise degree of immunity afforded me by my diplomatic plates. But nothing unfortunate had happened lately, and even war in the South Atlantic didn't seem reason enough to be called into the SG's office.

"I have no idea, Emil."

"Only I wonder, sir, who are we for in this war? *Englischskii?* That cannot be, we hate *Englischskii.* Then, what, is it Argentina? Who in Keshnev knows about Argentina?" His worried gaze sought me out in the rear-view mirror. "Which side do we go on, sir?"

Speculating on SG's moods and motives was exhausting. "The side of peace," I said, lapsing into bombast.

South of Central Park, congestion was especially bad. I rolled down the window and let city noise wash over me— jackhammers, car-alarms, epithets loudly exchanged, a splash of Calypso music. Less than a decade ago, New York teetered on the verge of bankruptcy, unable to meet public sector payroll or ensure that trash got picked up off the streets. The President of the United States famously told New Yorkers, "Drop dead."

Now, with the 1980s underway and a faded film star with an idiot grin seated in the Oval Office, things were looking up, faint stirrings of hope for the free market system, a new mercantile nip in the air.

"—events in the Falkland Islands gaining momentum beyond the Security Council's ability to keep pace?"

"Emil, shut that off."

Word of economic recovery hadn't yet reached Times Square. By day, it was hellish to behold, a parade of pimps and thieves, street preachers and drug addicts. Nestled in the Bentley's cushioned leather, I observe the pageant of degeneracy on

Forty-second Street, the junkies and con men, young runaways
sporting nose studs and spiked green-and-purple hair. Visig-
oths at the gate.

What was so damned important the SG required my presence on the day of rest? I had a moment of severe unease. What
if Minister Petrescu, a man I'd studiously kept at bay for years,
was somehow involved?

Escaping Midtown, we drove at a stately speed through
Tudor City. Spring sunlight drifted over the leafy neighborhood, lending a melancholy air to kids playing basketball in
Ralph Bunche Park. We passed a crew of moving men pushing
a baby grand piano up the steps of the Church of the Covenant.

"There is restaurant I hear about in Bowery," Emil said.
"They say there is real Keshnev food there. *Pulska! Stuknogy!*
We go sometime, yes, Ambassador?"

At an intersection, I watched a dimple-cheeked nun
waddle through the crosswalk, followed by a man in a bowler
hat walking a pair of sculpted black poodles.

"*A prescu et al,*" I said. You can't get that here.

Emil chuckled, a deep rumbling sound like thunder inside
his chest. In the same breath he cursed and leaned on the horn
as a bicycle messenger in red-white-and-blue Spandex cut us
off, speeding downtown.

4

REC

Russian Deputy Chief Delegate Sergei Litvinov was just as perplexed as Emil when war first broke out in the Falklands. One day early on, we stood before adjacent urinals in a men's room in the General Assembly Building. *Gabriel, you know the English, you lived among them,* Sergei said over the sound of our symphonic piss. *Going to war over a piece of rock at the bottom of the world—for what? Are they really capable of such folly?* Washing my hands at the cast-iron sink, I looked in the mirror at my old friend—a large man in a baggy suit with hyperactive eyebrows and a carnival barker's smile. *Folly,* I told him in the mirror. *It's in the air we breathe.*

"Ah, Ambassador Ash! How good of you to come."

Alfred Lundquist met me at the elevator on the 38th floor of the Secretariat Building. Formerly of the Swedish delegation, Lundquist was now one among many in the Secretary-General's entourage. He had light blonde hair and darting blue eyes; though slight in stature, he tried with his bespoke suit and imperious manner to fill a larger space.

But even on Lundquist's home turf, I had the better of him. In the corridor we crossed paths with a pair of North African delegates in flowing *djellabas* who greeted me warmly—*me*, not my official escort, to whom they were noticeably cool.

"I see your influence continues to grow among our Third World colleagues."

The sting of disapproval in his voice annoyed me. "Whatever influence I have comes from speaking for the will of the People."

"Of course." Lundquist held open the plate-glass door to the SG's office with the tiniest snort of disgust. "Please have a seat, sir. The Secretary will see you shortly."

The waiting room was quiet and empty. Scattered throughout were artifacts from the SG's country of origin—a jaguar's tooth resting on a shelf, arrowheads mounted in plaques, trinkets from Orinoco River Basin Indians placed here and there to catch the eye. On the far wall hung framed portraits of past Secretaries-General, visionaries like Dag Hammarskjöld and U Thant, together with their less-gifted successors. Last in line, our current leader, the pursed lips and owlish glasses suggesting a man deeply ill at ease with the tumult of world affairs. I noticed the frame containing his portrait hung slightly askew; staffers frequently passed by, but no one paused to fix it.

"Can I get you something, sir?" the receptionist asked.

"I'm fine."

Four months ago, a feud over scrap-metal salvage rights in the South Atlantic erupted into a shooting match between a tin-pot military junta and a once-proud global empire. As Security Council members scrambled to vote on a ceasefire resolution, Argentine forces invaded the mountainous islands they called *Las Malvinas*, known to the rest of the world as the Falklands—remote territory no one hitherto gave a damn about. Overnight, the island's scant populace of farmers and sheepherders woke to find themselves living under foreign occupation.

I glanced at my watch. Twenty minutes had passed.

Never mind that General Leopoldo Galtieri, President of Argentina, was a power-hungry gangster bent on distracting his citizens from a collapsed economy. Or that the Chancellor of the Exchequer could ill afford ransacking Her Majesty's Treasury for yet another colonial misadventure. Roused from its slumber by this act of naked aggression, Great Britain sent forth an armada of warships and submarines to punish the junta with a force roughly equal to the wrath of God.

To his credit, the SG worked hard promoting talks between the adversaries. But the two nations, previously sworn to peace at any cost, dropped all pretenses and declared war. Keshnev joined with other delegates in the Communist sphere, rejecting draft wording that pinned responsibility solely on Argentina, denouncing instead the *true* aggressor in this conflict—"a shopworn imperial power," I declared, "in the last spasm of glory." None of this went down well with the SG.

Thirty minutes!

I knew the great man didn't care for my politics, nor did he approve of my "wanton" ways. But making me cool my heels like this? It felt petty, even for him.

Finally, the door opened to an inner office. To my keen disappointment, Alfred Lundquist reappeared, smug and preening in his three-piece suit.

"My apologies, Ambassador. The Secretary is unavoidably detained and asked me to speak in his place."

"Today is Sunday," I reminded him.

"Yes, most regrettable." Lundquist guided me forward, arms outstretched, without a hint of physical contact. "Your forbearance is most appreciated."

A large kidney-shaped table occupied most of the conference room. Potted plants in the corners, a vintage Mercator globe mounted on a stand. What truly commanded the newcomer's attention was a magnificent view out of east-facing, floor-to-ceiling windows. From here, a huge tract of blue sky was visible, as well as rooftop patios and the skyscraper-tips of Manhattan's grand steel colossi. A perspective more often limited to birds and angels.

Why was *I* allowed in?

Alfred Lundquist looked at the conference table, a stickler-for-the-rules scowl on his face. Plucking a handkerchief from his breast pocket, he picked up the telephone and spoke curtly into the receiver.

"Send her up. *Yes,* immediately. The place is a disaster."

Disaster? The table settings—black leather brief books, Montblanc pens, cut-glass water goblets—looked impeccable. I'd worked with Lundquist a few times over the years, was familiar with his quirks and foibles. Insipid man, yet also a virtuoso sycophant, ideal traits for the SG's little flock of deputies.

"Please, Ambassador ..."

He indicated a chair at the table that faced the wall. What, and be robbed of the panoramic view? I sat on the opposite side, looking out—so high up you could touch the underbelly of clouds. Lundquist sat with his back to the window, a manila folder on the table in front of him unambiguously marked GABRIEL ASH, KESHNEV DELEGATION.

"I've been tasked with reviewing your portfolio," he said. "If you don't mind."

I sure as hell did. "Not at all."

"Tell me, Ambassador Ash, just out of curiosity—what sort of enemies would you say you have?"

"An odd question. Why do you ask?"

He tapped a manicured finger on the folder. "There are reasons."

Enemies? As a mental exercise, I ticked off possibilities in my head—a fair number, it seemed, accrued after a quarter-century of life within the UN diplomatic community. Husbands of past lovers. Spiteful delegates unhappy with the cut of my oratorical jib. Even that rat's nest of Keshnevite exiles holed up in Flatbush, bitter monarchists all.

I shrugged. "No one comes to mind."

The conference door opened, and a young Hispanic woman entered, wearing a blue pinstripe jacket and skirt. I couldn't help admiring her full red lips and the long raven hair she kept severely pulled back.

"Miss Alvarez, Ambassador Ash."

A chilly smile and handshake, then Miss Alvarez went about inspecting the conference table's lapidary surface.

"You know," Lundquist said, "up to now I had little idea of how deftly you juggle your American upbringing and the very different demands of an East Bloc country." He raised a hand, forestalling protest. "This may seem like going over old ground, but the Secretary wishes it done. He hopes we might find something of merit there. A clue, perhaps."

Clue? I had no idea what he was talking about. "Do what you must."

"Well, then," he said, opening the folder, "Let's just have a look." At first, he read in silence; then, more disturbingly, he spoke aloud, words and phrases snatched off the page at random moments.

"... brother's untimely death ... family uprooted ... spreading the Gospel in a remote corner of Europe ..."

Miss Alvarez worked her way along the length of the conference table, her heels clicking as she moved from one setting to the next, making tiny adjustments in the positioning of briefing books and fountain pens. The stealthy scent of her perfume was dizzying.

Lundquist kept on, apparently engrossed in my life story. Over his shoulder I saw a speck in the sky, the approach of some distant flying machine.

"... trained as a diplomat ... embassies in Krakow and Bucharest ..." He frowned, as if appalled by the bleakness of these postings, in which case he was right. "... named chief delegate to the UN ... a post held for many years with great—" His teeth chewed off the last syllables. "—distinction."

The tapping toe, the fingers flicking aside page after page —all this hinted at a girding of the loins for some dire pronouncement ahead. I looked at this deputy, this *minion*. Bad enough being dragged out of bed at the whim of the Secretary-General, but having to sit here like a lowly supplicant while Lundquist nattered on?

The telephone rang. Lundquist stared at it until Miss Alvarez crossed the room and picked up, turning away, and covering her mouth as she spoke.

"... serving twenty-five years in the General Assembly ..."

I strained to hear Miss Alvarez speak—her lips parting, the warm breath of her dulcet *sotto voce*—and hated Lundquist for his ceaseless drivel.

"... and, since last year, a rotating member of—"

"Enough!" I cried. "What is going on? You bore even the plants in this room with your talk—"

"Sir, I—"

"And *still*, you don't get to the point!"

Miss Alvarez paused in her conversation to listen to ours.

"Death threat," Lundquist squeaked.

"What?"

Behind him, I saw a flash in the sky, sun glinting off metal, the airborne vessel I saw minutes ago coming into focus. Police helicopter? TV news chopper?

"UN Security informed us only this morning," Lundquist said. "A threat made last night by an anonymous caller."

The idea of some lunatic conflating "death" and "Gabriel Ash" chilled my blood, but it wouldn't do to say so out loud. "Is *that* why I'm here? The Secretary wants to inform me of a threat on my life, but can't find time to do it himself?"

Justified or not, criticism of the SG caused Lundquist to sputter and fume. Quietly, Miss Alvarez hung up.

"This could have waited until tomorrow," I said.

"The Secretary thought it best to—"

"Look around! Do you see a Secretary here?" I lashed out, cleverly hiding my fear and confusion. "This is harassment. Punishing a junior Council member for daring to vote against the SG's wishes."

At that moment, the helicopter swept into full view of the windows on the thirty-eighth floor, a carbon-based dragonfly hovering perilously close, the whirring blades muffled by the Secretariat's industrial-strength glass. A darkened male figure stood in the chopper's open door, an object of some kind held aloft in his hands. Long-range rifle? Shoulder-held grenade launcher? Suddenly it seemed the death threat was real, a brazen attack on a UN delegate happening here and now, *inside the UN.*

"I assure you," Lundquist said, oblivious to the impending attack. "Our sole concern is your safety—"

I watched the helicopter bank on an updraft and land some floors down on a neighboring rooftop helipad. A man wearing a tuxedo emerged, followed by a blonde woman in spiked heels and a black evening gown. Close behind her, a fashion photographer wielded a weapon-sized camera.

Paranoia, pure and simple.

I stood abruptly, startling Lundquist. "When the SG's ready to meet in the flesh, let me know." I turned to his assistant. "Miss Alvarez, do you not consider this harassment?"

"*Ms.*"

"Pardon me?"

"*Ms.* Alvarez," she said, gently correcting her boss's error. "No, sir, it is concern for our well-being, as Mr. Lundquist says. Especially in the present crisis."

The telephone rang again. Faceless clerical staff began rushing in and out of the conference room. The Secretary-General was due back any moment from a high-level meeting, and His Nibs was reportedly in no mood to deal with the likes of me. Lundquist steered me out of the room, hands poised at a cautious distance. I looked back at Ms. Alvarez standing by the window with the Manhattan skyline behind her.

"Any chance you're free tonight for dinner?"

No response, just a glimmer of amusement in her deep brown eyes.

Death threat? That would be the least of my worries.

5

PAUSE

In captivity, I find some small comfort in *A Stranger's Welcome to Keshnev,* a dog-eared guidebook left behind by some previous castle resident. With jagged type and blurred snapshots of collective-grown beets and pumpkins, *A Stranger's Welcome* trumpets the splendid and mostly imaginary achievements of the People's Democratic Republic. Our nation has embarked upon a "mass expansion of agricultural output," resulting in record harvests of wheat and barley that are, in the guidebook's quirky English, "first to none." Other linguistic gems await.

Every house in Keshnev has
A roof. Some even more than
One door! Alcohol is not always
A problem.

As *A Stranger's Welcome* reminds us, a winding stretch of the Danube forms our northern border with Romania. Our

Bulgarian neighbors to the south shiver in the chill winds rushing off Keshnev's Lesser Alps. The capital city of Olt is "majestic in all degrees." In other words, a country roughly configured in the panhandle shape of Oklahoma, and land-locked but for a narrow strip of territory extending to the Black Sea coast.

Citizens in our democracy vote
many times. Everywhere you
look is total freedom!

In my lifetime alone, Keshnevites have endured grinding poverty during the reign of King Josef, a benevolent if distracted monarch. Then, brutal servitude under Nazi occupa-tion. And for decades since, misery and deprivation in the iron-fisted regimes of the Gray Wolf and Minister Petrescu. A work-er's state, as bleak and cold as anywhere in Europe.

Probably best not to share these thoughts with the Gentlemen of the Tribunal.

Goats on our farms do
Not complain. Like people,
They are happy. It is the
Law to smile.

A guard brings a jug of fresh goat's milk—a welcome relief, after days of molding bread and slimy broth. Tipping the jug with both hands, I drink milk down in a few greedy gulps. The sugary, astringent taste prompts memories of family life long ago in Rogvald. I'm ten or eleven years old, standing on a dusty patch of ground and facing off with the village goat known to all as Kaiser Wilhelm II. My mother and father are there, too—no longer the happy, smiling parents they once were, their missionary zeal deeply shaken by the death of my brother Willy. Wanting to amuse or distract them, I provoke a tussle, gripping the Kaiser's horns and wrestling the prickly creature into a headlock, but inevitably I'm sent crashing to earth on my backside. Father laughs and claps his big midwestern hands, even Mother wears a pained smile. A rare moment when despair gives way to simple human joy.

The guard takes the jug and leaves. In the cracked mirror, I see tears on my face. Tears! Is that what awaits me after speaking for hours and reliving the *sturm und drang* of my recent past? Sadness threatens to strangle these confessions in the cradle.

Of the husband-and-wife caretakers who reside in the castle—its sole occupants, beyond me and a rotating set of guards—Stefan is friendlier. In his fifties, thickset, with a large square head and a leisurely manner—won't walk, lift, or push anything sooner than he must. No one, including his long-suffering wife Anca, can make it otherwise.

As it happens, Stefan hails from the same mountain region where I spent my youth, fifty kilometers to the west. He remembers hearing stores about a missionary family living in Rogvald—*American* missionaries—but after 1939 and the German invasion, nothing more. "*Plukarsch*," he says, and spits on the floor. Pig-fuckers.

By contrast, Anca follows a strict etiquette of detention. When she comes to cook and clean, it's understood I'll keep a short distance apart. A slender woman, with green-apple eyes and long, unruly auburn hair. She wears a light-colored peasant dress and work boots—late twenties, I think, so not much older than my daughter.

"How are you today?" I ask brightly.

She sets a bucket and cleaning supplies on the kitchen counter. "Very fine."

Up to now, Anca's offered up little more than dismissive grunts in my direction. All I know about her comes from Stefan. She was born in Galuti Province, the daughter of a tram-driver and alcoholic mother, a girl who worked hard to study in *universitii*. *Smart girl*, her husband says ruefully. *Too smart for me.*

One morning last week, I caught her glancing at me from the kitchen, a look on her face of not-quite-disinterest. Any impulse to speak vanished when a guard walked in; since then, we've been mired in a world of acceptable distances and minimal eye-contact.

Today will be different.

First, though, our delicate dance of avoidance. She enters the cot-room, I retreat into the kitchen and watch as she drops a load of freshly washed towels onto the cot. Under the dirt-smudged face, she's pretty in a blunt, plainspoken way, nothing like the *femmes fatale* of Manhattan.

"Know what I wonder, Anca? I wonder if you'll talk to me today."

Intent upon folding towels, she seems at first not to hear. "OK, but English only. I learn more that way in my head."

I edge closer, hovering on the threshold. She flinches.

"Easy, Anca. I won't bite."

"Maybe," she says. "Maybe not."

"What does that mean?"

"A man who tries murder for Our Great Leader could be kind of man that bites people, eats them, too. Why not? Could be!" Towels snap under her furious folding. "What am I to know?"

It hurts to think I'm a mere criminal in her eyes. "So, you're certain you know what's going on. I'm jailed in this castle, ergo, I'm a killer."

"'Ergo'? What is 'ergo'?"

I'm seized by evangelical passion worthy of my missionary forebears. I want to shake this village girl out of her ignorance, make her understand something of the larger world.

"There are plenty of people out there with more on their minds than the Gray Wolf's well-being."

"Yes," she replies, anger building in her voice. "People in America and bags filled with money. Other people, what about them? People with holes in empty pockets."

I step into the cot-room, emboldened by her scorn. "Are you telling me life is better here?"

Anca stands her ground, spitting mad. "From each, according to, to—his ability ..." She stumbles on the words. "—to each, according to his—needs."

I laugh, surprised to hear Marxist dogma espoused in this medieval place.

"Why is this funny? I am not stupid. I have for one year study in *universitii* before, before ..." She waves a hand over my paltry dominion, the whole damp, poorly lit, barred-window world of it. "*This.*"

At that moment, the kitchen door creaks open. A squat, gap-toothed guard looks in, shocked to find the Enemy of the State standing close to the caretaker, precisely where castle rules forbid him to be. "Out! Move away!" I comply, staying out of reach of the guard's fists, with a glance back at the cot-room. Anca and her cleaning supplies are gone.

Twice a week I'm granted an hour of outdoor exercise, longer if the guard on duty feels generous with his time. These men rotate in and out of the castle; only by a biblical name scheme

—anointing each one with Old Testament names—can I keep track of them. Amos and Barabbas are long gone, replaced by Ezekiel who gave way to the current crop of guards, including a farm boy, Jonah, and Gad, an older man with a simian forehead and cauliflower ears. Gad relishes the unofficial perks of his job —verbal harassment, withholding food for no reason, once mock-shoving me against a wall. The other guards are harmless. It's Gad who worries me.

Today, Jonah—a scruffy youth who in fact looks like something coughed up by a whale—leads me out of confinement and down the winding staircase to the castle tower's ground floor. The door opens on a courtyard the approximate size and diameter of a two-ring circus, enclosed on four sides by tall stone walls. Passing the barn and stables, we come to the south-facing wall. Jonah climbs a ladder to the ramparts, leaving me to circumnavigate a well-trod path in the exercise yard.

On some days, the shock of the outside world feels pleasantly disorienting. If I squint just right at the sun, it's almost possible to believe I'm on a stroll in Central Park. Today, things are less cheerful. I twist my ankle in a pothole I never noticed before, and step on ground stained by Caruso's blood, not yet leached into the earth. The wind is brisk this morning, carrying a faint burning smell. Jonah up in the ramparts looks around in every direction, clearly alarmed by something; seeing me, he gestures that I should join him. I climb the ladder as quickly as my aching muscles allow, fearing at any moment a hail of gunfire from another guard's Kalashnikov. On the parapet I edge along the walkway and peer out where he's pointing. Down the mountainside, a jagged river divides the village and forest. A fire burns on the outskirts of the village, with enough luminous fury to be seen from our great height.

"Lightning," says Jonah, a man of few words.

For centuries, hunters have traipsed through that forest, rich in elk, bear, and wild boar. Archduke Franz Ferdinand gleefully shot wild game here just weeks before being gunned down himself in Sarajevo. Decades later, Hermann Göring, Reich Master of Forestry and Hunting, paraded about the area, a blimpish Nazi in jodhpurs and feathered cap. Far below, a gusting wind fans the flames. If winds carry the blaze across the river and up to the tree-line, fire could engulf us all.

"Time to go back," Jonah says.

The muzzle of his rifle prods me down the ladder. My last view of the world unencumbered by castle walls—a shroud of black smoke rising in the sky.

Hours later, I wake to thunderclaps rattling the tower. Rain pours down in a blind rage, pummeling the turrets and stone-and-mortar ramparts. The cot-room walls don't keep out much of the wind and rain. I huddle on the cot, my arms folded over my knees, as a thick, misty soup permeates the space. Smoke? Fog? Poison gas? It plays tricks with my eyes, melting away the edges of things.

After a career of dumb luck and witless folly, why should I be surprised to find myself here? I've been Keshnev's good soldier at the UN for as long as I can remember, consistently denouncing the West and praising Petrescu's regime at every turn? Over the years, I've been rewarded for my efforts—a roomy *pied-à-terre* with a wine cellar and a closet full of silk ties, Italian shoes, rows of wool and pinstripe suits, custom-tailored in Jermyn Street.

All in all, a fair exchange. I miss it badly.

Storm clouds unleash a final downpour and, like restless nomads, pack their things and go.

Dawn.

I grip the bars on the window, rising on tiptoes for a view down the mountain. The danger of fire is past, thanks to the storm, and the woods below twinkle greenly in the sun. A morning breeze sweeps in the smell of pine trees and brackish soil. I hear a distant crunch of underbrush and strain to make out the source—there! A massive brown elk emerges from the trees, antlers bent and twisted from some territorial dispute. The great creature trots to a ledge overlooking the valley and stands poised as if enthralled by the view, when of course it's thinking only about food and predators.

A sparrow-hawk keens in the sky. The elk retreats into old-growth forest. It has escaped, and so will I.

6

REC

The day after my disquieting encounter with Alfred Lundquist, I walked across UN Plaza in the grip of something like contentment. At a certain point in one's career, you earn the privilege of doing as much or as little as duty requires. My professional responsibilities weren't overly burdensome. Death threats notwithstanding, life was fairly routine and uneventful, just as I preferred.

Today, I chose the visitors' entrance on Forty-sixth Street, shunning the exclusive delegates' entrance two blocks away. Time would come soon enough for the hothouse world of United Nations bureaucracy—the countless legions of clerks, typists, interpreters, economists, civil affairs officers, as well as ambassadors from one hundred and fifty nations, and their ever-multiplying delegations. No need to rush things.

And sometimes I just enjoyed mingling with ordinary folk.

A line of tourists snaked around the perimeter of the Secretariat Building. Upon paying admission and undergoing a cursory body check, sightseers fanned out like crazed children on an Easter egg hunt. Visitors gawked at the Sputnik 1 exhibit, others ignored feeble barriers and left their grubby handprints on wall tapestries and the front of Chagall's enormous stained-glass "Peace Window." A hubbub of spoken languages echoed to the cantilevered balconies.

Across the lobby, I saw my old friend Sergei Litvinov guiding a tour of officials from the People's Republic of China, all of them wearing identical Mao jackets. Seeing me, Sergei shrugged from a distance as if to say, *Nobody knows the trouble I've seen.* Minutes later, I walked past a dapper American attaché of some slight acquaintance—was his name Powell? Peterson?—as he sternly admonished a terrified underling in front of an exhibit on global disarmament.

It was a morning of strange near-encounters. As I arrived at the bank of elevators, the doors closed on Francesca Cavour —a former lover whose heart-stopping Sicilian beauty looked in that split-second unchanged from three years ago—and whisked her away. I knew she'd recently transferred here from Rome, but I had yet to run into her in the flesh, as it were. This chance sighting triggered memories of a sunbaked villa on the Amalfi coast, our bodies slick from lovemaking, but also of shouting matches in the Delegates Lounge and jagged slash-marks etched into my office upholstery.

On the nineteenth floor, I nodded at passing delegates with a comfortable smile. Reaching for the door to the Keshnev Mission, I might even have been humming to myself.

My executive assistant stood there waiting for me—Vadim Murch, a thin, highly-strung Keshnevite in his mid-thirties wearing a gray, off-the-rack suit.

"How are you today, sir?"

"Very well, thank you."

"We have word, sir, of your presence here from yesterday. Had we been so informed beforehand, operations would be running when you came in." Vadim spoke in a self-taught English, overly precise and yet never altogether clear on meaning. He coughed into a sleeve. "If so informed."

Two years earlier, while working as a cypher clerk in our Hungarian consulate, Vadim Murch was tagged as "promising" and foisted upon me by the Foreign Ministry. As it turned out, he was good at what he did, running the Mission office smoothly in my not-infrequent absence. Lately, though, his eagerness to please and dedication to the State were getting on my nerves.

"It was nothing," I said.

I looked around at the waiting room décor, my sense of contentment fading fast. A well-worn sofa, poorly dusted glass table, and two spindly chairs. On the wall hung an oil portrait of the Gray Wolf, Hero of the Revolution, and his chosen successor, Minister Petrescu, both in full military garb, gazing out to sea and, presumably, a bright Socialist future. Oil portraits like these adorned every Keshnevite consulate from Havana to Moscow.

Hilda LaRue, my secretary, paused from typing to say hello —a diligent if excitable spinster from Queens. Apparently thinking I didn't notice, Vadim made urgent hand-signals at her to resume typing. *Tread carefully*, his gestures seemed to indicate. *The Ambassador today is out of sorts.*

"Sir, there are messages."

I stood outside my office, reviewing the notes he handed me. Apologies from the Nigerian representative for canceling a lunch appointment and asking to reschedule; an interview from some Lower East Side tabloid calling itself *Best Served Cold;* and several pleas via telex from a high-level official in the Ministry of Health, seeking help in obtaining "very best seats" for his mother, soon to arrive from Keshnev and dearly wishing to take in a matinée performance of *Cats.*

I grunted. "No, to all of them."

"Sir ..." Vadim glanced around nervously. "There is someone to meet."

"What? Who?"

"Please, this way ..."

He waved me down the hall like a dockhand guiding a clumsy barge into port. As instructed, I peered inside the file-room, hardly bigger than a broom-closet, where cabinets were filled to overflowing with Foreign Ministry directives predictably stamped URGENT. A man stood there in a thread-bare suit, an open folder in his hands. I felt a sharp pang of revulsion, as if I'd stumbled upon someone in a confessional.

Names were given, introductions made; I caught none of it. Shaking the man's limp hand added to my instinctual dread.

"... a Consul from the homeland, sir," Vadim said, "granted permission to visit us and only arrived yesterday. Sent to observe us for purposes of, of ..." He faltered, unwilling to look the newcomer in the eye. "I do not know."

This nameless Foreign Ministry official looked to be in his early thirties, with smudged eyes and dun-colored hair— features difficult for someone else to grasp hold of, more like the police sketch of a face, rather than the thing itself.

"Better word maybe is *support.*" The Consul's thin lips quivered as he spoke. "In times of great world affairs, this is important moment. For your advancing speech, things must be sure to run with smoothness. These are my instructions."

"I don't recall asking for support. Vadim, did we shoot a flare into the sky, something like that?"

Little shockwaves of fear rippled through my assistant's slender frame. Only now did I notice the makeshift army cot assembled in a corner of the file-room. Tissue boxes, a squashed tube of toothpaste and other obscene toiletries lay on the floor beside it.

"What the hell is this?"

"A little space," the Consul said. "For my comfort. Nothing of which requires your attention."

"You can't sleep here," I said.

"Only temporary," he countered.

"Are you listening? *Not here.*

Everyone seemed alarmed by my vehement tone, including me. Hilda stopped typing. Vadim clutched a folder to his chest, white as a corpse. The Consul grinned, or more accurately, offered a police sketch artist's rendition of a grin.

I turned on Vadim, wagging a finger in his face. "No calls, no interruptions. Understand?"

He nodded, too fearful to speak.

The décor in my inner office all originated in the old country. A frayed national flag, the gnarled lower half of an oxcart, a hunk of igneous rock from the Volstoc Hills. No portraits, oil or otherwise, of the Gray Wolf and his Mephisthophelean sidekick.

For a while I lost myself in paperwork, hacking through a jungle of unanswered dispatches and communiqués. The nearby presence of my briefcase—more precisely, the notes it contained for a speech as yet unwritten—nagged at me like a vexing in-law. My formal address before the Security Council was coming up in two weeks' time, but rather than cohere into lively rhetoric, the words and phrases I'd compiled thus far lay dead on the page. Of course, certain key points must be included. I had to denounce Great Britain for its long, bloody history of conquest and subjugation, while also condemning the United States, on general principles. I might toss in an anti-Zionist rant or two, just for the hell of it.

The rest of my forthcoming speech? Up for grabs.

After twenty years of these ritual denunciations, my belief

in the Petrescu regime had worn thin. I didn't know how much longer I could ignore the gap between Keshnev's cloistered worldview and, well, reality. My first preference was giving no speech at all, but this wasn't an option. Since the day of our ascension to membership on the Security Council, Minister Petrescu never tired of telling me, *Keshnev must be heard.*

Our last face-to-face meeting, ten years ago in the Minister's dank basement office, hadn't gone well. I was nearing the end of a trip home, eager to return to Manhattan and civilized life; such was the force of Petrescu's will, I felt obliged to linger. He was in his sixties then, with dyed black hair and a raptor's profile, his colorless eyes glinting with malice towards the world at large. We drank freely that night, which explains my blurred memory of events, but I knew this much was true: One minute we laughed over some drunken joke, the next a silver-barreled pistol appeared on top of his desk and Petrescu no longer seemed amused. Apologizing profusely without knowing why, I fled his lair at the first opportunity. It had never been spoken of since.

A knock at the door. Vadim's head poked in. "Sir?"

"Didn't I say, no interruptions?"

"Yes, but ..." He stepped inside, closed the door behind him, and sat in the chair across from me, each action shockingly unbidden. "It is your daughter, sir."

"Tess? What about her?"

"She has made contact in telephone call. I have message to give you, on her behalf."

Pause. "Well?"

"Yes, yes ..." He consulted his notes. "She requests lunch in two days' time from now. I take my liberties and reserve table of two at Waldorf-Astoria."

"All right," I said, pleased by my assistant's efficiency, but unwilling to show it. "Anything else?"

Vadim glanced around, his whitish pallor looking more consumptive than usual. "*Him,* sir," he said. "Contrary to your instructions, Consul makes camp in file-room. Why is he here, sir? What does he want? Is true his orders come direct from Minister for State Security?"

Since taking power many years ago, the Petrescu regime had earned a reputation for brutality surpassing its predecessor's. Shop stewards informed on factory workers, neighbors informed on neighbors, children informed on teachers and vice versa. This torrent of accusations and lies fed the hungry maw of Petrescu's elite secret police—*Securitaatpolizie,* or SPU—and likely would never stop.

So, yes, such orders were possible.

"Forget it," I said. "You're getting worked up over nothing."

Just then, an ethereal figure loomed up outside the smoked-glass door to my office. Vadim, made quick-witted by paranoia, turned just as the ghostly shape rapped actual knuckles on the glass door; he yelped like a frightened dog.

"Excuse?" the figure's muffled voice said. "Am I to come in?"

The door opened without permission and the Consul—whose name I no longer cared to know—waited as Vadim slithered out of the office. He sat in the newly vacant chair, a nondescript foreigner in a cheap suit. I doubted I'd be able to pick him out of a lineup.

"What do you want?" I asked.

The Consul reached into a coat pocket, produced a green requisition form, and smoothed it out on top of my desk. "I am needing signature of Comrade Ambassador. This makes authority for money I must spend elsewhere to live. Someplace not here, as your request was."

"You don't need money," I said. "There are shelters all over the city. Take your pick."

His eyelids blinked in rapid succession, but otherwise he didn't move. If my lack of compassion stirred any emotion in him, I didn't see it. Gradually, his stillness became a palpable, unnerving thing.

"Your speech, Comrade Ambassador. How does it come along?"

Impertinent little bastard! "It comes along nicely."

"In Foreign Ministry, they talk of this big speech you will give to UN. Many eyes are watching, many ears will hear. If you wish, I could look at your speech? I am told I am writer good as Hemingway."

The Consul's meat-grinder English made my head hurt. "No, thanks. Can I get back to work now?"

He tapped a poorly manicured finger on the green form. "Signature, please."

Vadim's terror of this man had amused me at first; now I found his audacity downright insulting. I was Permanent Representative of the People's Democratic Republic. Why should I care who the Consul was or who he claimed to work for? What did I have to fear from him, or, for that matter, from Minister Petrescu, holed up in a bunker office halfway across the planet?

I scribbled my name across the bottom of the form. "Signed. Now get out."

Such was my inability to contemplate the worst.

7

PAUSE

Among our little circle of castle-dwellers, I've lately gained a reputation as a good listener. Stefan lingers for hours complaining about his work, while a guard from the Jilka province—Amos, Habakkuk, who can remember all the names I give them? —confesses to a yearning for the family cow. Even Anca shares, in her way. Tidying the rooms, she grumbles about her childless marriage and the rigors of castle upkeep, year after dismal year.

From these and other encounters, I glean information about the village and forest below, which mountain passes might serve as the best escape routes. The more knowledge I acquire, the more options I have, or so I desperately hope.

Shouting erupts on the other side of the locked kitchen door. One voice is Stefan's, the caretaker, the other I queasily recognize as belonging to Gad. Their loud dispute seems centered around a meal Stefan is bringing me. The guard's request for a taste is sharply denied, angry voices arising in a flurry of regional obscenities. I fear the two of them will come to blows. I yell through the door.

"Gentlemen, stop!"

A moment of surprised silence goes by. Then a key opens the lock, the door swings open, and Stefan enters, carrying a bowl of homemade *furcersie* and setting it on the table.

Gad—squat, flat-footed, a surly dawn-of-man specimen—remains on the landing. His piggish eyes rake over me. Who am I, a mere *prisoner*, to dare intervene?

"What do we have here?" I ask. "Smells delicious."

Yes, Anca's baked raisin-and-date concoction is a welcome treat. I take a small bowl from the cupboard, ladle out a generous helping and place it in front of the foul-tempered guard. Seizing the bowl with both hands, he tilts the rim to his lips and slurps away. A moment later, a sated belch issues from deep within his small intestines.

Blessed are the peacemakers ...

REC

For a long moment after the Consul left my office, I pondered the situations at play in my life. Anonymous death threats. Minister Petrescu dangling his Consul-puppet in my face and—new for him—scheming from afar. The gossiping hens of UN member states, all the cliques and factions, endless intrigue and striving for power. Worst of all, for me, the ever-widening gap between what I proclaimed in the Security Council in defense of Keshnev policies and what I actually believed. The pen trembled in my hand.

What if I couldn't do this anymore?

I glanced at my watch—11:25 a.m. No more solace to be found in paperwork.

Gently I eased open my office door, hoping to sneak out

unseen. Hilda typed as fervently as ever while Vadim was berating a delivery boy for some reason. The Consul sat on the sofa, paging through a magazine with a glossy cover photo of the actress Natalie Wood, the caption underneath ACCIDENT? SUICIDE? MURDER?

"Sir?"

Vadim blocked my escape from this viper's den. "Not now," I informed him. "I'm going to the Delegates Lounge."

"But there are things that must be—"

"*What?*" I swung on him in full view of the others. "What's so damn important we need to do it right now?"

Vadim fell silent. Hilda stared at her keyboard. The only sound came from the briskly turned pages of the celebrity magazine.

"The Delegates Lounge," I said again, "if needed." Meaning, not.

If the goal was reaching my destination without bumping into some objectionable acquaintance, things didn't go my way. Approaching the Lounge, I heard my name called out. A man in a nearby alcove gestured for me to join him.

It was Inspector Pieter Best of UN Security.

I reluctantly complied, ending up at close quarters with him in a tiny alcove. Though I'm not a physically small man, the inspector towered over me—big chest, big head of tawny hair, impeccably attired in a dark blue suit and darker-blue silk tie. A former South African soldier of fortune turned international cop, Best had every right to ask me or anyone else in the vast UN complex to stop whatever we were doing and answer his questions.

You just didn't want to be the one so summoned.

"I understand," he said in a subdued Afrikaner twang, "there is a situation of some delicacy."

"You've been talking to Alfred Lundquist."

Best shrugged. "Such are my responsibilities."

"What's all the fuss about? I can't be the first delegate threatened by some crackpot."

"We don't take these things lightly," he informed me. "Nor should you."

Six months ago, a corrupt city official named Elwood Jenkins—fearing imminent arrest for tax fraud—leapt off the roof of a building in the Meatpacking District. Two floors down, entirely by coincidence, I was engaged in strenuous fornication with a big-boned Polish girl in what was once called a "house of ill repute." Police swarmed the premises, banging on doors and shouting, "NYPD! Open the fucking door!" The Polish girl ran off without a stitch of clothing, but I stood my ground in the black dress pants I'd worn earlier that night at a Yo-Yo Ma concert in Lincoln Center. Sometime later, outside on Fourteenth Street, a crowd of street people smirked and tittered at me from behind police lines. A plainclothes detective came over with a hostile look, but the laminated UN identity card I produced stopped him in his tracks. He instructed me to wait until someone "in authority" could be found. Someone turned out to be Inspector Best, greatly displeased to be roused from bed at that very late hour.

"This is just Lundquist," I said. "He likes pushing non-aligned members around. Who better than poor, defenseless Keshnev?"

Someone had left a newspaper on the small table in the alcove—above the fold, a photograph of SAS paratroopers with assault rifles aboard *HMS Sheffield* and the screaming headline BRITISH TASK FORCE SAILS ON MISSION OF WAR. Overwrought words and images reminding me, in case I'd forgotten, of all the world's troubles we in the UN were supposed to resolve.

"Would you consider the services of a bodyguard?" Best asked. "Temporarily, of course."

This death-threat nonsense was cramping my style. Delegates and staffers were gawking at me while I stood in hushed conversation with UN Security. I certainly didn't want some bull-necked goon on my heels all day.

"A bodyguard can't keep up with me."

"Perhaps you'll give this some more thought."

"No," I told him. "I'll take my chances."

"Unruffled, eccentric, scorning help from others." Inspector Best looked me over and then gazed off, as if across the scrub-brush terrain of the Rhodesian veldt. "You haven't changed a bit, Ambassador."

"Takes too much effort," I said, and with a minor feint, extricated myself from his presence.

Inside the North Delegate's Lounge—a two-tiered UN watering hole of not quite the highest order—the overhead lighting was weak, the Pinot Grigio lacked distinction, and waiters were often nowhere to be found. White-haired gentlemen in white linen suits sat around the place like grizzled expats in a Victorian outpost, downing gin slings and mourning the loss of empire. I did some of my best thinking here.

The message Vadim conveyed disturbed me, when normally a phone call from my twenty-six-year-old daughter, a celebrated photojournalist, should gladden my heart. Our last encounter, six months ago in a remote terminal at La Guardia Airport, went poorly. I had returned from routine business in D.C. and Tess was going to catch a flight to Paris, final destination Beirut and the Lebanese civil war. Had I been prepared to run into her, things might have gone differently—

fewer lengthy silences, less of the many things fathers and daughters can't abide about each other. We sat in hard plastic chairs in the airport lounge, looking down at our hands and saying little until a voice on the terminal loudspeaker announced, *"Dernier appel pour les passagers à l'aéroport de Charles De Gaulle,"* and off she went.

"Ah Gabriel. They said I'd find you here."

Sergei Litvinov hovered by the table, my old Bolshevik friend. A short man, thick around the middle, in a brown double-breasted suit with padded shoulders, a stylish look in Kremlin fashion circles. He gestured with an unlit cigar at the buffet on the lower tier.

"Are you hungry? I recommend the baked quail with apricots, and for dessert, strawberry balsamic tiramisu. Very good! *Harasho!*"

I looked at Sergei's square face and frosty eyebrows, not really in the mood for Russian conviviality. "Maybe another drink."

He sat, a laugh bubbling up in his chest. "Why not? It's almost noon!" Delegates at nearby tables cast disapproving glances our way. Age hadn't diminished the USSR deputy chief delegate's high-volume mode of expression, nor, at the age of seventy-five, his unruly shock of white hair.

"Those Chinese you saw me ushering around this morning? Difficult bunch, very grim and determined. A stroll through the General Assembly chamber becomes for them like the Long March."

Sergei was a survivor. Captured on the Eastern Front, interned in a German POW camp, later repatriated to Russia. Like all returning prisoners of war, he was labeled "poisoned" by Nazi imprisonment and therefore banished to hard labor in the Gulag. After Stalin's death and a general easing of government, Sergei's citizenship was restored, allowing him to join the diplomatic corps and serve the Motherland in peace as he did in war.

These days, he was a well-regarded figure, known for his gargantuan appetite and his skill in transforming Moscow's shameful human rights abuses into high-blown oratory. A survivor, but also my hero and role model.

"Gabriel, you're very quiet today."

"Just … reflective."

"Reflective?" A grin lit up his face, wrinkled and mucked-up by history. "That's not in your nature, my friend. What you're good for is chasing women and drinking before noon."

I squinted at him. "Didn't they bury Khrushchev in that suit?"

The waiter appeared. I ordered another Żubrówka, and with minimal encouragement, Sergei did the same.

"Gabriel, you are a bad influence."

How bad? I wondered. Bad enough to merit a threat against my life? To permanently alienate my only child? To draw the ire of Minister Petrescu and the Consul, his charmless, assembly-line police goon? On the far wall of the Delegates Lounge was an immense tapestry depicting the Great Wall of China, its serpentine ramparts and guard towers etched among sand-colored hills. As remote a place as anywhere on Earth. How I ached to be there.

"So, nothing to talk about?"

The petty babble of surrounding tables fell away. I considered telling Sergei about my meeting with Lundquist, and the jarring epiphany of barely an hour ago that I was no longer cut out for the diplomatic life. But if I couldn't confide in my oldest friend, who could I turn to? Or did the knot in my stomach that wouldn't go away suggest there were good reasons to keep quiet about the whole thing?

"Nope," I said, uncharacteristically concise.

The Delegate's Lounge was filling up, men and women departing the buffet line, trays in hand, and walking up the steps in search of a table. Among them was the tall, clean-cut American I'd seen earlier in the day in the Lobby, scolding an underling. What was his name—Parker? Pomeroy? I asked Sergei if he knew him.

"According to the US delegation, this individual holds the title of Deputy Liaison for Mission Support, whatever that means." His smile exposed blotchy, war-damaged teeth. "And who are we to doubt the US delegation?"

At that moment, the sharp-eyed Deputy Liaison spotted us. He headed our way, joined by a familiar-looking woman with long black hair. Sergei cursed under his breath, but produced a welcoming smile and invitation to join us.

"Gabriel, this is Mark Pearson. Mr. Pearson, my good friend, Ambassador Gabriel Ash."

Pearson looked to be around forty. Close-cropped hair, an athletic frame in a well-cut suit, and midnight-blue Yale Bulldog tie. His handshake felt a bit too gung-ho for my tastes.

"And this is Miss Alvarez, who I just met in the buffet line." His voice dropped into a stage-whisper, loud but not too loud. "She tells me she works for Alfred Lundquist."

"That's *Ms.* Alvarez," I said, earning her delighted smile.

"You know each other?"

In a pearl-white blouse and gray jacket, she looked as severely professional as the day before in the conference room. She sat quietly before a bowl of soup on a tray. "We've met," she said.

"Small world, huh?"

With that, Pearson tucked into a plate of veal chops *au jus* and Duchess potatoes. I looked him over as he ate—brisk, efficient, almost machine-like—made uneasy by the man's confident manner and the precise set of his jaw.

Sergei turned to her, asking after Deputy Lundquist's
health and well-being. "He must be under considerable strain
these days, with the Falklands business and all. Hard enough
in peacetime keeping the Secretary-General happy, let alone
when member nations are shooting at each other."

She rested a spoon from the soup bowl and looked at me, a
playful glint in her eyes. "Shall we ask Ambassador Ash? He
met yesterday with Mr. Lundquist."

Sergei looked at me, incredulous. "Yesterday? On a
Sunday?"

"Oh ..." Ms. Alvarez caught my disgruntled expression.
"You didn't mention it?"

Pearson looked up from his plate. "Mention what?"

I gazed at the tapestry on the far wall. *Oh, to be in the Gobi.*
"Go on," I told her. "Say what you want."

"Someone called in a death threat over the weekend," she
explained to the others. "A threat directed at Ambassador Ash."

The wounded look on my Russian friend's face tore at my
heart. *A death threat and you didn't mention it?* But Pearson
sprinkled generous amounts of pepper over what remained of
his *au jus*, grinning like an ape.

"Attaboy, Ambassador! Proud little Keshnev's playing in
the big leagues now."

What I'd chosen not to disclose was suddenly public
knowledge—and where's the waiter when you need him?
Serving as the target of someone's murderous intent wasn't
the ego-booster I might have hoped for; the death threat only
drew attention to me in unwanted ways. I was annoyed by the
young woman's guileless manner and, at the same time,
hugely attracted to her.

"This whole business is a waste of resources," I told Ms.
Alvarez. "Please ask your boss to drop it."

"Yes ..." Her smile weakened. "Of course."

"Don't let it get to you, Ambassador," Pearson said. "Some nutjob shoots his mouth off in a bar, somebody else calls it in —so what? Let's not get our panties in a twist over nothing." A mock-shy glance at her. "Pardon my French."

"Still," Sergei said, frowning at his unlit cigar, "these are serious matters."

This earned a sour look from Pearson. "I'm suggesting otherwise, Sergei."

Sergei chose not to answer, mysteriously cowed by this upstart American. Not me. "Mr. Pearson, didn't I see you in the lobby this morning, dressing down one of your subordinates?"

"You're mistaken, sir."

"Oh?"

"I've been in meetings all day."

Ms. Alvarez tracked us as we spoke, likely accustomed to staying silent in the presence of "important" men. Pearson's denial wasn't worth pursing, but—fearing a rival for Ms. Alvarez's affections—I couldn't let it go.

"Your Secretary of State, now *there's* someone whose health should concern us. Isn't he said to have a heart condition?" The Secretary of State, a respected military figure with presidential ambitions, had been much in the news lately. "Yet there he goes, leapfrogging from one world capital to another in search of peace. Putting his own delicate health at risk."

Pearson's smile stayed fixed throughout my remarks. "The Secretary is moving heaven and earth to broker a ceasefire in the Falklands. The state of his cardiovascular well-being isn't an issue."

"But the endless shuttle diplomacy must take a toll. Buenas Aires, 10 Downing Street, dinner in the White House with the Commander-in-Chief. Spurned at every juncture and still he comes back for more." I nodded at Sergei, eager to draw him into the fray. "Always the bridesmaid, never the bride."

My old friend didn't bite. The skin reddened around Pearon's throat.

"All due respect, Ambassador. Knock it off."

Why was it so much fun to rile him up? "Or what?"

"Or *what*? I'll tell you what—"

"My soup is cold," Ms. Alvarez announced.

All eyes fell on the spoonful of broth she held close to her lips. Pearson seemed especially shocked by the news. "*Cold*?" He snagged a passing waiter's elbow, causing the poor fellow to grimace and stop. "The lady's soup is cold. Get her more of that—what're you having?"

"Bouillabaisse."

"Got that?" he asked the waiter. "*Bouillabaisse chaud immediatement, merci.*"

Sergei, taking advantage of the kerfuffle, lumbered to his feet. "I must get back," he said, and bustled off with remarkable energy for a man of his age, weight, and penal history.

"Please, don't mention this again," I said to her. "There's no point in lending credence to the rantings of some—what did you call them, Mr. Pearson?"

Pearson lit up, like a smart kid called on in class. "Nutjobs."

Ms. Alvarez demurely arranged the napkin in her lap. I had the feeling she enjoyed this mild rebuke.

"You're right, Ambassador Ash. I should have said nothing."

He leaned over and slapped my shoulder, our little spat forgotten, once again all hail-fellow-well-met. I suddenly understood why Sergei had been so jumpy in his presence. Why didn't I see it myself? An old UN hand like me should know CIA when he saw it.

Pearson laughed, the sneering chortle of the privileged class.

"Women, huh?"

8

REC

Assuming the Gentlemen of the Tribunal lack familiarity with the Waldorf-Astoria Hotel, allow me to be your guide.

Enter the hotel on Park Avenue, that bastion roadway of capitalist excess. Pass through revolving glass doors and ascend carpeted steps to the spacious, sunlit foyer. Step into a world of hanging plants, dark wood, and tastefully subdued lighting. Guests mingle in the lobby like first-class passengers on an ocean liner. A magnificent standing clock dominates the space—nine feet tall, made of bronze and mahogany—with a miniature replica of the State of Liberty on top, the ceramic flame in her torch-bearing hand nearly scraping the ceiling. Continue up more carpeted steps on the left, fingers roaming over banisters of solid Caspian elm. A black man in a white tuxedo sits at a Steinway Grand on the Cocktail Terrace, performing music composed by the degenerate American, Cole Porter.

On this particular day, the Waldorf's bubbly, outdated ambience was charming. I walked into the Cocktail Terrace with a rare bounce in my step and found a table right away. It was a big occasion. My daughter was meeting me for lunch.

First things first. A glass of chilled Żubrówka—for the uninitiated, bison grass vodka imported from Poland—was promptly delivered. I sat and watched the lunch-time crowd, stockbrokers and city councilmen, a frowning dowager or two, a trio of silver-haired men at the bar having altogether too much fun. If, as it seemed, everyone was in the grip of end-of-the-week *joie de vivre*, the Waldorf's opulent setting was just the place for it.

I first met Eva Capshaw—blonde, wealthy, extremely fragile—at a Guggenheim charity event. Our breathless affair led to pregnancy with Tess, marriage following close on its heels. Six years of make-believe faithfulness went by and then I relocated to a new place on Seventy-Second across the Park. Amid much weeping and confusion on my daughter's part, I promised I'd visit regularly. I seldom did.

A bald, middle-aged man entered the restaurant, his hand on the arm of a younger woman with bountiful red hair. Her dress, I thought, was too short and "of the moment" for this louche crowd. The man and woman came to a nearby table, where he held out her chair and then took his own, launching immediately into some sort of diatribe, *sotto voce*.

Eva was a dutiful mother in our daughter's childhood and adolescence. She got Tess through Bronx High School of Science and Wellesley, indulging her obsessive interests in rock-climbing and action photography. In Paris in her senior year, Tess happened upon a crowd protesting hikes in student fees outside the Sorbonne. Riots broke out and she caught it on film—bloodied protestors, police batons cracking skulls, the glow of a burning *autocar* reflected in a street urchin's eyes. Reuters bought the photographs and soon magazines were sending her to cover famine in West Africa and civil wars in the

Southern Hemisphere. Not yet in her thirties, Tess had become an acclaimed photo-journalist, her work said to give viewers the sense they were witnessing historical events in the flesh, right there with her. It pained me knowing how little I'd contributed to her success.

"Sir?" the waiter asked. "May I get you something?"

"Another Żubrówka, please."

Eva and I agreed on very little, except for never telling Tess anything in-depth about our wedding day. On that memorable day, surrounded by overhanging willow trees and prized race-horses, we exchanged marriage vows on her father's bluegrass Kentucky estate. Hours later, separated by chance, each of us engaged in our first act of infidelity—she with a shaggy-haired limo driver, me with a coltish bridesmaid—reconvening again just in time for wedding cake, which we gleefully smashed in each other's faces.

Kitchen smells combined with those of the Waldorf's lunch-time crowd, a fetid mix of *haut cuisine* sauces, cigarette smoke, and cloying after-shave. None of this served to boost my appetite. I kept a tight grip on my bison grass vodka.

After Tess grew up and out of Eva's life, her demons came back to stay. On many nights, Tess later told me, her mother lay in a stupor of prescription medications, alternately worshipping me and cursing my name. Her circle of friends had by then dwindled to a select few, their chief pastimes being half-hearted deviant sex and the rampant use of intra-venous drugs. One night Eva came to rest alone in a cold-water flat, an empty barbiturate bottle nestled against the clawfoot tub. No suicide note, no farewell of any kind.

The tragedy failed to bring Tess and me closer. She threw herself into the globetrotting chase for news and never looked back.

The red-haired woman at the nearby table met my gaze,

even while her companion's shiny scalp bobbed up and down in fervent proclamation of something or other. Her wry smile in the face of withering abuse was impressive.

Murmurs from neighboring tables drew my attention. Tess stood at the entrance to the restaurant, all five-feet-nine-inches of her in pressed khaki fatigues and combat boots. Diners stared, bemused by the young woman in paramilitary garb as she trailed behind the maître d', forging a clumsy path between elegant tables. I stood and greeted her. She didn't return my smile.

"Sorry I'm late."

"That's all right." Nudging aside the maître d', I held a chair out for her. "Please. Sit." A waiter passed by with a tray of water goblets. Tess swooped one of them off the tray and drank the water in a single gulp. A startling sight on its own, but then she used the back of her hand to dry her lips! I asked if everything was okay.

"What? Oh, yeah ..." Only now did she notice the effect her feral actions were having on others. "Just thirsty."

Tess had her mother's pearl-white complexion, chilly gray eyes, and formidable cheekbones. Her hair fell to her shoulders, a moonless black. Meeting her for the first time, you might be put off by my daughter's stubborn self-sufficiency and humorless outlook on life. Things were more complicated than that. I knew Tess feared inheriting—beyond Eva's slim frame and ghostly good looks—a penchant for madness. It explained why she pressed such a hard-bitten version of herself on the world, a useful quality, I supposed, in her line of work.

Tess looked around, skittish and confused by her surroundings. Perfume and the aroma of *coq au vin* filled the air. A genteel bell rang each time an entrée was ready, and there was the hum of a hundred mouths at work, talking and laughing and masticating. From the baby grand came the decadent melodies of "I've Got You Under My Skin."

"What's this?" I asked, making a sweeping gesture at her outfit. I was more nervous than I'd expected. "Are you headed on safari or planning to drop behind enemy lines?"

Irritation flickered in her gaze. "I'm on a flight out of JFK right after lunch. No time to change clothes."

"Flight to where?"

This seemed to puzzle her. "I thought you knew."

"How could I know? Did you tell my assistant when you called?"

"Maybe." She blinked. "I thought I did. Maybe not."

I looked across the table at my striking, headstrong, socially inept offspring. How did she ever get through life? Then it dawned on me.

"The Falklands. That's where you're going."

Tess glanced around at the bankers and political hacks, the entire nakedly inebriated crowd. What she saw clearly made no sense to her.

"It's all happening so fast," she said. "My editor asked me to drop everything and go. Had to be now or never."

It, as I learned, included a ten-hour flight into Heathrow, then arrival at the Docklands via the Underground, and boarding the Royal Navy warship *HMS Invincible* no later than 0900 hours the following day. Hitching a ride on a vast armed convoy steaming towards hostilities at the bottom of the world.

"My editor is very demanding, only wants boots-on-the-grounds stuff." She shrugged, as if bemoaning her fate; in fact, her eyes lit up. "It's out of my hands."

The waiter approached, bearing menus. I watched Tess pore over the lushly worded items with all the apparent comprehension of a primate leafing through the *New York*

Times. I felt my teeth clench. A long moment passed, then I snatched away the menu and signaled the waiter.

"For the young lady, grilled trout almandine and house salad, dressing on the side. I'll have a New York steak, rare, *avec pommes frites.*"

The waiter left. Tess glared at me.

"I guess you always use whatever control you have," she said. "Some things never change."

The bald man at the nearby table suddenly came to his feet, threw down his napkin, and stormed out of the restaurant. With all eyes in the place on her, the red-haired woman calmly sipped from a glass of white wine.

"It's just that the situation in the South Atlantic is ..." I searched for the right word, not wishing to say, *Are you out of your mind?* "Heated, you might say."

"'Heated'?" She laughed, openly scornful. "I wonder if the crew of the *Sheffield* felt that way when an Exocet missile slammed into her hull."

"I'm just suggesting you reconsider the timing of this trip."

"In my business, Father, timing is everything."

Tess rarely called me "Father," and when she did, it never augured well. I drank off the last of the Żubrówka, stung by the coldness in her voice.

"Yes, get the news first," I said. "Always be first."

"What's news without pictures? That's only half the story."

"But we already know this story. Missiles, battleships, death at sea. We've seen it all before."

She frowned. "War is old news, is that what you're saying?"

"The news is, an empire is dying. You can't show that with pictures of dead sheep and maimed Falklanders."

"The hell I can't," she said. "And what about you and all your statesmanlike buddies? Make speeches. Draft resolutions.

Hang out in that fucking glass tower. That's pretty much it, right?"

What Tess said wasn't wrong. Still, I disliked hearing my own flesh-and-blood denigrate the institution from which I'd become so alienated all on my own. "The pictures you take, Tess, *all* pictures—they manipulate the viewer. What's left out of the frame is more important than what we see."

Angry color crept into her cheeks. She glanced around, taking in the lunchtime chatter, then leaned forward in her camo outfit.

"Who the hell are you to talk about manipulation?"

I stiffened. "What does that mean?"

"It *means*, I don't like being lectured by the man who manipulated my mother into an early grave."

I let this absurd remark hang in the air between us. We seemed predestined to be lifelong foes, like two armored figures astride horses on some medieval plain. It took so little —just a second-rate colonial war exploding halfway around the world—to bring out the worst in us.

"What you're trying to say is, I'm a bad man. Well," I said peevishly, "no argument here. Your mother married a bad man, thinking she could change him. She was wrong."

"Bullshit," she said. "I think you can live with being a 'bad man.' It's the other stuff—messy family stuff—you don't care for."

The waiter arrived, balancing a plate of garnished trout and a New York steak, rare, in respective hands. Tess looked up at the waiter as if unable to grasp the man's purpose, then turned and appraised me in much the same way. Without warning, she stood from the table.

"What are you doing?"

"I, I—" She fluttered her hands in front of her. "Have to go."

"Sit."

I clamped a hand on her wrist but seeing in her eyes the look of a trapped animal, I let go. The waiter stood in place, juggling hot plates.

"Don't do this," I said. "Don't fly to London, don't get on that boat. Don't willingly sail into a war zone."

"Since when do you care?" Grabbing a cloth napkin, she swiped tears from her face. "Fuck you, Father."

On her way out, Tess collided with numerous chairs and tables, leaving in her wake a whisper-storm of gossip. Following this memorable exit, the whisperers turned and aimed their disapproving gaze at me.

Is that it? I wondered. Are those the last words I'll ever hear my daughter say?

9

PAUSE

Rain falls in the mountain valley, a long curtain of gray bisected by bars in the window. It seems unfathomable, the gap between *then* and *now*.

REC

I sat for some time in the still center of the Waldorf's lunch-hour maelstrom. Waiters whooshed by. The pianist banged out, "Let's Do It, Let's Fall in Love." I heard munching and gnawing all around me, the full range of masticatory noises human beings can make. What if I suddenly erupted into violence, knocking over tables, and stabbing investment bankers in the chest with a butter knife? Would that really be so indefensible? All that kept me from severe misbehavior was the sight of the red-haired woman—herself a victim of some emotional outburst just moments ago—her attention drawn by my daughter's tearful exit from the premises.

In my experience, if you wait long enough, the good things

in life tend to win out. I came to my feet and approached her table, in some head-swirling mix of alcohol, deep filial regret, and slow-burning lust. The woman looked up at me—pale green eyes, a smattering of freckles across her face. Probably no more than five years older than Tess. A gaze that was measured yet inviting.

"What happened to your friend?" I asked.

"Difference of opinion," she said.

"About ...?"

"Oh, the usual. Good versus evil, Mets versus Yankees, Beatles versus Stones." She extended a dry, cool hand. "Hi, I'm Molly."

"Gabriel."

"Care to join me, Gabriel?"

I sat across from her, blatantly fixed on her mane of red hair—so brilliant a shade from a distance, more autumnal up close.

"Things looked pretty intense over in *your* neck of the woods," she said, nodding at my vacated table. "What got your young friend in jungle fatigues so hot and bothered?"

"Actually, that's my daughter."

"Oh." A hand flew to her lips. "Sorry."

"Have you eaten?"

"What with all the good versus evil stuff, we never got around to it."

I signaled the first waiter I saw. He approached, looking concerned.

"Have you not been helped, sir? My apologies! I am Philippe. May I tell you the specials of the day?"

Philippe was a short man, burdened with protruding eyeballs—a distracting specimen I'd normally dismiss in an instant. But I wanted, in these first heady moments with Molly, a witness to my good fortune.

"Proceed," I said.

"For starters, we offer a creamy lobster bisque and beef risotto cakes with orange *crème fraîche*—"

"Well?" I asked Molly. "Are you over him yet?"

"Who?"

"Your friend—the one with differing opinions."

Phillippe paused, looking confused.

"Go on," I told him.

"Uh, today's entrée, Tournedos Rossini, is served with roasted asparagus and leek mashed potatoes—"

"'Over him'?" Molly giggled. "God, yeah—ages ago."

"—and for dessert, your choice of poached pears with warm gingerbread or—"

"Not a soul mate, then," I said.

"—raspberry linzer torte."

"Not even close." She shifted in her chair. "Could we maybe go someplace less ..."

"Congested?"

"Yes," she said.

Phillipe paused to catch his breath. I regarded him coldly, as a prince might look over one of his serfs but figured my tip would make up for my unspeakable attitude. I was grateful, after all; as an oblique instrument of seduction, he had served his purpose.

"Your orders, sir?"

"No orders," I told him. "We're leaving."

As it happened, there *was* a less congested place—a grand suite on the Waldorf's seventeenth floor that I often reserved for visiting dignitaries. Damask curtains, silky coverlets, elegant *fin de siècle* furnishings. We disrobed in a hurry and collapsed on the four-poster bed, grappling for purchase, and flailing about in ways that seemed less like lovemaking, more like a barroom brawl, until—

Wait! What am I doing? Gentlemen of the Tribunal, please forgive me. You asked for testimony and now I subject you to, to ... *pornography*.

Picture instead, a short time later, a man of distinguished bearing and a woman twenty years younger, naked in bed, awash in Midtown's diaphanous, late-afternoon glow.

Molly dozed on her side, facing away from me—a perfect time to explore at length what I'd so frantically consumed moments ago. As my hand drifted over her body, youthful memories and associations of the old country came to mind. Her lips when my fingers grazed them as softly pliant as the tumbledown meadows of Mitk. Her breasts like the golden dunes of Sporba. The curve of her neck and shoulder like the gentle Levka hills. I kissed the glossy line of her hip and thigh, like sinuous bends in the Jaszy river, where—to my surprise and confusion—I left a path of tears on her flesh.

Daylight faded, our room easing into murky darkness. Sirens and car-horns rose faintly from Park Avenue seventeen floors below. I kissed Molly awake. She stretched and yawned, a feline grin of pleasure on her face.

"OK, now I can ask," she said. "Who are you, Gabriel? What's your story?"

"Let's hear yours first."

"Fair enough. How do you do?" She rose on an elbow and shook my hand. "My name is Molly Boyle, born in Hell's Kitchen, third-generation Irish-American. Currently residing in Brooklyn Heights."

I asked what she did for a living. Later I wondered, had I been warier, a bit less sated and at peace with the world, would I have noticed the split-second pause before she answered?

"Day-trading, mostly. Market's red-hot right now. A few good trades can keep me going for weeks." She traced a forefinger leisurely across my thigh. "I try not to think beyond that."

"Married?"

"God, no." She gave me a kiss, then leaned away. "That's enough for now. What about you?"

I was smitten. I saw no need to dissemble or lie outright about anything. Given every chance to fabricate a name and profession, I chose the most dangerous option. I told the truth.

"Wow, a toss in the hay with a UN diplomat! What an honor." Molly snuggled close, burrowing, with an animal need to occupy a place for sleep. "Where is Keshnev again?"

I spoke softly, as if telling a bedtime story. "Look for Romania on a map. Head south along the Danube to the Black Sea. If you hit Bulgaria, you've gone too far."

She closed her eyes, her breathing steady. "Hmmm ..."

And just like that, as if a switch was flipped, a surge of bitterness shot through me. All that I coveted about life in New York—my profession, my status, my various and sundry indulgences—all seemed at risk. Rather than settle into sleep, I felt compelled to whisper in the dark while Molly slept.

"Imagine a lesser circle of hell, where men of many nations —nearly always men—write speeches and issue draft resolutions ad nauseum, ad infinitum. I am one of those men. Wind me up like a mechanical doll and send me off to denounce every proposal, every motion, offered by the West. And," I said softly in the gathering gloom, "I've had enough."

A peculiar speech to make after sex, but these were peculiar and perplexing times. In a sense I no longer addressed the woman asleep beside me, but rather a ghostly audience lurking in the shadows of the hotel room. *This* was the speech I should give in the Security Council Chamber, but never would.

"The facts are clear," I told the unseen audience of statesmen and dictators. "Argentina seized territory that belonged to the Crown, an act of war they should have known would blow up in their face. Sooner or later, England will reclaim the Falklands, by dint of industrial strength and the brute force of a second-tier superpower. But not before many more lives are lost."

A service cart rattling down the corridor woke Molly. She looked confused about her location and time of day, and how it was I happened to be lying in bed beside her. Then, memory and a pleasurable after-glow caused everything to snap into place.

"What's it like, working for Communists?" she asked. "I mean, you're not one of them, right? You were born in the USA."

"Schenectady, New York, in fact."

"But why represent them?"

"That's just it," I said. "I can't do it anymore." Adding, with a teasing smile, "Weren't you listening?"

Molly stretched out again, a leg over my midsection. We lay close on the silk sheets, unseen and unknown to a world of insect-people far below, walking on their insect-feet and driving their insect-cars down Park Avenue. A world thrillingly indifferent to my good fortune and all the more amazing for it. Molly's fingers brushed along my skin, in search of more of the same.

"Some Communist *you* are," she said in my ear.

Later, inside the *cordon sanitaire* of the Bentley's plush interior, I noticed Emil's rigid posture behind the wheel, a twitch of his gloved hands on the wheel. Was he worried about my latest hijinks and bound by the universal chauffeurs' oath never to ask outright? As we journeyed uptown, I saw no reason to withhold *all* information from my old friend and countryman. I took Emil through events of the day, glossing over the painful lunch with Tess, lingering instead—in spirit, if not graphic detail—on an afternoon spent in the delightful company of Molly Boyle, day-trader.

Emil listened intently throughout. "I do not know if you like work you do," he said. "*Life* you like, this I know."

Traffic at Fifty-ninth Street and Central Park West was slowed by liveried carriages, the evening air enlivened by a feisty bouquet of cotton candy and horse manure. I felt moved to remark upon the contrast between New York in springtime and the same season in Olt, the capital of our nation, where it felt like winter all year round. Industrial smog and rows of Stalinist-era concrete towers.

"Here, we're like the beautiful girl who gets whatever she wants from life. Over there, we are the ugly sister wasting away in the corner."

Emil's neck stiffened. "If SPU hears you talking, there is trouble."

"Who's going to tell them, Emil? You?"

"Never," he said, sounding offended by the very notion.

I grew quiet, reflecting on my impulses and where they took me, on the erotic topography of Molly's body and my whispered speech before an audience of ghosts.

"Sometimes," I said, "I have a hard time keeping my mouth shut."

10

PAUSE

Lately I find myself engaged in a battle of wits with a cock-roach. Unlike others of his ilk, this cockroach is bold and impertinent—call him Franz—adorned with jittery antennae and a sporty yellow racing stripe down his back. Franz waits at my feet while I gnaw at dry bread. Any fallen crumbs are quickly retrieved and transported elsewhere; soon he's back for more. I tried luring him into an empty matchbox, anticipating hours of amusement observing my double-winged friend at work and play. Franz would have none of it. Inches away from entrapment, he snatched up the last scrap of bread in his ravening mandibles and scampered off on three pairs of legs.

Even a cockroach has more freedom than me.

REC

The day after my fling at the Waldorf, I called in sick. An unsettled feeling had come over me, a wish to be rid of death threats, office intrigues, and messy geopolitics. "Stress," Vadim offered by way of diagnosis when I first called in. "This I completely understand."

It was all I could not to shout at him over the phone. Idiot! Who asked for your understanding?

My daughter's parting words still haunted me. *Fuck you, Father.* Somehow, I had to locate her whereabouts and, in the heat of battle or not, make peace with her. Her editor, when I reached him, was slow to acknowledge me as his star photographer's actual father or a UN diplomat or anything but a possibly crazed stalker. Persuaded at last as to my identity, he remained unhelpful. "Where is she? Out in the South Atlantic would be my guess. Any message in case she calls in?"

I slammed the phone down. Idiots everywhere!

Attempts to contact Molly Boyle were equally futile. When I called the number she gave me, a monotone male voice repeated back the number I'd just dialed, and then the line went dead.

Emil, at home in far-off Queens, seemed unsurprised to hear he had the day off. "You are needing from me nothing, sir?"

"Maybe tomorrow. We'll see."

By mid-afternoon I sat in an outdoor café on Columbus Circle, sipping Espresso and reading about the war in the *International Herald-Tribune*. News from the Falklands was bad. Hundreds of Argentine sailors dead after a Royal Navy torpedo sank the cruiser *General Belgrano*—this in response to Exocet missile strikes killing troops aboard *HMS Sheffield*. The military junta, anxious to expunge all trace of British colonial rule, issued directives for the newly conquered Falklanders. From now on, Spanish was the official language. Port Stanley was rechristened *Puerto Argentino*. And in a wonderfully petty snub at Queen and Country, motorists now had to drive on the right side of the islands' windswept roads.

Later, my spirits dampened by the warlike tide of human affairs, I ducked into an art-house theater on Bleecker Street in search of distraction. Fumbling to a seat in the dark, I strained to make sense of the images flitting across the screen, a surreal landscape of dancing bears and loin-clothed fire-eaters. Over this strange land a boy-king reigned, foppish and demented, nothing like the flesh-and-blood monarch I was once privileged to know.

The film did nothing to boost my morale. I took a cab to Bryant Park and walked aimlessly. Over dinner in a Lebanese restaurant in the Theater District, I watched as spring showers ambushed theater-goers emerging from a matinée performance of *Fiddler on the Roof*. The seasoned New Yorkers among them, already armed with umbrellas, nimbly hailed cabs, and made their getaway. The crowd they left behind—hefty corn-fed Midwesterners all, by the look of them—huddled under the dripping marquee like frightened pack animals.

I remembered the first time I saw King Josef—atop a white horse, in a village square—and the last time, in his Mayfair flat in '42 or '43. The doddering old soul, once a handsome monarch, lived in exile, still grieving the deaths of his Queen and Princess, killed by the Nazis. In his last days, King Josef praised the virtue of his former subjects, the peasants and farmers and shopkeepers, the land they lived and worked on. *Y glash se kelp*, the old king would tell me. *You don't own the land, the land owns you.*

Playing hooky from work on Monday had been a spontaneous act; doing the same on Tuesday felt more like a necessary thing.

Vadim left urgent phone messages, irked by my refusal to check in. *Paperwork piling up! Overseas cables demanding responses!* When I leisurely called back later in the day, I remarked that all this frenetic activity on his part presumed anyone outside of our homeland gave a rat's ass about what Keshnev had to say. This was met by stunned silence, as if I'd just branded Lenin a child-molester.

Rain fell most of the day, and the day after that, a downpour that kept me immobile by the window and sealed off from humanity. Water cascaded over the ledges of rooftop gardens and pelted the tiny heads of civilians far below. I poured my third, possibly fourth Żubrówka of the day, and tried sorting out the benefits and drawbacks of my current situation.

Luxury dwellings, a position of status and influence, easy access to the city's round-the-clock epicurean jamboree—all these must count as *pros*.

But little *cons* popped up like the heads of prairie dogs in the holes of my good fortune. A rupture with Tess on the eve of her departure for the Falklands. My Security Council speech, still unwritten. The nameless Consul, who showed up out of the blue, and through whom I felt Petrescu's hot breath on the back of my neck. What if he got fed up with my mischief? I could be recalled to Keshnev at any moment.

All *cons*.

From my last visit home, I recalled old women queuing up on the winter street for government-issued bread, while loudspeakers blared out our tin-eared national anthem. Molly's body had evoked in me a sudden fever for the old country, but the thought of a trip back, even a short one, was too depressing to think about. How could I ever manage to *live* there?

Cons, cons, cons.

Emil appeared the next morning, concerned about my reclusive well-being. When I greeted him in my bathrobe and slippers, he reminded me of our plans for lunch at Vlek, the hole-in-the-wall Keshnevite restaurant south of Houston. I tried begging off, but he wouldn't budge, clearly believing I mustn't be left on my own.

Later, on Spring Street, we found an empty space in a commercial loading zone, where NO PARKING signs sprouted like weeds. Such restrictions were, in my case, happily irrelevant. As we exited the conveniently parked Bentley, passing motorists shot us dark glances; pedestrians, too, frowned enviously at our diplomatic plates. I was unfazed. Years of servitude to a police state should entitle me to park wherever I want in Manhattan, or what was the point?

On Broadway, sunlight dispelled the last of yesterday's rain showers, and foot traffic was brisk—stockbrokers jostling with Hasidim, wild-eyed beggars curtailed by cops on horseback, street vendors peering out from the malarial fog of their hot-dog stands. Everyone seemed oblivious to the stench of days-old garbage, and to the dagger-in-the-ear *ping ping ping* of delivery trucks moving in reverse.

Inside Vlek, another world—smoky, window-less, ill-lit; old men occupied a handful of tables, indistinguishable by their white hair and rumpled suits. The honeyed tang of barbecued goat meat filled the air, mingling with the death-stink of East European tobacco. A sad mazurka played on the fifties-era jukebox.

"There." Emil pointed at a table nearby. "We can sit."

Several minutes passed. The muted silence that greeted our arrival became faintly hostile. A man in a chef's hat dropped menus in front of us and skulked away through a beaded curtain, after touching two fingers to his lips and pressing them on a tattered flag nailed to the wall—black stars against a band of gold, Keshnev's *true* flag, not seen in the old country for many generations.

"These men," Emil said, nodding at the tables around us.

"They know who you are, who you work for. I am sorry. Is my fault to come here today."

Yes, these surly fossils were the last to recall Keshnev's prewar golden days, when gentlemen in top hats and women twirling parasols strolled the boulevards of Olt, the so-called "Paris of the East." In the long decades since then—forced into exile by the very people I spoke for in the UN—they sat and drank with the hollow-eyed stare of men defeated by history.

"Never mind, Emil. What's for lunch?"

The grease-stained menu featured such exotic fare as *stuknogy*—potato stew with cheese balls—and *vesa cuche*, a meat pie spread across cabbage leaves. Around us, murmuring among the expatriates grew louder. Why have we come to Vlek? What does Petrescu's lacky want from us? The chef reappeared, poured us each a glass of *slavka*, and walked off.

I raised my glass. "*Luk se prenum.*" Our feet will walk again in King Josef's land.

Emil nodded gravely. "*Luk se prenum.*"

For the first time in years, I tasted the plum brandy of my adopted country. A sip of its jaw-numbing sweetness evoked memories of village life, the horticultural sounds and smells. By now, the low-level babble had turned to hostile chatter. It seemed our toast to the homeland had enraged the other patrons. Emil stood, glaring into darkness at our anonymous accusers.

"What is this?" he demanded. "What do you do here?"

Silence. Old, stony faces.

"We are come to eat, not for bad looks and—"

"Emil," I said.

"—mumbles at our faces!"

"Go somewhere else, then," a scratchy voice said.

Emil squinted into the shadows. "Who says this?"

"Go," said a brittle figure at a corner table, his voice hoarse with age and loathing. "No Communist *plukarsch* wanted here."

Emil stomped to the table, fists clenched, a barrel-chested strongman in a chauffeur's uniform—just the sort of evil godless thug these decrepit exiles believed us to be. I laughed. Did that old coot just call us *pig-fuckers*!

"Do you know who is this man?"

"All right, Emil—"

"Yes, ambassador for UN, sure, but when he was boy, you know what he did?" Emil looked around. "*Do you?*"

No one spoke.

"He is boy who saves King Josef."

A wave of toothless gasps swept the restaurant. Everyone knew the legend of the missionary boy who foiled an attempt on their beloved king's life; but blinded by hatred for the Gray Wolf and Petrescu, they never made the connection until now. Here was a chance to meet the legend in the flesh. The exiles struggled to their feet, one by one, wincing and grunting as if they'd been nailed to the chairs for years. They crowded our table, shaking our hands, patting us on the back.

The old crank who called us *plukarsch* seemed most shaken of all. He fell to his knees, weeping and blathering in some garbled tongue.

"... sorry, he says," Emil translated, "very sorry ..."

The aged émigré kept on, choking back tears.

"... he is one who calls UN ... leaves message someone will kill you soon ..."

I couldn't help laughing again. *This* was the death threat that so vexed Alfred Lundquist. "No matter," I said, raising my glass. The chef uncorked a fresh bottle of *slavka*, pouring all around, amid much thrombolytic laughter and shared memories of Keshnev's golden days.

"Long live King Josef!"

"One day Keshnev is ours again!"

Upon our departure, Emil and I received the traditional farewell embrace, long since banned by the Revolution. One man grips the other man's shoulder, pulls him close as if for a lover's kiss, and they touch forehead-to-forehead. We left Vlek amid cries of sadness and longing.

Inside the Bentley on the drive home, both of us were too moved to speak at first. Then Emil mentioned something one of the exiles told him, about the Ambassador's mother and father and the tragic circumstances of their deaths years ago.

"What about them?" I said. "The Nazis killed my parents, crushed them under a tank."

"Yes, but old man says—these are words I remember —'such is not case.'"

"*And?*"

"That is what I say! *And?* Old man shakes head, says, 'If I talk more, SPU puts bullet in my brain.' I cannot make him think otherwise." Emil glanced at me over his shoulder. "Ambassador, what does this mean?"

I leaned back in the Bentley's lavish interior, unwilling to relinquish the good feeling born of *slavka* and our ecstatic reception in Vlek.

"Pointless gossip," I told him. "You know how these old men like to talk."

PAUSE

An upsetting event took place yesterday.

The batteries powering the TEK-3RX failed and I had trouble extracting them from the device with my large, maladroit fingers. I heard a guard's thudding footsteps and, made slightly mad by frustration, yelled through the door, "How about some help in here?" The door swung open and

Gad stood there—thick and squat, Neanderthal in gait and profile—reeking of *slavka*.

I held out the dead batteries and asked for fresh ones. In response, Gad swung at me, weak in force and accuracy, but not from lack of trying. I flinched, the batteries fell from my hand and clattered to the floor.

"What the hell!" I shouted.

To Gad, my outrage was a source of high amusement. He staggered off laughing, a sound like small arms fire.

Today, Stefan delivers a fresh box of AA batteries.

11

REC

As it happened, the adulation of crackpot émigrés wasn't as spiritually rewarding as I'd hoped for.

Back in my apartment, I drew all the shades and drank bison grass vodka in the purgatorial light of late afternoon. Given enough Żubrówka, I could almost forget my daughter's parting curse at the Waldorf or my own waning interest in the job of chief delegate. I might even chuckle over some crazy exile's death threats.

Late in the night, the telephone rang. I lay stretched out on the sofa in old clothes, unshaven, with a painful kink in my back and alcohol-impaired night vision. The ringing telephone might have been a thousand miles away.

"Sir, are you there?" Vadim's plaintive voice rose from the answering machine. "Please, sir! Is essential we speak."

"Sure it is," I grumbled from the sofa.

"—Consul, sir, your orders of which he disrespects and, and ..."

Among Vadim's most aggravating traits was an inability to get to the point. "Spit it out!" I shouted in the dark.

"—takes residence in file-room, makes of it a home, sir. Hilda yesterday finds him washing armpits in sink. Very upsetting for her, for everyone! We wish your speedy return to make right of things."

I took a last swig of the bottle, thinking, *Who needs this crap?* News of the Consul's bold actions was very disturbing. Whatever his intentions, they were first and foremost Petrescu's intentions, too. And meanwhile, my feckless daughter steams south aboard a British warship, farther away with every passing moment.

The alcohol consumed thus far this evening proved inadequate to these challenges; more would be needed to get through the night. I stumbled barefoot across the hardwood floor to the kitchen, where a fresh bottle awaited me in the refrigerator. I had only to pull open the door and retrieve it.

No Żubrówka.

Impossible! Nothing on the shelves or cupboards or drawers. A second desperate search of the premises confirmed the unthinkable. My entire apartment was devoid of vodka, a calamity on par with the sack of Rome.

In most cities of the world, if you want specialty liquor at two a.m., you're pretty much out of luck. In *this* magnificent city, even here in my neighborhood, the all-night bodega on First Avenue had just what I wanted. Getting there, of course, meant leaving the sanctuary of my apartment against which my dulled instincts screamed, *Bad idea!* Either I headed out for reinforcements, or stayed here in the dark, defenseless against a storm of sadness and regret.

In some drunken manner I couldn't later recall, I made the journey from elevator to ground-floor lobby and out the front door without incident. On most nights, this was a quiet neighborhood, middle-of-the-night silence occasionally broken by police sirens or a burst of amplified rock music. Tonight, as I made my way on foot, the buildings and parked vehicles seemed particularly hushed and vacant. No one took note of a tall, distinguished-looking gentleman in an alpaca coat, designer pajamas, and rubber-soled plimsolls.

Inside the bodega, colorfully packaged items throbbed with life beneath the glaring fluorescence. Stacked discreetly in the back of the spirits section was a single bottle with the forest-green label, proud gold lettering Żubrówka, and stylized rendition of the creature for which it was named. I rapped on the glass partition at the checkout counter and, for the cashier's benefit, pointed out the signature blade of grass resting on the bottom of the bottle.

"See? Bison grass! All the way from Poland!"

The cashier, a heavy-lidded Black woman, looked bemused by the weirdly precise tastes of Caucasian New Yorkers. "That'll be twenty-five ninety-five." She pressed back change for a fifty through an opening in the partition, her gold-lacquered fingers perched on the edge of the bills lest they come in contact with me. I laughed. I wanted to say, *Don't you know who I am?*

The task ahead looked simple—re-enact the three-block voyage that brought me here, in reverse. But the after-hours milieu no longer seemed benign; a wire-haired terrier with a Hitler mustache lunged out of an alley on Second Avenue and narrowly missed sinking its teeth in my ankle before it ran off yipping into the night. A half-block later, I came upon a Raggedy Ann doll hanging from a noose atop a NO PARKING sign, its limbs slack, stuffing coming out of its mouth. Near my building, a rosy-cheeked *au pair* pushed a baby stroller uphill as if it was a cart of rocks—at three a.m.!—and grinned at me, exposing fangs.

The distinguished-looking gentleman made it home, but just barely, clutching the bottle for dear life.

I woke late in the morning to a punishing hangover. A locomotive roared through my head. My eyes felt like eggs cracked and sizzling in a fry pan. The telephone rang—or, from where I lay on the sofa, howled like a banshee—and Sergei's gruff voice spoke from the answering machine.

"They tell me you're out of office all week, but no one says *why*. No matter! Meet me outside the Fulton Street Hotel, one o'clock." An impatient pause. "Do you hear me, Gabriel? I won't ask twice."

A solo expedition into the larger world seemed ludicrous, but how could I refuse an old friend? I rinsed my face clean of at least one layer of execrable hangover, put on the first semi-presentable clothes I could find and left the apartment; a curt wave to Javier at the front door, then strolling briskly and hailing a cab on Third Avenue. As I was climbing in, a man in a black tracksuit jogged past, something familiar in his haughty bearing and dust-colored buzz-cut. The jogger slipped a hood over his head and loped out of view.

Pearson?

"Hey!" the cabbie cried. "You comin' or not?"

On the drive downtown, I recalled an evening with Sergei Litvinov twenty years ago, early in our friendship. We had a shared antipathy towards authority figures, and often indulged in less-than-worshipful talk about our respective bosses. I bemoaned Keshnev Foreign Ministry idiocy, while he mocked the fat cat *nomenklatura* living outside Moscow in fancy dachas. In 1960, when Nikita Khrushchev came to town to address the UN, Sergei and I elected to watch the proceedings not in the

General Assembly where we belonged, but on bar-stools in a blue-collar bar off Delancey Street. On the cracked screen of a black-and-white TV, the First Secretary of the Communist Party of the Soviet Union waved a ham-sized fist, working himself into a froth over "imperialist stooges and their genocidal policies." In case anyone missed the point, Khrushchev banged his fist on the podium, shouting, "We will bury you!" Sergei, riding high on his fifth or sixth Stoli, smacked his own fist on the hardwood counter, crying out, "We will bury you!" in a pitch-perfect impression. The bar's clientele was great amused by his antics, and I doubt I've laughed so hard at anything since.

The weather had lifted, clear skies over South Street Seaport. Vast numbers of tourists on and off the boardwalk, cramming into gift shops and maritime museums, threatened to undo my re-entry into society, as did the unwelcome smells of raw fish and salt-water taffy. I turned to flee.

"*Boizhe moi!*" a voice rang out behind me. "You look terrible!"

Whereas *he*, Sergei Litvinov—in white pants, navy-blue blazer, and Bahama loafers—was fitted out like a Connecticut yachtsman.

"Beluga caviar," he said, explaining his mission here. "My wife wants only the best, which she says comes from this fish market and nowhere else. Obtaining the delicacy is now my task since no one else in the household can be trusted to do it. Not the maid or the doorman, certainly not—and here I agree with her—our moronic teenage son. Just me."

We joined the crowd of sightseers on Schermerhorn Row, tourists breaking off for video game arcades or fish-and-chips shops. Sergei's booming voice felt like SWAT team stun grenades going off inside my head.

"These days, all I hear is, what's happened to Ambassador

Ash? Has he been kidnapped? Taken into police custody? Where oh where is Ambassador Ash?"

"And yet," I said miserably, "it took all of one phone call to find me."

"*Da,*" he said, eyeing my disheveled attire. "Just in time."

We walked on, the hobo and weekend commodore, in what otherwise might have been companionable silence. Today, weighed down by Sergei's displeasure and my own self-loathing, it was a brave front I couldn't maintain. I came to a sudden halt outside the Fish Market, repulsed by the slime under my shoes, the stench of fish guts and sawdust, and the cries of the men inside the market hawking their wares.

Flounder! Cod! Halibut!

Sergei, at last noticing the depths of my torment, guided me to a park bench. "Tell me what troubles you. The caviar can wait."

Gulls flocked above our heads in cartwheeling disarray. A gaggle of schoolgirls in ballet outfits cavorted on the gangway of the sailing ship *Peking*, moored at Pier 16.

"I have a daughter who hates me," I told him "A man sent by Petrescu is camped out in my office. And a woman ..." No, better leave Molly Boyle out of this. "Next week I'm giving a speech in the Council chamber except, so far, there *is* no speech. And I have reason to think Mark Pearson is following me."

"Who?"

"Your CIA man, Sergei. Remember? We had lunch with him in the Delegates Lounge."

His face took on a pale, fish-colored hue. "I don't recall saying such a thing."

"On the plus side—that death threat we got all worked up about? Turns out, just empty talk from some windbag expatriate in Flatbush."

We fell into silence, watching the ballet girls romp aboard *Peking*. Sergei turned to me.

"What is it you want, Gabriel?"

"Yesterday, I thought it might be time to go back to Keshnev. Can you imagine?"

"That was yesterday, my friend. Today you see things differently? How much have you been drinking?"

"Not enough."

A rubber ball bounced down the path and rolled under our bench. A little girl in a pink tutu and grass-stained slippers chased after it. Seeing us, she pulled up short. Sergei smiled at her—in a child's eyes, surely, the wrinkled face of an elephant without a trunk.

"What is it, little *dushka*? Did your ball go missing?"

She pointed at a patch of scraggly grass. "There."

"Yes? Let's see."

Sergei reached under the bench and, with his free hand, rummaged inside a coat pocket; like a vaudeville magician, he produced both the ball and an after-dinner mint wrapped in shiny foil.

"Here, *dushka*," he said in a voice thick with emotion. "And something extra, too."

The ballerina snatched the rubber ball and after-dinner mint in one hungry swoop. "Thank you!" she cried, running off. I looked at my old friend, surprised by the sorrow in his eyes.

"A daughter is special," he said. "Do you know what my idiot son wants? He wants to be a TV game show host! You're lucky, Gabriel, whether you know it or not. Whether your *daughter* knows it or not."

A woman strolled by with a Dachshund on a leash and a red balloon tethered to the dog's collar, trailing in the air behind him.

"These things you mention," Sergei said. "Let me look into them. In the meantime, can you do one thing for me?"

"Just one?"

"Stay out of trouble," he said. "This is all I ask. Can you do that?"

"Sure." I genuinely believed I could. "Listen, I really appreciate you calling and getting me out of my—"

"Stop! Another minute more and you'll have me bawling big fat Russian tears." He stood from the bench, smoothing the pleats of his yachtsman's trousers. "Come, let's buy some goddamn caviar."

In those days I could sink into despair yet somehow rouse myself after a good night's sleep. I woke Monday morning feeling refreshed, cleansed of existential despair. I showered and shaved, put on a charcoal-gray flannel suit with a white oxford shirt, cranberry-red silk tie, and mother-of-pearl cufflinks. Ready to take on the world.

Javier greeted me in the lobby, holding open the door and saluting with a tip of his visor cap. "*Buenas días, Embajador.*" Outside, a spring breeze whipped the canvas awning that extended to the street. As always, the gunmetal Bentley idled at the curb; as always, Emil stood patiently beside the open rear door.

Routine is good, I thought. A lot can be said for routine.

We spoke little on the drive downtown, neither of us referring to what I already thought of as my "lost week." At Forty-third Street and Second Avenue, I instructed Emil to pull over.

"A nice day. I'll walk from here."

In Ralph Bunche Park, I felt a quickening of my pulse, a lift in spirits, much as I did many years ago when approaching the UN complex for the first time. A curving staircase led downhill from Tudor City Place to First Avenue. Midway down stood the Isaiah Wall, with wording engraved in granite and soaring with biblical eloquence—yet all in all, dead wrong about the human condition:

> THEY SHALL BEAT THEIR SWORDS INTO
> PLOUGHSHARES. AND THEIR SPEARS INTO
> PRUNING HOOKS. NATION SHALL NOT
> LIFT UP SWORD AGAINST NATION. NEITHER
> SHALL THEY LEARN WAR ANY MORE.

Uplifting sentiments for a young, idealistic diplomat newly transplanted here from the heart of East European darkness. Behold the looming steel-and-glass behemoth by the river, a world body conceived out of the ashes of war. A shining light, a beacon of hope, the Parliament of Man.

I had no idea what I was walking into.

12

PAUSE

Time is fuzzy here. One day dribbles into the next like water in a lazy mountain stream. Some days I sit at the table for hours, waiting for Stefan or Anca to appear. On other days, they seem to come and go every ten minutes.

In these dire times, *A Stranger's Welcome to Keshnev* offers a measure of relief:

Everywhere in Keshnev there
Is total freedom to speak. OK,
Old joke says, but not too loud!

Franz visits often, lighting up the place with his quivering antennae and dash of yellow streaking his forewings. Having cleared the territory of rivals, Franz acts as though I, and these rooms I inhabit, belong solely to him. He waits at my feet for long stretches, tiny compound eyes gazing upward lest any crumbs fall his way. When they do, his puckish mandibles grab all they can hold, and he zips off through a tiny hole in the wall.

A clear-cut, food-for-companionship deal. I prefer to think of it as *friendship*.

There's solace as well in memories of a cliff-top villa in Corfu, where Eva and I honeymooned soon after our perfidious wedding day. In my rose-colored memories, Eva lounges poolside in a whisper of a bikini, while I occupy a deck chair and muscle my way through *Crime and Punishment*. When she removes her bikini top, exposing tanned and lightly scented breasts, all thoughts of Russian winters and ax-wielding murderers flee my brain. We fall into each other's arms, shiny new husband-and-wife, each of us ignorant of the miseries ahead.

Corfu! Who would think to look for me there?

Perfect for asylum, for falling off the map. The money needed to underwrite this escape plan resides in a Credit Suisse numbered account in Zurich. Years ago, at a drunken state dinner, the Minister of Finance divulged to me the existence of a secret repository of "surplus" government funds. I remember the password he shared in his cups, an acronym combining letters from our national motto—*Lep y Topkis*, "Power for One, Good for Many"— with lyrics from a folk song about Helga the Pure, a legendary Keshnevite warrior-queen. Armed with this information, all I must do is get out of the castle, bluff my way across the border into Bulgaria, and make my way to Switzerland. Claim the secret funds, then vanish forever into the island-rich Mediterranean.

Is it wise to openly announce my intentions to escape, while in REC mode? These days, I feel cast aside by the Gentlemen of the Tribunal. Weeks have passed since my arrest and confinement; a mountain of pre-recorded cassette-tapes sits on the shelf, hours and hours of my testimony, and no sign anyone's coming by to collect and transcribe them anytime soon.

Sleep is erratic. There are long stretches of open-eyed limbo or, conversely, I sleep like the dead. I have dreams of men in death's-head masks screaming at me in the Security Council chamber. These days I dread the prospect of bedtime; too little sleep is unhealthy, too much conjures up demons I'd just as soon forget.

Facing the cracked bathroom mirror this morning, how different I look! Gray has gained traction in my scraggly black hair. I can see my noble profile fading, the patrician nose and strong blue eyes, all drifting away. Women in New York often said I looked ten years younger, a man in his mid-forties. I ate well, exercised when I could, was vain enough to care about what others thought. What good is any of that now?

Restricted movements, prolonged confinement. Add to this, sporadic fears for my life. All very stressful, and injurious to my good looks.

In Keshnev visitors are greeted
with our hands wide open. Look!
No dagger inside coat. We smile
a lot and so will you.

REC

For someone who'd been out of office for a week, I expected more fuss would be made upon my return. Vadim was mired in a phone-call and Hilda typed as fervently as always. At least the Consul wasn't around, but I couldn't ignore the little shantytown he'd made for himself in the file-room—rusty hotplate, pockmarked transistor radio, dirty socks and underwear heaped in a pile.

Considerable paperwork had accrued in my absence. I attacked the correspondence with untypical zeal, no bureaucratic matter too trivial to attend to. I even jotted down notes for my speech—words clinging to the Party line, but imbued, I hoped, with a subversive charm. All this effort took up most of the morning and I was glad for the distraction.

At noon, a commotion outside my office drew me away. Phones were ringing, Hilda fielding calls with a look of mounting panic. Vadim hurried towards me, a rolled-up magazine in his hand.

"Sir ..."

"What's going on?"

He held out the publication, as if presenting a severed body part. "*This.*"

Not really a magazine, more of an oversized tabloid under the banner *Best Served Cold*, a self-described "counterculture rag," printed in the East Village. I dimly recalled turning down the tabloid's interview request weeks ago.

Per Vadim's instructions, I opened to the center page. Amid a jumble of photographs and strident left-wing headlines, one banner stood out:

FOLLY IN THE FALKLANDS
One Diplomat's Shocking True Confessions

The caption beneath a square-inch photo identified the author of the article as "Molly Carmichael." But it was Molly Boyle's fair-skinned Celtic beauty greeting me on the page. Dread trickled down my spine like drops of cold water.

"Sir ...?"

I looked up at my executive assistant. Suddenly I saw

myself through his eyes—a moody, brutish employer forever skirting the limits of acceptable conduct. I didn't like what I saw.

"Get her," I said.

"Sir?"

"Get *this woman* on the phone."

In my office I scanned the article again—columns of ink strewn across the page, an unflattering photograph of Gabriel Ash in formal dress having a grand old time at some public gathering. Keshnev's chief delegate was described as "polished and articulate," "a diplomat's diplomat" who served "one of the planet's most oppressive regimes."

What followed was a dismal rehash of past crimes and misdemeanors, not all of them inaccurate. Street-corner disputes with NYC meter maids. A rumored association with an elite uptown escort service. The strong suggestion that I'd funneled money from my home government to support a lavish lifestyle in the city. The article stated I'd had an affair years ago with the wife of the president of the International Monetary Fund, when *in fact* it was a World Bank vice-president's wife, on the brink of divorce when I entered the picture. Also, it claimed I lost twenty thousand dollars in a single afternoon's betting at Belmont Park, when *in fact* the amount was closer to ten grand, and I was acting as proxy for a higher-up in Gracie Mansion who couldn't be seen laying bets at the parimutuel window.

The phone rang on my desk, Hilda announcing *this woman* was on the line.

"Nice of you to take my call," I said.

"You're upset," a liltingly familiar voice said. "I understand."

"Upset? Because you're not who you said you were? I'll get

over it, Miss Carmichael, Miss Boyle—what name do you go by these days?"

"Let's stick with Molly," she said. "You know, there is an upside to this."

I laughed, out of sheer bewilderment.

"All the speeches and politics, that UN bullshit you guys do? No one cares about that. But when you get in trouble for shooting your mouth off, readers can relate. It's what Americans do. Getting in trouble makes you one of us."

"*That's* the upside?"

"That's what makes it fun."

"I'll sue your goddamn tabloid," I told her, "And you, while I'm at it."

"Last time I checked we had three hundred bucks in the coffers. There's a Treasury bond or two somewhere, you're welcome to them."

"Molly," I said softly, so as not to shout. "Meet me for a drink. Let's talk this out."

A pause, fraught with unknowable meaning.

"We're all adults here," she said. "We had a good time at the Waldorf, I know *I* did. But no one forced you to say or do anything."

"One drink, OK?"

"Sorry, Gabriel. Not a good idea."

Click. The handset nestling in my grip like a small woodland creature seemed indifferent to my fate. I told hold of the cord, yanked it out of the wall-socket, and flung the phone at the far wall. Its plastic casing shattered on impact.

In the outer office, all sounds ceased. Would someone come to investigate? Minutes passed; no one did.

According to *Best Served Cold*, the quotes in this piece were taken verbatim from a chance encounter with the reporter at the

Metropolitan Opera House—where, "for reasons of his own, UN delegate Gabriel Ash freely shared his scandalous views on world affairs." Yes, the sentiments expressed sounded like things I might say, or perhaps already did in the darkness of a hotel room. Here, on the printed page, the words looked very bad.

On the Security Council: "A lesser circle of hell is reserved for men like these, who knowingly mistake words for actions. In our esteemed international organization, nothing happens quickly. Entire species have gone extinct in the time it takes Council members to finish a thought."

On Argentina's invasion of the Falklands: "England has every right to avenge her honor, with all the warships and jet fighters she can muster. *Argentina?* When soldiers dressed up like Hollywood extras tramp in and occupy any country they want, there will be a thousand Falklands to come."

On Cold War relations between East and West: "Empty sword-rattling may buy us some time, but for how long? Which superpower will blink first? The men we call 'leaders' are more like children squabbling over toys on the playground. Except *they* come armed with thermonuclear weapons."

I put down the tabloid, a parade of dire consequences marching through my head. First, I must make a strongly worded denial to the press. I should also expect a sharp rap on the knuckles from the Foreign Ministry. Other scenarios involving Minister Petrescu and assorted gadgets of torture were too awful to contemplate.

A knock at the door. The accursed Consul peered inside.

"We hear noise, Comrade Ambassador. Is trouble in here?"

I gestured at the wreckage in the corner. "Phone's not working."

Vadim appeared, squeezing past the Consul, and flinching at their incidental contact. "Sir, I—"

"Vadim, please inform our guest he can relax his surveillance. Tell him to take the afternoon off."

The Consul's dark eyes flickered, a snake sighting its prey. Vadim, on the other hand, looked drained of blood.

"Sir, another overseas call from Foreign Ministry, of extreme importance."

Could they have already heard about the article? Bad news rarely penetrated the Ministry's fortress-like walls back in the old country. Still, this was a summons I should heed.

"Tell them I'm busy."

"Sir?"

"*Go.*"

The Consul remained poised in the doorway. Standing by my desk, I reflected on the consequences of poor decision-making, on women as instruments of betrayal and disgrace. I thought about the yawning gap, big as a fjord, between the words I expressed on behalf of my government and what I truly believed.

The Consul's lips twitched in a feeble semblance of a smile. Then, having made his point or simply lost interest, he left. The air itself felt unhinged by his recent presence.

That's what makes it fun.

PAUSE

Voices wake me late at night—cursing, laughing, braying like mules. Men are drinking *slavka* around an oil-drum fire in the courtyard below.

The damp night air sparks memories of spring showers in New York, long-legged office workers squealing as they run for cover. Emil spent many lunch hours watching these beautiful professional women stride down Wall Street in their short skirts and heels, sunglasses perched on their flawless noses. It was something we shared, Emil and I, a love of women caught in the wind-tunnels of Lower Manhattan—swept along, as it were, into our waiting arms.

Footsteps thudding up the tower steps interrupt my thoughts. A key fumbles in the lock, then falls on the landing, accompanied by loud profanities. I inch my chair away from the door. Why would anyone come visiting at this time of night?

At last, a key works and the door opens. Gad lurches in, fat and sloppy, reeking of *slavka* and day-old vomit. He plops into the empty kitchen chair and points a grubby finger at me.

"They talk to you," he says, slurring his words. "They come here, tell stories."

"Who?"

"Guards. Caretakers. Everybody. They talk, you listen."

Something's agitating him. He tugs at his tunic, as if in desperate need of oxygen. Slowly I stand from the table, doing my best impersonation of a calm individual seeking a safe corner. The kitchen has suddenly become very small.

"I'm here for you, too," I tell him. "Didn't we once share a bowl of *furcersie* like great old comrades?"

He pulls on his tunic, runs a paw through his bristly hair. "I am border guard up north, OK? One day, wife of farmer walks to me in field—not so beautiful, but still, a woman. We go for stroll. Big sun, no clouds in sky, easy for clothes to come off.

We make *yaki-yaki* in field, OK?" Pump-thrusting a fist in the air, in case I miss his meaning. "Farmer hears about wife, comes for me. We argue. Then we fight."

Gad's crooked teeth grind every word coming out of his spit-riddled mouth. I find his need to confide in me very disturbing.

"Yes, well, things happen," I tell him. "Marriage can be hard for any—"

"I beat farmer dead. No more living. Forever."

I freeze. The kitchen, the tower, the castle—for all I know, the entire spinning planet—go still.

"For this thing, they punish me," Gad says. "What I did they say is wrong. To kill a man is wrong."

Great heaving sobs erupt from his chest—pent-up sadness or, less likely, remorse for his deeds. I watch in horror as his face collapses in on itself, bushy eyebrows rendezvousing with scalp-line, nose and mouth squeezed together like the bellows of an accordion.

"What for am I put here in castle? I am not castle guard, I am border guard! Is all I know!"

"All right," I say, as if to a wounded animal. "It's not as bad as that."

"One thing keeps me here, not at border where I belong." Again, the sausage-thick finger is raised and pointing. "*You.*"

"What? No, no. You'll be sent home soon, I'm sure."

Gad shifts his haunches and lets out an enormous fart. This seems to propel him towards a decision. "If you are gone from castle, where is reason for me to stay? No reason! They must send me back to border."

He staggers to his feet, takes a gun from his holster—an antique revolver, with a short barrel and grip—and drunkenly aims the barrel at my chest.

"Down," he says, with frightening composure. "On knees."

I'm more insulted than alarmed. "Hey, let's not get—"

"*Down.*"

Fear kicks in, slowing my blood like a dulling narcotic. The journey I'm ordered to take—from the chair to the floor, from sitting to kneeling—lasts for eons.

"Did I offend you somehow? If I did, I'm sorry."

"Gone," he says, the gun wobbly in his hand. "No more you."

Is this where your life flashes before your eyes? All I see in my last seconds are the faces of people I've wronged, living and dead. Gad steps closer, enfolding me in his barnyard smell. I close my eyes. Any protest I might hope to make is lodged in my throat.

"Gone."

There's a sharp *click!*, and the echo of an empty chamber. Gad laughs, his mouth issuing pig-like grunts. I look up. I'm not dead.

"Well," I say weakly. "You got me."

But the madman isn't finished—another step in, the gun-hand steady now, the muzzle placed against my forehead— cold steel on flesh, a precisely localized sensation.

"*Gone,*" he whispers, and pulls the trigger again.

Click click click.

Each time I await my own messy death, a supernova of exploding bone and brain matter. Nothing happens. There's only Gad's psychotic, never-ending pig-laugh.

No more!

Rising to my feet, I charge him. Sheer momentum on impact propels the guard against the far wall. The back of his head strikes stone, a vile sound, enough to knock any mortal senseless. Gad merely stands there, blinking in surprise and rubbing a sore spot on his head. Dazed with rage and adrena-lin, I fail to notice the sudden descent of a gun-butt in his hand. When it strikes my left temple, pain of withering intensity drops me on the floor with a deadweight *thud*.

Splayed out at ground-level, I detect scuttling motion in the corner of the kitchen. Franz has emerged from his lair to see what all the fuss is about. Spotting me, his trusty meal-ticket, Franz sets forth on a collision course with Gad's tree-trunk legs. I choke out a warning, but it's too late. Gad lifts a mud-streaked boot and squashes my bold arthropod friend.

Tears flood my eyes—for a cockroach! Then I pass out.

13

REW

I remember the moment I looked at my brother lying in a hospital bed—thin, pale, a scarecrow version of his eight-year-old self—and realized, with sickening clarity, it could have been me.

Treatment of tuberculosis wasn't especially advanced in the 1930s. Our search for care took us from the scrublands of Arizona to Narragansett's sea-salty air. Doctors poked and prodded Willy, offered cryptic diagnoses and quirky cures. This quest was subsidized by our fellow parishioners in the Mission Church of the Nazarene, but after months of fruitless travel, our resources were nearly exhausted. Enough funds remained to pay for Willy's care at a sanitorium in upstate New York, run by a renowned TB specialist who sometimes took on "hardship cases" like ours.

I was the older, and presumably wiser brother, but on these journeys, I felt neglected, punished as it were for my own good health. Willy's suffering, at such a young age, undercut my parents' notions of a merciful god. For a budding twelve-year-old philosopher, the loopholes in theology looked big enough to drive a truck through.

Given the circumstances, I kept these feelings to myself.

Two months into Willy's stay, we visited him at his "cure cottage," a ground-floor room in a boarding house just beyond the clinic's perimeter. It had none of the amenities of the cottages on the sanitarium grounds, where the wealthy patients lived.

Recent rainstorms had brought unseasonably cold, damp weather to the region, forcing a cancellation of our plans for an outdoor family picnic. Instead, Mother, Father and I sat outside on deck chairs, our backs to the Adirondack Mountains, while Willy stayed in his room, separated from us by a sliding glass-door and a thick mesh screen.

Things felt awkward and stressful, given the bad weather, abandoned picnic and Willy's endless struggle with disease. Mother, a raw-boned woman in a plain summer dress, traced her finger on the pages of the Bible in her lap.

"'Behold, I will bring health and care and I will cure them, and will reveal unto them the abundance of peace and truth.' Jeremiah: 33:6."

Father in his over-eager way kept trying to amuse us with bad jokes and goofy faces. Red suspenders and flannel trousers filled out his act, as did the straw boater atop his head. A large man, he spoke much softer than you'd expect, and the handshake he offered strangers felt limp, so as not to cause harm. In twenty-odd hard years as a traveling shoe salesman, these traits had endeared him to some, moved others to bully and betray him. When he finally had enough of accommodating strangers' feet, he found solace in the Mission Church of the Nazarene in Schenectady, New York. Julia Cummings was already a congregant there—his future wife, my future mother—a thin, nervous woman who'd fled the Dust Bowl for the spiritual comfort in the Nazarene Christ.

Memories of my mother and father as entities apart from one another are few; they were always together, bound as witnesses to God's work and by the terrible scourge affecting their youngest son.

On the other side of the mesh screen, Willy reclined in a second-hand chaise lounge. A frayed tartar blanket covered his legs and feet. Scattered around him were the detritus of convalescence—mentholated cough drops, half-eaten Vanilla wafers, a flotilla of Kleenex boxes, two dog-eared paperbacks in Edgar Rice Burroughs' *Red Planet Saga*. Ever the informative host, Willy described for us the simple idea behind the clinic's famous "wilderness cure"—prolonged exposure to upstate New York's crisp mountain air, eight or more hours a day resting by the shores of Saranac Lake or in day-beds on the clinic grounds. Patients rich and poor followed this open-air policy, taking the cure regardless of the weather.

"'And the prayer of faith will save the one who is sick, and the Lord will raise him up.'" Mother gazed at Willy, her beloved, the most innocent of lambs. "And if they have committed sins, they shall be forgiven.' James 5:15."

From elsewhere in the boarding house, FDR's high-pitched voice wafted over a wireless radio, exhorting Americans to fear nothing but fear itself. Suddenly I felt flooded with pity, a foreign emotion in my self-absorbed youth. What sins could Willy have committed to end up here? Each day I despised my faith a little bit more.

"I want to go to the lake," my brother announced.

Father leaned close to the mesh, pretending he hadn't heard. "What was that?"

"I want to see the lake. It's two months already I've been

here and nobody lets me. Nurse Bishop says I can go if I get permission first."

Any activity requiring more exertion on Willy's part was cause for concern. "Soon," Mother assured him. "You need to be good and strong for that."

"I am!"

Of course, the ravaging disease had left its mark—this eight-year-old boy weighed half of what he should—but today, wearing freshly laundered pajamas and a red scarf tied around his neck, Willy looked as healthy as I'd seen him in a long time. The nurse had trimmed and combed his straw-yellow hair, and there was color in his cheeks. Not a demanding boy by nature, Willy startled us with his insistence.

"Really, it's OK—lots of patients go!" He paused. "Gabe could take me."

Mother swiped nervously at her graying hair, which retained the whirl and madness of Okie dust storms.

"It gets pretty cold down there this time of year," Father said. "Wind comes hard off the water. A fellow could get a chill."

"So what? I'm not going to fall in."

"But what if you did, pal?" That was Father, the gentle giant, making a joke of things. "I bet your doctor wouldn't care for that."

Late-afternoon shadows crept into my brother's little room, obscuring the bed, night-stand and mess on the floor. On the wall was a sepia portrait of the founder, a stern-looking man with a high-domed brow and mutton chop whiskers.

"Look how much better I am!" He waved both arms like a stranded explorer hailing rescue planes in the sky. "Look! I can even—"

A coughing fit erupted—long, ragged, hacking sounds that caused Willy to double over in the chaise lounge. We watched the panicked intake of breath, the attempts to suck at whatever air his consumptive lungs could handle. I turned away, gazing at the wet spruce and cloud-covered Adirondacks in the distance. I was just beginning to grasp the dimensions of his world, the endless days of boredom, the all-encompassing restrictions, the weakness, and affliction. *It could have been me.*

The coughing stopped. Willy breathed steadily again, as if by sheer force of will, and soon all trace of the wracking cough gone. He sat up with a shaky smile, pressing his small white hands on the mesh screen between us.

"See? I'm better."

Father grinned broadly. Mother wiped tears from her eyes. It did seem like something of a miracle.

"'And heal the sick that are therein,'" Mother said, "'and say unto them, the Kingdom of God is come nigh upon you.' Luke 10:19."

"Amen," Father and Willy said in unison.

A paternal hand nudged my shoulder. "Amen," I said.

The day's last burst of sunlight broke through the clouds. Patients emerged from their cabins in white robes and slippers, a pageant of ghosts across the wet open ground.

Two evenings later, buoyed by Willy's improved condition, my parents took a rare night off to visit cousins in Saratoga Springs. Within minutes of their departure, the cook's daughter hired to watch us asked if I thought I was "old enough" to tend to my brother for a few hours. The Saranac Lake Festival was happening in town, and she and her gangly boyfriend just *had* to go. "Sure," I said, offended by the question.

Now Willy and I sat on the boarding-house stoop, free of mesh screens and other protective measures, quietly violating clinic rules. Moths beat papery wings against the porch-light.

From inside the boarding-house came a jaunty refrain, "Puttin' on the Ritz."

"You have to take me," he said.

"What? Where?"

"Ernie says there's a canoe tied up to the jetty. We can take it if we want."

"Who's Ernie?"

"The gardener," Willy said impatiently. "No one uses it. It's OK if we do."

True, my brother in his robe and striped pajamas didn't look bad at all. What was wrong with taking a quick spin on the lake and getting him back, unnoticed?

Willy, keenly intuitive even in poor health, sensed my imminent surrender. "OK, Gabe? Can we go?"

In my memory we raced downhill to the lake in no time. First, though, I bundled him in a watch cap, two layers of sweaters and a thick winter coat; then we crept to the woods like jail-breakers. Armed with a kerosene lamp, I led the way, tiptoeing past half-lit cabins from which arose disembodied wheezing and panting sounds. I remember the smell of pine needles crushed under our feet, stars dappling the night sky, creatures of darkness rustling in the trees. Willy stopped to catch his breath, but raw excitement pressed him on.

The trees parted. The light of a quarter-moon skimmed over waves in the lake, their ebb and flow making a *shhhh* in the darkness. I watched my brother rush happily to the shore-line and thought my parents wrong to limit his activity. The wilderness cure was working, you could see it for yourself. A few minutes on Saranac Lake wouldn't hurt, and I'd do all the paddling.

"No! No, no, no!"

Willy stood at the end of a jetty, ten or twelve feet out from shore. I saw no canoe, no water vessel of any kind, tied up there. I ran over to him. Tears streaked his face.

"Ernie said it would *be* here—!"

Another coughing fit came over him, worse than before, twisting his delicate frame like a corkscrew. He tried covering his mouth but couldn't hold back the murky yellow sputum coughed up by his lungs, spilling over his mittens and boots. This time, willpower alone didn't bring these spasms to a halt. The coughing fit ran its course until finally he breathed regularly again. Snippets of froth hung from his lips.

I felt somehow betrayed. "You said you were getting better."

"I *was*," Willy said.

We stood on the jetty, my brother and me. A breeze off the lake set bulrushes murmuring and a loon cried out, very clear and somewhere close by.

"Gabe, I don't want to live here anymore."

"What do you mean? The boarding-house looks nice."

"I'm sick of it," he said. "The clinics and doctors—all the rules! All the fresh air I breathe, I should be better. But I'm not!"

I touched his shoulder in what I hoped was a brotherly way, lacking any other response. It seemed to calm him. He stared at the water beneath the jetty.

"It's late," I said. "Let's go back."

He stifled a cough. "Yeah, OK."

The planks of the jetty creaked underfoot as I walked the short distance back to land. If we were quick about it, I could get him back to his room and into bed before my parents returned. I stepped on shore just as a white-winged heron shot out of the bulrushes and glided across Saranac Lake.

There was a splash behind me. I turned. The place on the

jetty where my brother just stood was empty. Circles rippled across the dark water.

"Willy!"

What happened next has, over time, assumed dreamlike qualities—biting cold water in my nose and mouth as I forced myself down, a sliver of moonlight illuminating my brother's slow descent. Grabbing his shoulder and then his waterlogged torso, I pushed upward, my chest ready to burst. When we surfaced, Willy's head bobbed out of the water, his hair soaked and dripping, a smile on his face until he realized he wasn't dead.

I got him to shore and led him back through the woods and into the boarding house. The cook's daughter—fearing for herself as much as for her two charges—agreed to stay quiet about our forbidden excursion. She washed and dried our clothes, drew a hot bath for Willy and, after settling him in bed with warm pajamas over his trembling frame, ran off into the night. Willy clutched my wrist and pulled me close.

"Promise," he whispered. "Promise you won't tell."

A month later, only days before Willy's death from a pulmonary artery infection, the founder of the clinic paid a visit, drawn by professional curiosity to observe the effects of a particularly virulent strain of TB on young William Ash. The old man thumped his knuckles on my poor brother's chest and shook his head in defeat.

After that, only flashes of memories—the small pine coffin, the orchids' sweetly nauseating smell, Mother's frenzied grief, Father's permanently startled expression. I felt too guilt-ridden to join in mourning, as if by my actions that night, I'd forfeited the right to grieve. All I had to honor Willy was the promise I made, keeping the one great secret of his cruelly abbreviated life.

14

PAUSE

Opening my eyes unleashes searing pain, like a box-cutter blade drawn across the ridge of my skull. Even sitting upright is too great a hurdle to overcome. I'm seized by a terrible chill, my limbs contracting beneath the sole tattered blanket in my possession. Adrift in the ocean, rocked by waves of fever and nausea.

I am alone here.

REC

Days passed in the full glare of the public eye. Tales of my misconduct jumped from *Best Served Cold* to the pages of *The Village Voice*, and into the *Times* Metro Section ("East Bloc Envoy Fumes at Toeing Party Line"). A legion of readers and columnists took turns raking me over the coals. "Guilty of mind-boggling hypocrisy," one reader wrote. "Spawn of the Communist devil," wrote another. "American? Keshnevite? Either way, call him *traitor*."

I hunkered down, taking no calls, declining all requests for interviews. Beyond a statement I had Vadim issue to the press —"The People's Democratic Republic condemns this gross intrusion into the chief delegate's private affairs"—nothing came from my office. Nor did I respond to a blizzard of Foreign Ministry calls and telexes. How could I make those simpletons understand the context behind my published remarks? It seemed a hopeless task.

Oddly enough, the Consul proved the most sympathetic to my plight, arranging his face in a facsimile of concern. Vadim and Hilda acted like parents flummoxed by their problem child's behavior. Among my so-called friends and colleagues, reactions were equally distressing—glances averted, whispers chasing me down the corridor. To some, I was a source of amusement, to others disdain. But all despised me for the infamy I'd brought down on their profession. This led, as in Amish country, to a general shunning.

Several days after the event, in mid-morning, I felt in need of a drink. I slipped from the office and headed for the Delegates Lounge. Translators, advisors and technical experts hurried by in the crowded hallway, as if even fleeting contact might prove harmful. A European Union official in a pinstripe suit actually *pointed* at me. Steady on, I told myself. One drink and I'll be fine.

It wasn't meant to happen.

A portly middle-aged man blocked the entrance to the Lounge—Gunter Kleist, a West German cultural attaché about whom I happened to know a dark secret. The woman standing beside him was Francesca Cavour, wearing a sleek black jacket and chambray pencil skirt. The contrast between her sharp-featured Sicilian beauty and Gunter Kleist's pale Nordic complexion was striking.

"*Mi amor!*" she cried. "It has been too long!"

In her forties now, slender and youthful-looking, her dark hair shortened and flecked with gray. I recalled our urgent trysts in shadowy UN antechambers during our affair three years ago—but also, near the end, a sunny outdoor buffet on the Eleanor Roosevelt Lawn when she snatched a knife from the carving station and hurled it at me.

"It's not possible," I said. "You're more stunning than ever."

Francesca smiled demurely. "It is my curse."

Gunter Kleist began circling me, a big fat grin on his big fat face. After serving together over the years on General Assembly subcommittees, we'd developed a healthy dislike for each other. He'd taunt me about Keshnev's backward ways, I suggested turning Auschwitz into a theme park. The predicament in which I now found myself—a victim of self-inflicted wounds, harried by the gutter press—was, for him, too delicious to ignore.

"How famous you are, *Herr* Ash. Newspapers, television, radio—such *tumult*! For a person of high standing like yourself, the public scrutiny must be—" He worked himself into giggles over this. "—*intolerable*."

Representatives of nations, friendly and hostile alike, passed us, intent on queuing up for lunch. Worse than the notoriety caused by my published remarks was the idea that a mediocre hack like Gunter Kleist now deemed himself superior to me.

One glass of Żubrówka, I told myself, and all will be well.

"Everyone makes mistakes," I said, smiling not at him, but into the eyes of my ex-lover. "Some of us more than others."

"What do they say in your Foreign Ministry, *Herr* Ash? Did they know your true feelings about the British and the war before or after reading the papers? Don't tell me they're *gemütlich* with the news." Bubbles of peptic mirth seeped between his lips. "Nobody looks to Minister Petrescu for a sense of humor."

"Not like you rollicking Huns," I said.

But the detestable little man was right. Petrescu, unburdened by notions of a free press, could never grasp what was happening in New York—only that, by my actions, Keshnev once again looked foolish in the eyes of the world. In some Warsaw Pact countries, offenders were imprisoned for blunders like this; in my adopted homeland, you could be executed for far less.

Francesca watched me, knowing I don't suffer fools gladly.

"I think, for you, all this publicity is something new, *tutta questa publicita*," she said. "Upsetting, of course, but still you manage to, to ... what is the word? *Revel* in it."

She reached out and placed a hand on my cheek, heedless of passersby. Instantly, I was transported across time and space to the deck of a sun-drenched yacht off the Amalfi coast, our bodies after lovemaking slick as seals. The touch of her fingers created a private erotic zone within the lunch-time crush.

"Gabriel Ash in the spotlight!" Gunter clapped his hands. "How the mighty have fallen!"

Was this mockery the price I must pay for my indiscretions? One look at the West German's grinning, porcine features and I decided, *Nein.*

"Gunter, how would you like to be in the spotlight, too?"

His eyes glittered with confusion. "*Ja?*"

"Think back to your salad days in Göttingen all those years ago ... the incident at the *gymnasium?*" I paused to let this sink in, adding in a confidential tone, "They tell me there are photographs."

Gunter's face turned violently red. Judging by her blank expression, Francesca had no idea what I was talking about. The only reason *I* knew anything was because a friendly Bulgarian commissar had once shared intelligence gleaned from Stasi files, including snapshots of a respected official of the Federal Republic cavorting in the Black Forest with naked high school boys.

"Isn't it time, *Herr* Kleist? Time for *you* to claim the spotlight! Take it from me, confession is good for the soul."

Few in the crowd noticed Gunter's knees buckle, how he buried his face in his hands, shoulders quivering—a thing truly wretched to behold. Francesca rushed to shield him from the scorn of bystanders, saving her most poisonous glare for me.

"Why do you say such things? You have not changed."

I watched her lead the Social Democrat pedophile away, both pleased and horrified by my own handiwork.

"Gabriel."

Sergei Litvinov stood there, a scowl on his leathery face, the white hair boisterous as ever. He grabbed my arm and guided me to an alcove outside the stream of humanity.

"I understand you are under considerable stress," he said. "But your words and actions are too extreme. Look how you hurt that poor man for no reason."

"No reason? Sergei, he's *German.*"

A blunt scarred finger wagged in my face. "Remember that day in the Fish Market, when your life was so miserable, when you pleaded for my help? One thing I requested of you, *one thing.* Stay out of trouble. And see what's happened."

Shame threatened to mar my moral triumph over Gunter Kleist. "Forget it," I said. "I can take care of myself. Whatever happens, I'm still smarter than they are."

"Who? Your bosses in the Foreign Ministry?"

"Yes."

"Smarter than the Minister for State Security?"

A shiver of hesitation. "All of them."

The old Russian's jaw tightened, turning his lips a blood-less-white. I realized I'd never seen him so angry before.

"Pray it won't come to that," he said.

Celebrity faded, as it must. Reporters fell away, chasing other stories. I resumed official business, though my heart wasn't in it.

After several days' surveillance, Emil called with news from a phone booth on the Lower East Side. The woman I knew as "Molly Boyle" had just left the shabby offices of *Best Served Cold*, headed uptown on foot. Emil's next call came from Union Square, where he reported seeing her enter a restaurant on Seventeenth Street. "Don't move," I said. Arriving by taxi a short time later, I found him glumly situated behind a street-corner fruit stand, looking in his bland suit and chauffeur's cap all too conspicuous among the plantains and cantaloupes. Surveillance was never his thing.

He brushed aside my praise for a job well-done, nodding towards *Tropicale*, the restaurant across the street. "What is your plan?"

"Plan?"

Emil frowned, a very unhappy employee of the month. "For *her*."

As if on cue, *Tropicale*'s doors opened, releasing into the night air potent aromas of Chanel No. 5 and catfish gumbo. Molly appeared in a short fur jacket and marble-green miniskirt; at her side was the short bald man who'd verbally abused her over lunch at the Waldorf. He wore a white suit and barely came up to her chin. A valet handed him the keys to a silver Lexus parked at the curb. Accepting Molly's playful kiss on top of his head, the bald man jumped into the Lexus and shot off for the West Side.

"No plan," I hissed at Emil. "Get out of here."

Moments later, on a quiet side-street, the late-in-the-day glow seemed in thrall to our surroundings, one of those rare moments when the city holds its breath and assumes a peculiar calm. Warehouses and office buildings muffled the noise of traffic. The evening air smelled blessedly free of the East River's primordial stink. At this twilight hour, Molly stood at the curb and lit of a cigarette. *I'm of this place,* her confident stance in Manolo Blahnik heels indicated. *I can handle whatever comes at me.* She started walking uptown.

Was there a plan?

I followed at a safe distance as Molly passed in and out of haloed streetlights, her shiny red hair muted by the dusk. She went into a Duane Read and came out tucking a fresh pack of cigarettes inside her purse. In this way I observed a curious mannerism on her part—aside from one briskly carnal afternoon, what did I know about Molly Boyle?—that is, stopping to light a cigarette and then, in violation of every New Yorker's unwritten pedestrian code, walking to a curbside receptable and depositing the match.

A liar and a schemer, but also a model citizen!

Molly's long-legged stride caused men on the street, and not a few women, to turn and look. No one took note of the tall gentleman in an alpaca coat trailing behind. Should I accost her out in the open? Feign a mugging that left her injured or worse? What punishment fit the crime of tarring my good name and jeopardizing my status with Minister Petrescu?

Turning the corner on Nineteenth Street, I pulled up short. Molly stood among a group of spectators, staring at the radiator-hissing aftermath of a fender-bender between a Checkers cab and a rusted pickup truck with Nebraska plates. The cab's front bumper had sustained a nasty dent and there were spiderweb cracks in the pickup's front headlights. Nothing terribly fraught, it seemed to me, but the motorists involved— a dark-skinned Sikh with a turban and a beefy man wearing overalls and a GO CORNHUSKERS cap—chose not to address the matter in a civilized way. Curses in overheated English and Punjabi flew back and forth, the driver of the pickup pointing at the cabbie's turban as if it were somehow at the core of their dispute. Just as a siren-blaring squad car arrived, Nebraska Fat Man sucker-punched the Sikh and dropped him to his knees. A bunch of New York's Finest engulfed the assailant, onlookers delighted by all the free entertainment. Molly snapped open a compact and studied herself in the tiny mirror, indifferent to the fracas around her.

You had to admire that.

A short time later, in a leafy and more sedate neighborhood, I came up from behind and lightly tapped her shoulder. A small fist came rocketing around, missing my nose by inches. I caught her fist and held it in my grip.

"*You*," Molly said in a hushed voice. "What the hell do you want?"

"Let's start with an explanation."

She pulled free, glancing up and down the street. "What's to explain? You like talking after sex. Big deal. I just wrote it down."

"You claimed to be a day-trader."

"Did I?" She seemed struck by her own inventiveness. "You know, I think this is all just a big misunderstanding."

"Whatever you call it, everything I said that day was off-the-record."

"Why?" Her eyes flared with the same ravening appetite I saw that day in the Waldorf. "Because you *fucked* me?"

I stood over her, my own fists clenched, feeling in that

moment a strongly violent impulse, while remaining, of course, part of a global peacekeeping organization. Molly, clever girl that she was, sensed my hesitation. She smiled, the smile that first drew me in, the smile of the wicked and opportunistic.

"Come on," she said, taking my hand.

We cut across Twentieth Street and came to Gramercy Park. Lights flickered on in brownstones and carriage houses. A wrought-iron fence kept the park off-limits to all but a select few, Molly Boyle apparently among them. At the locked gate, she flourished a large, gold-plated key.

"Live nearby?" I asked.

"Sublet," she said. "Charming two-bedroom, two-bath on Irving Place." The key slid in the lock and the gate swung open. "Owned by a classics professor at NYU who stays twice a year in Majorca, chasing Andalusian pussy."

We followed a path of crushed stone, flanked by willow trees and cast-iron streetlamps. At this evening hour, the park was pleasantly shadowed and quiet. No dog-walkers, no nosy passersby—a magical place, like something out of the city's Gilded Age. What are her intentions? I wondered. What are *mine*?

Without warning, she backed me up against a tree close by the statue of Edwin Booth, 19th-century thespian and famous assassin's lesser-known brother.

"All kidding aside," Molly said, "I like what I see."

We kissed with a fervor I didn't mistake as a desperate woman bargaining for her safety; easy enough to maneuver around and trap *her* against the tree, caressing her throat with one hand and with the other reaching up under her skirt. My fingers slid along her inner thigh, pressing gently where the bright pulse of life throbbed beneath the skin. Molly gasped in my ear, normally the most arousing of sounds, but something else drove me on now, a mix of patience with cunning, a dish *best served cold.* She pushed against my hand, her head back, hands clutching my arm, seeking all the pleasure that was her due, not immediately noticing how my grip had tightened around her throat. She opened her eyes, began squirming, fighting for air even as her body, swept up in its own dark drama, edged nearer to climax.

Then I let go.

"What—"

I took a step back. The disheveled young woman massaging her throat was the same conniving journalist who'd seduced me days earlier—even as I thought I was seducing *her*—lipstick smeared, red hair unruly, green eyes still glazed with lust.

"You don't get to ruin my life," I told her. "That privilege belongs to me."

Walking up Fifth Avenue a short time later, I felt at ease with myself for the first time in weeks. The Bentley's precision-engineered hum rose above the dull roar of evening traffic. I slowed my pace, allowing it to catch up. My trusted driver sat upright behind the wheel, appearing hugely relieved to see no blood on his employer's hands.

We made a great team, Emil and me.

15

PAUSE

A glass of murky water appears before my eyes.

"Drink."

I look around, clueless as to time of day. The cot-room walls are a pale larval gray.

"Drink," Anca says again.

She sits beside the cot in a flannel shirt and old jeans, her hair pulled back in a single long strand. She tilts the glass so water can trickle through my lips—a grainy taste, like mud—a look of concern on her face I haven't seen before.

"How long have I been out?"

She smiles faintly. "'Out'?"

Pain trudges through my body like Napoleonic foot soldiers in retreat from Moscow. "Asleep. Unconscious."

"Oh ... some days."

Two days and part of a third, I'm told, during which my pistol-whipped head wound grew infected. Antibiotics found elsewhere in the castle lessened the damage, but the fever still had to run its course—including, by her account, bouts of nausea and delirium that only recently came to an end.

"My *bubbka* is smart old woman, she has remedy for this," she says. "Mix cup of slaughtered pig blood and ashes from dead fruit bat. Cook on fire three hours, then drink fast—it will sting! Next day, *bubbka* says, you are better than brand new."

I drift a while in these sweat-soaked clothes, my vision blurred, the few surrounding objects—cot, chair, barred window —awash in shimmering colors. I remember Franz being crushed beneath Gad's boot, the ugly sound of the guard's skull striking the wall. A hand gently props me up to drink more water. Anca, intent on the task at hand, senses my gaze and turns away, nodding at the moribund recording device on the kitchen table.

"What do you say on so many tapes? About America, I bet. Big guns and fast cars. Gangsters! Hot jazz!"

Sleep tugs at me, pulls me under. Waking later, I see her standing at the window and bathed in moonlight, gripping the bars as if *she's* the one imprisoned here. Which, of course, she is.

"... my father is tram driver, my mother always drunk, easy for her to die ..." It seems while I wander in and out of dreams, Anca's been talking about her life. "I do not stay in village, I go to *universitii,* far away. Sit in classes, read many books, before I —I am *flehvic.*" Letting go of the bars, she rests a hand on her flat belly. "With child."

The child's father, a heartless graduate student, ran away and was never seen again. Anca returned to the village, gave birth to Ursula, and raised her there, a beautiful little girl with a bright smile and red cheeks. For five years, despite their hardships, mother and daughter had a perfect life together.

"One day, man runs through village—robber, killer, I do not know—and here comes *polizie* chasing after him, big angry guns in hands. I come out of bakery holding hand of my daughter, I remember she is laughing, there is frosting smeared on her face. Such a happy child!" Anca looks out the window. "*Polizie,* if you give them guns, they will shoot every bullet they have. Better chance that way to hit something. But it is Ursula who gets bullet *here*—" She taps a spot below her rib-cage. "And *here*—" The pulsing artery in her neck. "She dies very fast, my little girl. On that day, my life ends."

I think of Tess at that young age, never imperiled by anything more than a tumble on the playground. "I'm so sorry."

"Stefan is good man, which sometimes I forget," she says. "Who else would give pity on unmarried childless mother like me? We marry, he says, go work in castle. I think, why say no?"

Sleep is impossible to resist, days and weeks of it, a lifetime might not be enough. When I next wake up, Anca kneels by the cot, placing a damp towel on my forehead.

"You do not feel like it maybe, but you get better."

"If so ... thank you."

"Oh, more than me—Stefan, too! This is job for us, what they tell us, we do. Care for bad man who hurts Our Great Leader. Make sure he stays *not dead.* Prisoner not allowed to die before they say so."

Wincing, I prop up on one elbow. Our faces are inches apart. Up close, I see her shapely, intelligent eyebrows, and a faint meteor shower of freckles across her nose. In her eyes is a look hard to decipher; where before there was rancor, now her gaze suggests something like a childlike fascination with me. I clasp her wrist—warm flesh, blood coursing just beneath the surface.

"Things can be different," I tell her. "No more of this."

She doesn't pull away, though she easily could. "We get

warning you will talk words like this. Do not listen, they tell us, to what bad man says."

"But you *are* listening," I remind her. "You're listening right now."

She smiles distantly. "Maybe, I am under spell of you."

Footsteps echo in the stairwell. Anca stands and gathers up the bucket and cleaning fluid, just as yet another troglodyte guard unlocks the door and steps inside. "Lock-up!" he barks. At the door she looks back at me and frowns, as if realizing I might not be a blood-sucking demon after all.

In the absence of a clock or calendar, time slows to a crawl. *A Stranger's Welcome to Keshnev* still offers passing distractions —*"Inside caves of Lothia, bats feed on naughty children"*—but mostly I pace from kitchen to cot-room and back again, pausing to gaze through the bars at an ashen sky. Rotting timbers creak in the tower. In the forest below I hear wolves attack and loudly eviscerate their prey.

I've stopped shaving, since what's the point? I eat little, decline weekly exercise. My body, dressed in tattered prison garb, is many pounds lighter than on my last day of freedom, five—or six?—months ago. In the cracked mirror I see the ravages of confinement, a splotchy beard with more gray than black in it, eyes flat and lusterless like the sea in horse latitudes.

Tonight, the sky darkens early, a sign of impending rain. From the courtyard come the grunts of livestock being herded to shelter. I hope for rain of such ferocity it washes away all habitation in its path, water seeping through fissures in this wall, forming puddles of ice-cold rainwater rising to my knees. Good, let it happen, anything's better than this.

Dark clouds pass by overhead. I cower in my flea-bitten

clothing, a frayed blanket tugged around my shoulders, seeking comfort in the memories of women I've known—Eva, my doomed wife, Francesca Cavour and her whiplash temper, Molly Boyle's sexy, deceitful nature.

Lightning blazes across the cot-room like floodlights at a crime scene, catching its sole occupant in the gloomy act of self-abuse. Gentlemen of the Tribunal, behold your loyal servant, a hand in his pants, in tears, in prison, in the rain.

16

REC

During the night, someone left a cryptic message on the office answering machine. Male voice, unidentified, asking to meet Ambassador Ash in Central Park at one p.m., "for advice on his current situation." Vadim argued strenuously against any such meeting, and I was doubtful, too. But feeling dazed by my recent scandal, I yearned for moral guidance of any kind, however dubious the choice.

At lunchtime, I slipped out of the Secretariat building, unseen by two photojournalists dozing in a parked car and another dissolute member of the Fourth Estate standing on the pier and contemplating God knows what in the clouds above the river. Minutes later I reached the Bentley, idling on Second Avenue, no one the wiser.

Emil smoothly navigated midtown traffic, circumventing stalled panel trucks and slow-moving buses. He didn't inquire about my escapades with Molly Boyle, nor did he express curiosity in our destination today. And I, for once, managed to keep quiet myself.

As instructed, Emil pulled over at Fifty-ninth and Madison to let me out, then drove off with a worried look in the side-view mirror. I entered Central Park, brooding over the identity of my mystery caller. What about the black-hooded jogger I spotted days ago outside my building? It was Pearson, the cocky, dapper CIA man, I was sure of it. Maybe *he* requested this meeting. I kept walking, more attuned than usual to my surroundings. Pearson might be close by, disguised as the ice-cream vendor plying his trade in Grand Army Plaza or the patrolman ticketing a double-parked limo in front of the Sherry-Netherland.

Did Sergei Litvinov leave the phone ominous message, or someone calling on his behalf? *Lesche et de molt,* as they say in the old country. Ask questions and you can die.

Soon I stood near the Arsenal, a squat Gothic Revival structure with creeping ivy on the red-brick walls. Box kites floated in the air, a dog chased a frisbee down a hill, and girls in miniskirts sunbathed by a cascading fountain. Springtime in New York! Given such bucolic conditions, it seemed insane that my own life might be teetering on the brink of collapse. How could misery and paranoia thrive in a world like this?

The designated meeting-time came and went, no sign of Pearson or Sergei or anyone else with "advice" for me. I struck out on a path around the Pond, not especially dismayed by the harmless prank. A day in Central Park—birds and flowers, diamond-shards of sunlight peeking through the branches of sweetgum trees—was far preferable to office work.

On Gapstow Bridge, a man approached from the opposite side, clipped me in passing, and kept going. I rushed to catch up with him, though little effort was required; the culprit had stopped on the grass, bent-over, panting. Mustard stains on his rumpled suit, dung-colored hair in wild disarray. One black shoe and one brown shoe, lacking laces.

It was the Consul, but nothing like what I had seen of him before.

"What the hell is this? What are you doing here?"

He belched loudly. "Why not? Is free country."

"You're drunk."

The Consul shook his head, a motion that seemed to further undermine his upright position. "I admit nothing. If only world will stop spinning ..."

Lurching forward, he collapsed on a park bench. I stared down at the bedraggled police agent. Either the encounter was coincidental or this man, Minister Petrescu's slovenly operative, left the anonymous phone message. Was it worth sticking around to find out?

A neighboring park bench stood just out of range of the Consul's odors of whiskey, flatulence, and unwashed flesh. Against my better judgment—and, lately, wasn't that always the case?—I sat down nearby.

"Friendly city this New York, but not always," he said. "Last night I go to Times Square bar, end up in bed of strangers with two, maybe three American prostitutes. Next minute, their *pimpisch* jumps out of closet, knocks me on head, steals wallet. I am in street alone, no hat, no wallet, five a.m. in morning. Is bad for me! Very bad!"

The Consul's nose drooped, bits of grime and dirt smeared his face. The features I'd dismissed as humdrum had, due to his misadventures, acquired some character.

"A sad story," I said. "To be honest, it's nice seeing someone else in trouble for a change."

"My job, what they send me for, very simple," he said. "Watch ambassador, what he does right, what things go wrong. Which for you is a lot." He looked at me, then down at his own befouled suit. "See what happens! What goes wrong is *me*."

A short woman in a grubby cardigan drew near, pushing a shopping cart filled with empty beer cans.

"In Olt," he went on, "I have mother in wheelchair and sister who never marries. From me they need money to live. But when Foreign Ministry hears about American prostitutes, I will lose job. They will put mother and sister in prison, then shoot me and—*Hey!* Old woman!" The Consul glared at the woman in the cardigan sweater. "You make eavesdrop on us? What for? Sell to SPU, get us killed, what?"

The woman, who knew crazy when she heard it, scurried off. The Consul's ragged, forlorn turned to me.

"What do I do? How do I get out of trouble? Please, you will tell me."

Wasn't the real question, *why am I still listening to this?* "You could always defect," I joked.

In the ensuing silence, it seemed one of us should laugh out loud. No one did.

"Defect ..." A cracked smile broke through layers of facial dirt. "Great idea! Super-great idea!"

"No, I'm just—"

"Very much there is for me to tell America! You will talk to people for my behalf, OK? Important people! They will asylum me, for sure."

I glanced around. Was anyone within earshot listening to this absurd exchange? Not the young couple strapping on rollerblades, or the long-haired youth stretched out on the grass reading a dog-eared copy of *The Hitchhiker's Guide to the Galaxy,* or the harried mother of triplets attempting to feed her stroller-bound progeny all at the same time.

"I am not so stupid," the Consul said. "I know where are your beliefs and where they are not. Maybe once you have belief in Party. But now? Nothing, I think."

A chill tiptoed down the back of my neck. If this strung-out, hoodwinked police agent could so easily discern my core convictions—or lack thereof—what chance did I have explaining myself to Petrescu?

"Really," I insisted, "I'm a loyal servant of the State, just like you."

His breathing grew choppy. He tugged with both hands at his thinning hair. "If I go back, they shoot me! You must give help to defect!"

Must I? I pretended to mull it over, inwardly bemoaning the loss of my idyllic afternoon. It would be simple enough to usher this pathetic creature into the office of the US delegation and let them take it from there. Here was a man clearly in fear for his life. How could I deny him assistance?

"No," I said finally. "I don't think so."

"You will not help when I ask?"

I watched mallards glide onto the surface of the Pond, envying their blissful ignorance. "What's your name, again? I never did get—"

Without warning, the Consul went into a body-length seizure. His limbs twitched and shuddered, his eyes rolled up in his head, his spine made cracking sounds. Epilepsy? The DTs? In horror I watched his body liquefy, turning briefly invertebrate as he slid from the park bench to the ground. His legs quivered, as if absorbing bursts of high-voltage electricity.

I looked around. Amazingly, our little *mise-en-scène* had yet to get anyone's attention.

"Get up," I said, not without compassion.

The Consul struggled to his knees and sprawled across the bench, like something washed up by a giant storm surge.

"You will do nothing for me?"

"I won't report this appalling anti-socialist behavior to State Security," I said. "That's something."

A French bulldog waddled up the footpath, pursued by a

woman in a floppy sunhat. "Suzi!" she cried. "Come back here this instant!" The Consul stared at Suzi's ungainly getaway, and then, before my disbelieving eyes, breathed deeply and sat bolt upright, smoothing the wrinkles in his suit, even using a forefinger to wipe debris off his lace-less shoe. A completely different man.

"What the hell?"

He smiled, exposing blackened teeth. "Call it test."

"Test?"

"Of allegiance you have for People's Republic."

My first impulse was to leap over the bench and beat him into a vegetative state. He was the one who left the overnight message, hoping to entrap me in a scheme that would end my career. The act of defection—or helping others to defect—was, in Minister Petrescu's eyes, the worst of all sins.

"Well?" I asked. "Did I pass?"

Rollerbladers swerved between pedestrians like clever winged gods. The long-haired youth dozed in the grass. The mother of three gave in to her squalling brood, aiming the stroller for the nearest cotton-candy stand. Just another day in the park.

"You did not fail," he said.

The following evening, I traveled uptown and delivered trade papers to the Albanian delegate, a gruff, solitary man who chose to live in Harlem, as he put it, "among the capitalistic oppressed." Six muggings in the past year—only six!—proved that the local community was warming to him. I conducted our business as quickly as possible, then rejoined Emil in the Bentley parked a block away from the delegate's rat-infested hovel.

"Morningside Heights, please."

Dusk fell. Neon flashed to life above pawnshops and pizzerias, rib joints and hair salons. What was the purpose of this fundraising cocktail party anyway? Either Vadim had neglected to tell me, or, more likely, I'd forgotten. All that really mattered was showing up, announcing by my presence alone, *I'm still here, unbowed by recent events.*

"Excuse, sir ...?"

"Yes, what is it?"

"We know each other how many years?" Emil said. "All that time, I do not say, *Go home to Keshnev.* How can I tell you go home? *I* never go home." He shifted uneasily in the driver's seat. "Maybe for you now is time."

I reminded him of the Foreign Ministry's abiding displeasure with me.

"Yes, yes, but this is what you do good. Make words to get out of trouble. If you go home and talk, they will listen." Emil's voice dropped to a whisper. "*He* will listen."

Return to Keshnev? I imagined the criminal charges I might face there, everything from defying orders and treating delicate matters of state like pillow talk to embracing a style of life far beyond what a true servant of the People required. Was there *any* way of explaining myself to Petrescu that wouldn't lead to imprisonment or death?

Some obstruction up ahead had traffic completely stalled. I glanced at a dark-green sedan idling in the next lane over. The front-seat passenger's handsome suit and firm-jawed Episcopalian profile were visible in the growing twilight. As I stared in disbelief, Mark Pearson turned and smiled at me.

"Pull over," I said.

"What?" Emil looked around. "Why? Where?"

I pointed at a fire hydrant on the far corner of the intersection. "There."

He guided the Bentley through a lurching U-turn and

careened to a halt beneath a NO PARKING sign. I had the rear door open and a foot on the pavement before we reached a full stop. As expected, the green sedan cut across a line of cars and pulled up ahead of us at the curb. No one got out.

A chilly evening in a part of town I seldom visited. I walked over and rapped on the tinted glass. The window rolled down with a maddeningly sedate hum.

"Evenin', Ambassador. How's it going?"

"You have to stop this," I said.

"Huh?"

"This is harassment! I represent a sovereign nation and you are violating my human rights." His blameless grin infuriated me. "And let's drop the pretenses, shall we? Admit you're CIA and be done with it."

"CIA?" Pearson addressed the driver, a figure in shadows, and together they shared a crude laugh. "Calm down," he told me. "No one's rights are getting violated."

I thumped the flat of my hand on the car-roof and took satisfaction in seeing both occupants jump in their seats.

"Is that calm enough for you?"

The car door opened, and Pearson got out, roughly equal to me in height and weight, but a good ten years younger—and, if push came to shove, in far better condition.

"OK, you're outraged," he said. "Duly noted."

Only now did I notice we had an audience. Across the street, three young men in dark glasses, basketball jerseys and backwards-facing caps sat on a stoop, watching events unfold.

"What is it you want from me?"

Pearson scanned the neighborhood, taking no special interest in the youths eyeballing us from the stoop. His Pierre Cardin tie—midnight blue with thin translucent strips sewn into the silk—was distractingly perfect.

"It's not what we want, Gabriel—can I call you Gabriel? It's what *you* should be wanting from *us*."

"I can't think of a thing."

"It's important to understand something," he said. "To your bosses back home, you're a liability. An embarrassment. Clowning around like you did at the UN makes the bosses look stupid and nobody wants to look stupid."

An older man appeared on the stoop, flaunting estimable body mass beneath a gray puffer coat. His rowdy acolytes pointed at the two white guys in business suits having it out on 122nd Street. The man in the puffer coat folded his arms, staring at us with undisguised malice.

"Here's what I don't get," Pearson said. "You're a mouthpiece for one of the nastiest satellite nations in Eastern Europe —but at least you get to live *here*! Walk our streets, breathe our air." He waved proudly at a graffiti-scarred telephone booth. "New York, New York! Why oh would you ever mess with that?"

Good question, I thought. And asked far too late in the game.

"Some muckety-mucks over at State think you're well-placed to offer strategic intelligence vis-à-vis your charming Warsaw Pact buddies. They also believe you could profit enormously from the generous nature of the United States. Especially since, as we see it, you don't have a whole lot of options. Just two, in fact."

"Enlighten me."

"First option? Cut and run."

"Cut and—?"

"Jump over to our side," he said. "Join the rest of us poor slobs in the Free World."

The grim humor of the situation—being strong-armed into defecting on a Harlem street-corner, only a day after talking myself out of a similar situation in Central Park—caused me to laugh out loud.

"Option two," Pearson said, unruffled. "Go home to Keshnev and spill your guts to the Minister for State Security. See how far that gets you."

"Strange," I said. "My driver just suggested the same thing."

"Is that so?" The smile he produced could cut glass. "Personally, I don't give a fuck what happens."

"What do I get in return?"

"Witness protection, my friend. Best in town."

This was the moment the man in the puffer coat chose to confront the interlopers in his midst. He stepped into the street, adjusting the hitch of his gait, and incidentally flashing a hitherto concealed weapon. Pearson, who'd shown no prior interest in the man or his crew, turned to meet the encroaching menace head-on. Puffer Coat got halfway across the street when something in the white man's hardened gaze and Langley-trained body language made him think twice about his intentions. He backtracked, grinning excessively, and rejoined his baffled crew on the stoop.

Suppose I *did* cut and run. Whatever "strategic intelligence" I possessed had limited value at best. Then what? Left to rot in a farmhouse on the Oklahoma Panhandle—no women, no three-hundred-dollar suits, no bison grass vodka. Slow death in the heartland.

"It's simple, Gabriel. You're in or you're out, with us or against us. What's it going to be?"

Pearson was wrong; I had a third choice. Signal Emil in the Bentley, then step aside as he walked the short distance to the green sedan and, with an unlicensed gun in his gloved hand, fired a bullet in the CIA man's forehead.

"Your offer is insulting," I said. "On behalf of the people of Keshnev, I reject it."

"Well, hell ..." He stepped in close, no longer smiling. "Maybe take a goddamn minute and—"

A sharp command issued from inside the car, like the bark of a seal. Pearson took a deep breath, opened the passenger-side door, and climbed in. I stood there, dizzy with adrenalin, almost faint with righteous indignation. And still, it wasn't enough. Before I could move, the tinted window rolled down with that same nerve-wracking hum. He looked at me with the blue-eyed gaze of a true believer.

"What if we wanted to fuck you up, Ambassador? I mean, *really* fuck you up. How hard do you think that would be?"

I took a deep breath and told him I was headed for a gathering near Columbia, then home to finish some paperwork. "I promise you, the schedule won't change."

"Fine," he said. "As long as we understand each other."

I turned and began walking away.

"Hey, Ambassador! Gabriel! One more thing!"

No more things, I thought, and kept walking. Scornful laughter trailed in my wake.

17

REC

An old dancehall had been rented for the occasion. By the time I arrived, a hundred or so guests were milling about in tuxedoes and evening wear. Waiters glided by with appetizer trays of *dolma* and *falafel*. A pianist in top-hat and tails played a Chopin *etude* on the baby grand. Festive gatherings like this offered a rare opportunity for those in attendance—men and women besieged in their daytime professions by the dogs of war—to let off some steam. The high-ceilinged ballroom thrummed with cocktail chatter.

I downed a glass of Merlot, then snatched a second off a passing tray. From some artful eavesdropping I learned the fundraiser had something to do with restoring the Giza Pyramids, employing state-of-the-art laser technology. More importantly, in my button-down suit I was glaringly underdressed. Normally, this would be very irksome, but I was too rattled by the encounter with Pearson to care. How foolishly I'd incited the younger man to the brink of violence! More wine was needed to calm my nerves.

Across the ballroom stood Ms. Alvarez, stunningly different in appearance from the last time we met in the Delegates Lounge. Her jet-black hair hung unfettered down her naked back, and her off-the-shoulder black cocktail dress covered a barely acceptable part of her lithe, petite body. I saw her flirting with a tuxedoed frat-boy goon and wished him dead.

"Gabriel! Thank you for coming."

The Egyptian ambassador greeted me, a tall, finely featured man in a sleek tux and wing-collar shirt. His pomaded hair gleamed in the light of the chandelier.

"Ambassador Fayed, thank you for the invitation."

"It is my honor." Stepping nimbly aside, he presented his wife. "You remember Halima, of course."

"Of course. A pleasure to see you again, Mrs. Fayed."

Long fingernails skimmed across the palm of my hand and withdrew. I sensed the ambassador's wife—a wafer-thin Cairene of a certain age—disapproved of my presence here.

"So happy you could make it," Halima said, meaning *I wish you hadn't.* "The word is, you've been in hiding."

The ambassador sighed wearily. "Darling, please ..."

Years ago, facing huge losses after a spectacularly bad day at the races, Abdul Fayed came to me for help. I offered to do what I could—in fact, a single call to a friend at OTB made the problem disappear—thinking I might someday find myself in similarly perilous straits and need assistance. Fayed had remained loyal ever since. Despite the media hoopla, he didn't hesitate to ask me to his lavish pyramid-restoration *soirée.*

"My husband and I strongly believe in the sanctity of the diplomatic corps," Halima said. "Statesmen who toil on behalf of mankind should not be subjected to abuse in the press."

"Hear, hear." I raised my glass, more than a little tipsy.

"On the other hand, people assume if they see something

on TV or in the newspaper, it must be true. In this way, one person's bad conduct can tar an entire profession."

The pianist, who up to now had performed waltzes and sonatas, launched into an improbable ragtime. A bevy of grand dames in sequined dresses led their octogenarian spouses onto the dance floor.

"I admit to a lapse in judgment," I said. "The rest is history."

"Yes, yes," Fayed agreed. "All in the past now. Water under the bridge."

Halima's laugh sounded like the birth-cry of some prehistoric creature. "Almost a flood!"

Sergei Litvinov emerged from the crowd, grinning broadly at Ambassador and Mrs. Fayed. My heart swelled with hope at the sight of the old Russian with wild white hair and cummerbund straining to hold back his girth; Sergei was the only person who could understand what I was going through. He greeted the hosts warmly, then shook my hand with markedly less enthusiasm.

"Good to see you, Ambassador."

Guests on the fringe of our little group began recognizing the infamous celebrity in their midst—*me*, that is. Little cloudbursts of gossip spread from debutantes to dowagers to captains of industry.

"Please forgive our painfully indiscreet guests," Fayed said. "You've set a spark to the festivities, for which we're grateful."

Halima nodded, clearly doubtful as to my overall entertainment value. "Oh, yes, immeasurably so."

"There's a lot to be said for discretion," Sergei said. "And, for that matter, conducting ourselves in the public eye with a little more humility."

We all shared a laugh over this minor impertinence, but the barbed underpinning of Sergei's remark disturbed me. Was he really so upset over some unfortunate quotes in a tabloid? Or seeing me browbeat Gunter Kleist outside the Delegates Lounge?

"Discretion is overrated," I said. "The same goes for polite discourse and the rule of law. Remember, it's a jungle out there. Beat swords into ploughshares all you like, but man's inhumanity to man wins out every time."

"We are diplomats for precisely that reason," Sergei said.

Fayed nodded. "And very good ones."

"Except," Halima said, "when you're not."

Guests had gathered around the baby grand, clamoring for music from their various homelands. With admirable *esprit de corps,* the pianist launched into "La Marseilles," followed by "When Irish Eyes Are Smiling," and a sampling of Hungarian folk songs.

"You are too prideful," Sergei told me in front of the others, "out of all proportion to your place in the world. I hope Ambassador Fayed and his lovely wife will forgive my bluntness, but the time has come for you to shut the hell up."

Halima laughed. "Hear, hear!"

I was too stunned to respond. Never in our long friendship had Serge showed me such blatant disrespect.

Fayed, trained to snuff out discord, hastily intervened. "We're all of us guilty of excessive pride, aren't we? Pride in our people, our culture, in each country's natural splendor ..." He trailed off, with the same stricken look I remembered from the dark days of off-track betting. "Sadness, too, at being such a great distance from the ones we—"

"Darling, look! The Paleys are here!" Halima grabbed her forlorn husband's wrist and led him across the dance floor. "Hurry, darling!"

Hava Nagila, "Camptown Races," Fly Me to the Moon"— the beleaguered pianist played on. I scowled into my wine-glass, even as Sergei was scowling at me. He pressed close, out of earshot of others.

"If you're so damned pure, why not fly home to Keshnev and make a clean breast of it with Petrescu?"

So-called friends and adversaries had been hammering this point home all day. *Go back, maybe now is good time. Go back, see where that gets you.* A wave of memories swept over me, abrupt and unasked-for—the smell of fresh-cut hay, the way mud slushed under my shoes walking to school. The cliffs of Pomanzek on the Black Sea coast, where I said goodbye to my mother and father before sailing to England, none of us imagining it was for the last time.

"A dog is tied to a post," Sergei said. "Every day the little boy from next door comes and teases this dog. Makes faces, pokes it with a stick. But always the boy stays out of reach of retribution." He looked at the guests writhing amiably on the dance-floor. "One day the dog breaks free of the post and lunges at the boy, tearing the skin from his face. Then it attacks his family and everyone in the village. All this, because of one little boy."

Loud, discordant noises came from the baby grand. The exhausted pianist lay slumped over the ivories.

"Which one am I, Sergei? The little boy or the rabid dog? Maybe the post in the ground."

"You, my friend, are a colossal pain in the ass."

"Yeah, well—I can live with that."

He looked at me as if I was complaining of a stubbed toe in a hurricane. "You don't get it, do you? I am wasting my breath."

I watched Sergei push through the crowd, too consumed by my own troubles to follow. It was time to leave the party, even if that meant running the gauntlet of Abdul Fayed's guests, sanctimonious jerks one and all. As I turned to the side-door, a woman's delicate hand fell on mine.

"Ambassador, do you remember me?"

It was Ms. Alvarez—up close, even more striking than before, her black hair draped over her shoulders, her dark-brown eyes too large for her face and yet achingly perfect.

"My problem, Ms. Alvarez, is I never forget."

"Won't you call me Luisa?"

After our first encounter—back when anonymous death threats were the biggest problem in my life—I dug around into Luisa Alvarez's background. Reports of exemplary consular service in Tegucigalpa and Mexico City, but also rumors of a turbulent affair with her supervisor in Havana, and a "reassignment reprieve" to the UN in New York. Nothing about marriage or children.

"In due time," I said.

Lights from the chandelier lit up her face. For whatever reason—alcohol, the high-spirited party—Ms. Alvarez seemed no longer timid in my presence.

"You may have heard, I've been promoted to the Secretary-General's office."

"No more Alfred Lundquist? Impressive."

"Thank you," she said. "I can't believe it myself. It's all happening so fast."

I signaled a waiter to replenish our drinks, then toasted the young woman's advancement.

"What secrets have you unearthed about the SG? Wait," I said, "let me guess. He's fond of a hearty breakfast of poached eggs and Canadian bacon. One day he hopes to skydive over Machu Picchu. And he harbors a secret passion for romance novels."

Her laugh sounded purer than anything produced on the baby grand. "That's not like the Secretary-General at all."

"I only know what I hear."

"Well, *we* keep hearing about you." She stepped closer in

her preposterous heels. A sweet almond scent rose from her lightly clothed body. "The article that woman wrote, the things you supposedly said ..."

"Lies," I told her. "A howling pack of lies."

"Yes, of course, but—how did she get you talking? Was a simple smile all it took? Or maybe more was involved?"

A strand of hair fell over her face, and I gently brushed it behind her ear. Over her shoulder I saw Fayed's shrewish wife scanning the crowd and instantly knew who she was looking for.

"Let's get a drink somewhere," I said. "You can hear all about it."

Ms. Alvarez smiled. "Your reputation precedes you, Ambassador, and not all to the good. I wonder if getting a drink is a good idea."

I spread my arms wide open, as if to proclaim, *Nothing up my sleeves.* "Why not? What could go wrong?"

Halima Fayed swooped in, her lacquered bird-claw encircling my young friend's tiny waist. "Luisa! Look who's here! JFK Jr.! You must come meet him." And, with a look for me of precisely calibrated disdain, she whisked Ms. Alvarez away.

Caught out in the press as a two-faced figure of state. Sparring with demented police agents in Central Park. Almost coming to blows with a CIA man on 122nd Street. Even three sheets to the wind, I could see things for what they were—a life, *my* life, spiraling out of control.

PAUSE

In the morning, Anca and Stefan arrive under the supervision of a new guard, a dullard like all the rest of them. The guard smokes a cigarette on the landing, ignorant of how odd it is for this husband-and-wife caretaker team to be working together at the same time. Anca heats up leftovers on the stove, Stefan twirls a mop across the floor. I smile at his approach, and he recoils as if I was spitting flames. Anca sets a bowl of *stuknogy* on the table in front of me, then retreats to a corner.

The bubbling grayish stew tastes like ashes, but what else do I expect or deserve? When I raise a second spoonful to my lips, some sixth sense cautions against it. *There*, floating in the broth, a scrap of parchment no larger than a fortune-cookie note. I look around. My caretakers are busy washing dishes and restocking toilet paper. I unfurl the parchment and read the ink-splotched message inside:

Ne sta ovlutti.

The guard on the landing takes note of my suspicious behavior and clomps into the kitchen. The ugly sound of his boots triggers the panic I felt when his sadist-predecessor held a gun to my head. *Click click click.*

This time, I don't cower or tremble with fear. "What do you think you're doing?" I yell from the table. "Can't you see I'm eating?"

The guard falters, shocked by my impudence. Behind him, Stefan says, "We are finish," Anca nodding beside him. Soon their footsteps echo down the stairwell. The guard glares at me, probably under strict orders *not* to harm the prisoner, but dearly wishing he could. I hold my ground, keeping the soggy parchment balled-up in my fist. He's first to back down, kicking the chair against the wall on his way out.

Ne sta ovlutti, the message says.

Be ready.

18

REC

An air of tense expectancy hung over the Security Council chamber. Delegates milled around in tight groups—nearly all men, nearly all wearing dark Brooks Brothers suits—talking and smoking beneath a dome of constellation lighting. Entering from a side-chamber, I passed through a fog of dueling dialects and warring colognes.

Earlier in the morning, I'd had episodes of sudden chills, the first scratch of a raw throat. Now, still a bit *off*, the chamber's color-coded seating arrangement briefly confused me. Red chairs for "Interested Parties," including observers and technical advisors. Along the north/south walls, three rows of chairs in a sickly beige, reserved for clerical staff. At the famous horseshoe-shaped table, delegates of the Permanent Five Nations—US, USSR, Great Britain, France, China—sat in blue, elegantly upholstered chairs, alongside representatives of ten other rotating member-states. A brass nameplate marked my place at the end of the U-shaped table: PEOPLE'S DEMOCRATIC REPUBLIC, KESHNEV.

As soon as I took my seat, Vadim leaned in behind me from the staff section and tapped my shoulder. He wore his best suit for the occasion, but as he handed over a sheaf of papers, I noticed his hastily combed hair and grime under his fingernails.

"What's this?"

"Changes, sir. To your speech."

He tilted his head towards the Public Gallery, where row upon row of tiered seating fanned upward as in a movie theater. The Consul sat there, no longer the drooling misfit of Central Park, nestled among civilians in his thin gray suit. A shark in a wading pool.

"What the hell is he doing up there?"

Vadim kept his eyes down. "He wishes to be with masses."

The pages given to me weren't "changes" so much as a freshly composed screed against the West, harsh even by Stalinist standards. I looked again at the duplicitous little shit, half-admiring his brazenly false smile. Vadim sank back in his chair, exhausted from fear of this man.

"How long, sir? Until he is gone?"

Stenographers and transcriptionists set up shop at a narrow table, sunken between the prongs of the horseshoe table. I had no answer for him.

The chamber filled with advisors, administrators, delegates and their lackies—tourists, as well, with fanny packs and hideous sunglasses. The bottom row of the Public Gallery was reserved for members of the international press, a larger-than-usual contingent on hand today, in case Keshnev's headline-grabbing chief delegate chooses to make more news.

My nose itched. Something tickled in my throat, a cold coming on.

"Water, sir?"

My assistant hovered close by, holding a carafe of ice water and a glass of cut crystal.

"Go on," I said, annoyed by his unsteady hand. What did *he* have to be nervous about? "Careful with that!"

Vaguely I recalled the idealistic thrill of those first days at the UN, a young man in his thirties desperate, after years of diplomatic indentured service, to finally *do* something. Time passed. Wars raged on, poverty and disease went unchecked. I came to understand idealism had no place here—impractical at best, often dangerously naïve.

This morning, the air inside the Security Council chamber was thick with cigarette smoke, odors of varnished wood and male perspiration, the smells of *realpolitik*. The blue-silk damask wallpaper looked particularly drab, and Per Krohg's towering Mural of Peace on the east wall—scenes of toil and servitude giving way to a rising phoenix and other symbols of rebirth—felt more oppressively inspirational than usual. The powers that be always kept the heavy floor-to-ceiling curtains closed during deliberative sessions, thus concealing from us a vision of the East River, Queens, and points beyond. Room without a view, an apt description for this blinkered world body.

A Swedish diplomat, presuming familiarity on the basis of very little acquaintance, tapped my shoulder as he walked by.

"Looking forward to your speech!"

"As am I."

In those early days, the mere presence of Perm Five members left the fledgling statesman awestruck. Their modern-day counterparts settling in behind their respective nameplates were, by contrast, an unimpressive bunch. The British ambassador—natty, pompous, in line for a knighthood —was notoriously indifferent to living conditions in Third World countries. His Jordanian colleague, with steely black eyebrows and blow-dried hair, was said to have a wife in Amman and another in Atlantic City. Seated side-by-side, the representatives of Mexico and Guyana formed a pair of well-tailored, nearly identical marionettes.

Bad timing on my part to give a speech in front of *this* lot, and so soon after my moment as *cause célèbre*.

Other arriving members included Turkey's corpulent envoy, and the Filipino chief delegate, advanced in age and mostly deaf. That I must suffer the moral censure of men like these left a taste in my mouth as bitter as the ashes from which the phoenix rose in the Mural of Peace.

Last to be seated, the USSR Permanent Representative, stooped and jowly, trudging to the conference table like a farmer in a muddy swamp. When he bumped the chair where the American ambassador sat—"Madame K," as everyone knew her, a schoolmarm type given to finger-wagging lectures —she smiled tightly and turned away. The Russian's chief deputy, Sergei Litvinov, walked behind his boss, not deigning to glance my way.

At the center of the horseshoe table was the Secretary-General, a small, dapper man seated impassively while a horde of assistants whispered in his ear. Most of the time, the SG toiled away in solitude. Thrust into the limelight by the Falklands war, he had the world's attention but didn't seem to know what to do with it. I wondered if he'd stick around for my speech.

As if reading my thoughts, the great man's large, silver-haired head turned towards me. I felt the full brunt of his trademark cold-fish stare, a stare reserved for special occasions and magnified behind horn-rimmed glasses. *No trouble*, the SG silently admonished me. *We want no trouble from you today.*

"Ladies and gentlemen, may we please come to order?"

The Acting President, a genteel if short-tempered delegate

from Zaire, rapped a gavel three times on a pad on the table, a thing he seemed to enjoy doing. "We will begin with a reading of the draft resolution, there being no objections." He waved the gavel pre-emptively. "So decided."

The draft resolution under discussion today sought to "request" the mandatory UN protection of civilians trapped in a war zone—a straightforward-enough idea any outside observer might think all member states could easily agree on. That observer would be wrong. The French ambassador draw our attention to "ambiguous and misleading language" in Paragraph Five, secondary clauses 3.c and 4.b., where, he added, alterations in the text were "regrettably necessary." This set off another round of tedious debate.

Not for the first time, I thought of the village elders in Rogvald, the village of my youth, those rough-hewn men who straddled wooden barrels and spit tobacco while arguing over the issues of the day. The draft resolution discussion dragged on and on. I gripped the pen tightly, wishing to get on with the vote and fumble my way through a speech and wanting to put the whole thing off forever.

"There being no further objections in the wording, the Council at this time calls for a vote."

In the Public Gallery, Francesca Cavour smiled down on me. In her blue dress and with her long black hair swept over her shoulders, she looked as smartly fashionable as any woman on the Via Veneto. Her tart smile lifted my spirits, until I saw Mark Pearson sitting in "Interested Parties" with his arms crossed and a facial expression set in neutral. As if he had no stakes in these proceedings, as if he'd never tried to entice a Security Council member into an act of treason.

"The draft resolution is put to a vote. All in favor?"

A show of hands, all fifteen members—Keshnev's chief delegate included, looking a little green around the gills—

boldly supported the safeguarding of helpless men, women, and children in wartime. The Acting President rapped his gavel.

"So decided."

Even the village elders reached consensus faster than this; when faced with some civic infraction, they argued over the criminal's sentence—a beating in the woods, public shunning —then happily celebrated their verdict with plenty of *slavka* and roasted boar meat. 'd debate the verdict and come upon the right punishment for the crime—public shunning, a beating in the woods—then celebrate their verdict with *slavka* and grilled boar meat. By contrast, the men seated around the horseshoe table were fat, long-winded, and bereft of charm. Who were *they* to sit in judgment of *me*?

I have wasted my time here, I thought miserably. I have wasted my life.

Vadim's cough alerted me to a growing silence in the amphitheater. Apparently, the Acting President had invited me to speak, though I never heard the request. He did so again, less politely this time. I felt eyes on me from above, where glass booths high up on the north wall housed desk-bound inter-preters, each face lit from chin up, a jack o'lantern in the dark. Also, in the chamber at large, the eyes of my fellow delegates, their deputies and advisors, and of course, row upon row of rubbernecking spectators and members of the vampire press.

"Thank you, Mr. President. I—"

My mouth went Mojave-dry. The glass of water Vadim had poured was thankfully within reach and I took several restora-tive sips, flagrantly buying time. Then I set the glass down, spent a moment adjusting the flexible neck of the microphone in front of me, and began.

"Ladies and gentlemen, esteemed visitors, representatives of the soulless press ..." A snigger from the bleachers. "It is an honor to address you on a day that incidentally marks the one-year anniversary of my country's ascent to membership on the United Nations Security Council. To be seated at this table, the setting for so many historic events and decisions, is for me and the Keshnevite people, a source of great pride."

These opening remarks were heartfelt, more or less; not so the marked-up pages in my hands, my own empty rhetoric soiled by the Consul's left-wing claptrap. I looked up in search of the author. There he sat in the Public Gallery, gazing down at the proceedings, maybe smiling, maybe not, a bargain-basement sphinx.

"Lately, I've reflected on my first days here," I told the assembled crowd. "A newly-minted delegate overwhelmed by a newfound sense of duty, of purpose. Of being part of a global mission that transcended outmoded notions about *borders* and *nations*."

So far, nothing new or exciting. Delegates around the table yawned, smoked cigarettes, fiddled with their headphones.

"Who can say when the first glimmers of reality poked through? What caused me to start seeing clearly through my idealistic haze? It might have been the Suez crisis, or civil war in the Congo, maybe the endless cycle of bloodshed in the Middle East."

I heard Vadim behind me, rifling through his copy of the speech, trying in vain to match the printed words with what was coming out of my mouth. *Well?* I asked myself. *Do I give the Consul's prepared speech or not?* I noted with pleasure the pained expression on the seedy police agent's face, as I crumpled the pages in my fist.

"Let's be realistic," I said. "The world perceives this hallowed institution as structurally incapable of solving problems. Yes, peacekeeping forces defuse conflicts from time to time. Stave off famine with emergency food supplies. Just enough humanitarian effort to reassure ourselves, we are who we claim to be, international custodians of hope and justice. We cling to the belief our words have *meaning*, if we somehow arrange them in the right order, we can stop bullets in mid-flight, even raise the dead." I paused, waiting for the pounding to subside in my head. "And what a wrenching shock to discover, time and again, none of it is true."

I savored the heat of hundreds—thousands!—of eyeballs upon me. At the sunken table, stenographers looked up like tiny birds Stenographers at the sunken table looked up at me like tiny birds demanding more of mother's disgorged tidbits.

"It's happening now, as we speak. A Third World nation invades a rocky outpost under British dominion. Outraged, the guardians of Empire—that's *Empire* with a capital *E*—go on immediate war footing. Soldiers are mobilized, frigates and destroyers hauled out of dry dock, a whirlwind of militarism that leaves the rest of the world scratching our collective heads and wondering, Why not leave it alone? Why send a flotilla of warships to retake by force what your own government seized for itself a century ago?"

The British ambassador's left eyebrow seemed to lift on its own, a display of mounting irritation.

"Let's not overlook the achievements of Empire," I said. "Take, for example, the international slave trade, at one time a hugely profitable enterprise. And, at the turn of this century, there was the thorny problem of how best to confine a large group of people while you're busy occupying their country. From the wizards of Empire came forth *barbed wire*, miles and miles of it, highly effective in keeping thousands of Boer men, women, and children in place." I aimed a forefinger, *j'accuse*-style, at the East German delegate, sitting there minding his own business. "Look how far concentration camps have come since then!"

Murmurs rumbled in the chamber. The British ambassador stood and quietly exited by a side-door, well-coiffed and digni-fied to the end. The USSR's chief delegate looked forlornly at the now-vacant chair beside him. Sergei leaned in and whis-pered in his ear; whatever he said calmed the elder statesman.

"Empire begats Empire, and our host country hasn't failed to pick up the mantle. At one time, some damn good slave traders themselves." The sight of Madame K's sour-lemon face cheered me on. "A republic that's always buying or manufac-turing state-of-the-art killing machines. A republic that equates *might* with *right*, a republic stunned to find itself trapped, not so long ago, in an unwinnable jungle war."

Now it was Madame K who rose to leave, but with none of her transatlantic colleague's style and grace. Documents were loudly stuffed inside an attaché case, there was the nasty scrape of a chair-leg and the staccato effect of sensible heels marching out of the chamber. The press section hummed like a hornet's nest, reporters busy scribbling away. I felt feverish, and curiously out-of-body, ready to say anything that came to mind.

"And of course, our friends in the East, a vast superpower reigning over one-sixth of the Earth's surface. A cobbler's son from the Caucasus rises to become General Secretary of the Communist Party, sowing terror and repression across the Empire on an unimaginable scale. Millions of citizens lost to famine, torture, and execution. All to appease a cobbler son's madness—" Surely, I didn't have to say, *Josef Stalin.* In my voice, I heard something like passion, something I might even believe in. "One man! Millions dead!"

The Russian chief delegate lumbered to his feet, wheezing on the way out. Francesca Cavour smiled down from the Public Gallery, always one for *épater la bourgeoisie*. Pearson in "Inter-ested Parties" looked far less pleased.

"What of the subject nations," I said, "the former colonies and protectorates, scraps of Empire scattered around the globe? How do they fare in our post-colonial times? If we answer honestly—and today, ladies and gentlemen, I propose we be brutally honest—the answer must be, *not well.* These ex-colonies are rudderless. They behave less like sovereign entities and more like battered children, angry and resentful, most of all bewildered by the chaos Empire has left behind."

The murmurs grew louder, little pockets of disruption throughout the amphitheater. I felt hyper-alert, my heart pounding. Even if I wished to retract every word I'd uttered so far, it couldn't be done. I was just a vessel for the message.

"All along, we've assumed our mission is putting an end to Empire. It's right there in the charter, isn't it? Strive to foster self-determination for all people, everywhere. The question we must ask ourselves today—"

The Secretary-General abruptly pushed away from the table, obliging his startled underlings to carve a path for him out a chamber door. *Press on.*

"The question we ask ourselves today is, What if the charter is wrong? What if Empires still serve a purpose and self-determination isn't such a noble goal, after all? I mean—" Scanning the unruly audience for any friendly face. "Aren't subject nations *subject* for a reason?"

"Objection," said the delegate from Ireland.

"Request to intervene," the Japanese delegate said.

The Acting President banged his gavel. "Order!"

"Be it Allah or the Vatican, Bolshevism or the Chamber of Commerce—"

"Traitor!" a voice called out, and another. "Communist scum!"

"—everyone bows to a master, it's what we crave—"

"Liar!"

"Degenerate!"

"—as a species—"

The microphone emitted a smoker's cough and died in front of me. Objects of alarming shapes flew past my head—ashtray, brief book, a woman's shoe—while a voice on the loudspeaker pleaded for calm. A Polish attaché, evidently maddened by my words, took a swing at a NATO observer. Scuffles broke out in the Press Section, where the beat reporters and UN clerical staff, long-suffering adversaries, cast niceties aside and began trading blows. Then an ear-splitting alarm system made everyone forget their differences and leave the chamber *en masse*. Somehow in the commotion the Consul had attached himself to Francesca Cavour; in a cold fury I saw his vile hand resting in the small of her back, guiding her to safety.

The alarm shut off. The chamber was quiet and empty. I sat at the table, giddy and morally reinvigorated. For a quarter of a century, I'd tumbled down the UN rabbit hole to no good end, and now I finally told the truth. *My* truth, not some Petrescu-approved version of it, consequences be damned.

A red light flashed on the telephone. I picked up.

"Quite a performance, my friend."

Sergei Litvinov occupied his boss's seat at the horseshoe table. He held the receiver to his ear and stared out at the empty galleries.

"What are you doing, Sergei?"

"One thing I am *not* doing is talking to you." He kept his gaze fixed on some inscrutable end-point. "Did the Foreign Ministry approve this grand speech of yours?"

I giggled like a lunatic. "Not a word."

"This was you, then, Gabriel Ash, speaking from the heart."

"Well—"

"Sleeping with journalists. Ignoring death threats. And now, *this*. What has happened to you, old friend?"

My pleasurable after-glow was fading. Reality loomed, and things didn't look pretty.

"I could defect," I said. "Pearson claims that by jumping over, I solve all my problems."

"Impossible," Sergei said. "The Minister for State Security would never permit it. All evidence to the contrary, you still serve a purpose for him."

"I'll resign and *then* defect. Sell my story to Hollywood and live out my days on the Cote D'Azur."

My old friend sighed, centuries of Russian woe in his voice. "Impossible."

"Goddamn it, nothing's impossible when you—"

The phone went dead, like the microphone. Sergei came to his feet and walked out of the chamber. I felt friendless and abandoned, and yet, due to the power of my own soaring oratory, cured of illness.

19

PAUSE

Be ready.

Days have passed since the mysterious message surfaced in the stew. The caretakers resume their individual work-shifts, washing, mopping, and cleaning without a word for me. At times, when the bored guard turns away, Anca or Stefan could edge close with details of the escape plan—*if* such a plan exists. But nothing gets said.

Cockroaches emerge from under the door, but none with the panache of the late lamented Franz. Each time I sprinkle breadcrumbs on the floor, his timid successors take their multiple eyes off the prize and scamper off, empty-handed, as it were. Who can replace a legend?

A Stranger's Welcome to Keshnev doesn't offer consolation or solace as it once did. All the punishing malapropisms and garbled flights of fancy are too much to bear:

In Keshnev, ice is useful as funeral
gift. Guns unallowed in playground,

but other places? A-OK!

Last night, faint knocking woke me from sleep. The knocking stopped, then started up again, barely audible even in the silence of the night. Friend or foe? "Who is it?" I whispered. "Who's there?" I imagined Anca crouched on the landing, her ear pressed to the door just as mine was. A guard's shout elsewhere in the castle spooked my unseen visitor into a quick retreat.

This morning, Anca heats a pan of leftover *comyika* on the stove. The guard smokes on the landing, indifferent to the prisoner seated at the table. "Was that you last night outside my door?" I whisper as she sets a plate in front of me. "What's the plan?" She moves on, no words, no eye contact. My hopes dashed, I stir a fork through the lukewarm casserole of snake eggs and pig's bladder—in search of a message, any message, like *not much longer* or *rescue comes soon.* There's only *comyika.*

> *Cows grow safely here. Babies*
> *in Keshnev can keep every limb.*
> *For old people, less choices. Life*
> *does not go on forever.*

REC

On the day after my flameout performance at the UN, the phone started ringing at 6 a.m. Insolent questions from media jackals rang out from my answering machine. *What is the response from Minister Petrescu? Do you expect to be recalled to Keshnev? Are you currently under psychiatric care?*

Also, on the machine, Vadim's anxious query: "Sir, television people ask will you go on and talk to man of anchor? Please, sir, give me your reply."

From Alfred Lundquist: "Too bad I missed your speech, it sounds like one for the ages. And did you know there is a motion to censure you in the works?"

From the Consul: "Ministry reports severe displeasure. You are commanded hereby to give reasons for your actions."

Yes, it was possible I'd overstepped myself. The vivid image of crowds fleeing the Council chamber no longer felt as liberating as before; now it was one more reason to bring down the hammer on me. Over the weekend, I succumbed to gloom—eating little, sleeping poorly, pacing around the apartment like a caged big cat. On Sunday, I looked out the window to check conditions on the street. The batch of reporters clustered at the curb looked like germs from my vantage point, poorly dressed bacilli seeking to infect the host. *Me.*

On Monday morning, I woke as I still occasionally did, cleansed of despair. I showered and shaved, chose a Hermès tie of robin's-egg blue along with a cream-colored shirt and black Armani suit. At the kitchen table, I sipped coffee and paged through the *Times*, avoiding the front-page account of my Security Council meltdown—UN DIPLOMAT IN HOT WATER AFTER BIZARRE SPEECH—and seeking out instead news of the Falklands war. Two photographs accompanied the featured story, both credited in miniscule lettering to *T. ASH.* In one photo, a Sea King helicopter lifted dramatically off the deck of the warship *HMS Brilliant.* In the other photo, shot on the heels of invading British forces, SAS paratroopers in camouflage gear and night-vision goggles marched across a windswept landscape. I pictured Tess in her khakis and combat boots hunkered in a ditch as bullets flew by. If I'd been a better father, she might have chosen a more conventional career, or at least one not so precariously life-and-death as this.

"Enough," I told the surrounding appliances.

Starting today, things were going to change. I would adopt a suitable air of remorse, mend fences with my disgruntled colleagues, and devise a face-saving way out of my difficulties. The hell with Minister Petrescu, buried in his basement office thousands of miles away, waiting to claim my soul. There was still time to turn my life around.

The elevator arrived seconds after I pressed DOWN. On the tenth floor, a small man in a tweed jacket and tortoise-shell glasses entered and stared at me throughout our descent. To be expected, I thought, my face being in the news and all. Best to turn the other cheek, endure the gawking of others, and move on. But upon reaching the ground-floor, I did a quick two-step and invaded Professor Tweed's personal space. "Boo," I said, inches from his face. The startled little man fled across the lobby.

The doorman's desk happened to be unoccupied at the moment, Javier likely out somewhere fulfilling a tenant's eccentric request. Bismarck was lurking there, of all places, the elusive yet strangely well-fed feline resident of 345 E. Seventy-second Street. The tiger cat's spine melted under my touch, a vibratory hum building in his chest. "You're not supposed to be here," I whispered, glancing up for a split-second to make sure no one was coming. When I looked down, something had changed; Bismarck cringed from me, ears lowered, hackles raised. There was fleeting contact between his claws and my hand. But even though the scratch was minimal, a deeper psychic wound came from knowing Bismarck was now aligned with all the others—only *homo sapiens*, up to now—joined in writing me off.

Javier appeared, doorman of distinction, holding the lobby

door open for me. Pinned to his lapel was a tiny brass replica of his stateless colony's national flag.

"*¡Embajador! ¿Cómo está hoy?*"

"Never better," I said, my hand stinging a little from Bismarck's baffling attack. "And you?"

"*Sí, sí,* never better."

Together, we stood outside under clear skies on Seventy-second Street.

"What's the press situation, Javier? Where did all the bastards go?"

The doorman grinned, eager to share good news. "I heard one man say there is a fire in Crown Heights. A synagogue, I think, maybe? *La presa* jump in their cars, go chasing after that."

On this quiet Monday morning, the world of the Upper East Side seemed more crisply defined than usual. Clouds shaped like puffy white schooners sailed above the river. A cherry-red Maserati gleamed in the sun. Across the street, old men and nursing students sat on a bus-stop bench, while a pair of schoolgirls giggled over a half-naked mannequin in the tailor shop window.

The Bentley arrived. Emil emerged in his uniform of faux Habsburg design—gold buttons, epaulets, a medal or two of dubious origin pinned to his chest. A sudden breeze rushed down the block. As I tugged at my coat-collar, a woman wearing a full-length chinchilla coat strolled past the building —dark-haired, slender, fortyish, and walking a black-and-tan King Charles spaniel on a jeweled leash. I was looking forward to the luxury of the Bentley's interior, but when the woman in furs and I exchanged a cordial smile, new purpose entered my life.

The spaniel tugged her towards a bevy of odors on Third Avenue. She stopped at the corner, fumbling a lighter from her purse and trying to light the cigarette in her mouth. It was hard to get much done, between the unruly dog and the burrowing wind. With a quick nod at Emil, I walked over and offered my assistance.

"Thanks." She smiled, surrendering the lighter. "It's a lot to deal with, all at the same time."

Later, I wondered, What made me do this? Women in countless numbers crossed my path every day in New York and I didn't act on it. Why now? Was it just knee-jerk chivalry or a last-ditch effort to glom onto Old World money? At the very least, I figured, a little unforeseen encounter might delay the public humiliation waiting for me at the office.

The woman's gloved hand touched mine, cupping the lighter's flame. She had arresting blue eyes, thin yet sensual lips, patrician features that looked blessedly free of cosmetic surgery. I asked where she was off to on this lovely spring morning.

"Manicure," the woman replied in a wealthy drawl. "It's a weekly thing. But first—" The spaniel strained at the leash. "*Someone* has to have his little walk."

"And after?"

The leash became entangled around her leg. "Well, I—"

"Have lunch with me. I know a great Italian place near the Frick."

"Lunch ..."

The woman frowned, deep in thought, as if contemplating a life-and-death decision. A half-block away, Javier had joined Emil standing by the Bentley; the sight of driver and doorman in complementary uniforms was strangely touching. I smiled and shrugged, as if to say, *What can I do?* Shaking his head, Emil climbed in behind the wheel.

"Yes," the woman said. "Lunch would be nice."

"Wonderful! My name is Gabriel. It's a pleasure to meet you."

"I'm Sofia." She struggled in vain to prevent the dog from peeing on a mailbox. "And this frisky fellow is—"

A wave of concussive sound washed over the street. I felt myself lifted from the ground and thrust violently backwards, like a sack tossed from a moving train. Ordinary objects, things normally inert and earthbound, took flight with me—a man-hole cover, airborne tires, brick-and-plaster shrapnel—bodies, too, hurtling through space, just like mine. Then I struck my head on some hard, unyielding surface and fell to earth.

I could see things happening around me, but all without sound. A gushing, beheaded fire hydrant, the Maserati engulfed in fire. I touched the back of my head and came away with blood-streaked fingers.

Then sound came roaring back—sirens, screaming children, an aria of car-horns. Clouds of ash, dust, and other nameless particulates. The shop-window dummy was covered in someone's blood. A schoolgirl stared open-mouthed at her scorched and mutilated hand. Flames shot out of the Bentley's mangled chassis and two men lay nearby, one-face down, the other in a charred fetal ball. I slowly realized I was sitting in a puddle, a rising noxious tide of sewage and bodily fluids. And there was the woman Sofia—whose cigarette I lit only seconds ago in some other, saner world—on her knees by the bombed-out storefront, great chunks of her lips and tongue torn away, wailing to the sky for her unnamed spaniel, now a mass of bloody fur and bones in her arms.

20

REW

Another time and place ...

Autumn, 1936. Rumors of a surprise royal visit had swept through the village of Rogvald all day. Last night's year had thoroughly muddied the grounds, which some villagers took as a bad omen. My father, a perennial optimist, hoped the King would be impressed by the crisp mountain air of Keshnev's Lesser Alps.

In my twelve-year-old imagination, King Josef stood proud and resolute in battle, a stirring, almost mythical figure in a brilliant white uniform. As I later learned, he never saw a day of combat. For my father—a large man nearing fifty, with slumped shoulders and prematurely graying hair—this visit was a once-in-a-lifetime chance to express gratitude for His Majesty's benign attitude towards foreigners preaching the Gospel on his native soil. In many East European countries, brigands and thieves set upon pilgrims with impunity; things were different here, thanks to His Royal Highness and Imperial

Majesty, Sovereign of the Lower Danube, and Emperor of Keshnev.

The town square was the rumored destination, a small enclosure flanked by plane trees and low stone walls. The crowd had grown throughout the morning.

"C'mon, Gabe," Father said. "Let's try getting closer."

He insisted on holding my hand as we maneuvered through the crowd, which felt demeaning and undignified, but after we wiggled past bodies and neared the stage, he released me with a stern admonition.

"Don't wander off."

Familiar faces abounded in the square. The village handyman and his buck-toothed daughter. A middle-aged bachelor said to excel at games of chance. Rogvald's last surviving Great War veteran, the left sleeve of his scruffy uniform hanging empty and limp. When we first came to Rogvald, I looked down on these people, but their unflinching warmth and good humor—qualities absent among our spiritually frostbitten brethren in upstate New York—won me over. Rogvalders practiced a strain of Christianity less heated and more accommodating than our own, and after months of failed conversions, my parents came to accept this. Father became a sympathetic listener, trusted advisor, and occasional lender of money. Mother reinvented herself as a healer and midwife. On this day of the King's visit, her skills were required elsewhere, in a hut by the river where a Magyar girl was struggling to survive a breech-birth delivery.

Heavy clouds lingered overhead like guests who won't leave the party. Questions bounced from villager to villager. Will the King really show up? Is another storm coming? I felt certain King Josef would appear just as I imagined him, astride a great white horse, brandishing a sword of justice. I couldn't recall ever wanting something to happen so badly in my short life.

But when I saw Mina in the crowd, all thoughts of royal pomp and circumstance fled my brain.

Just days ago, hanging around a campfire with ragtag village kids, this dark-haired girl four years older than me had unveiled the ecstasies of the French kiss. Tongue on tongue! For the son of God-fearing missionaries, it was a discovery on par with the invention of fire. She quickly lost interest in my sentimental education, drifting off with a girlfriend, the same chubby companion beside her now. The square was tightly packed, bodies confined on all sides by the low stone walls, but I could only see Mina, with her ringlets of brown hair and small breasts in a loose-fitting peasant dress.

As if conscious of my scrutiny, Mina turned and saw me. I looked away, my cheeks radiantly hot.

"I'll be right back," I told my father.

"What? Gabriel! Where are you—wait!"

Under threatening skies, I squeezed past more familiar faces. The town's top-hatted patriarch with his dowdy wife and cross-eyed son. A pair of orphaned fraternal twins, one tall and lanky, the other squat and obese, each burdened by a bereft-of-parents stare. Even Madame Yerkes, the village governess, was there, in her customary widow's weeds, the sole French exile and *cosmopolite* in all rural Keshnev.

Mina spotted me coming. She laughed, took hold of her friend's hand, and vanished into the crowd. Rain pattered down, the bodies around me damp and slippery. I kept on. All that mattered was burrowing through ever-shifting gaps in flesh, inching past a knee here and a shoulder there, so I could lay claim to more of Mina's kisses.

Suddenly, the talk and laughter of the morning was gone. Clattering hoof-beats broke the silence. "Make way! Move aside!" Three Hussar foot-soldiers in jackboots and spiked helmets cleared a space, scowls on their faces and black truncheons in their hands. In the commotion, I was hemmed in, unable to move, even with Mina so maddeningly close.

Then the crowd parted and there he was.

King Josef—tall, ram-rod straight in the saddle, in a white uniform and naval commander's cap—far eclipsed my feeble notions of monarchy. The white-maned creature he rode was too majestic to be labeled a mere "horse." Together, cantering smoothly into the village square, they formed a seamless fusion of man and beast. The pungent smell of purebred horse-flesh filled the air.

We, his awestruck subjects, crowded as close as the ill-tempered Hussars would allow. I could see the King in greater detail now, his fierce black beard and benevolent smile, a salad of medallions pinned to his chest for wars never fought. A man long accustomed to the adulation of others.

The rain let up and clouds abruptly gave way, bathing the sovereign and steed in a golden light.

Mina! Where was she? *There*, squeezed in between the orphaned twins, on her face the same rapturous gaze as everyone else. Villagers shifted in waves to welcome the royal presence and soon she was lost from view. Pushing around bodies with renewed zeal, I heard a single voice rise above the collective cheers—a man in a work shirt and black suspenders, shouting in a hostile, unknown tongue. The Hussars, busy stiff-arming the crowd, didn't notice. No one saw the man raise a short-barreled revolver in the air. No one cried, "Gun! He's got a gun!" I ducked my head and pressed forward like a battering ram, grunting and twisting in just enough time to leap up and sink my sharp adolescent teeth in the gunman's meaty forearm.

The howl he let out caught everyone's attention. He jerked

free, slapping me away and firing the gun into empty air. The white horse reared up in terror, a look on His Majesty's face of dumbfounded surprise. Can someone be shooting at *me*? The man was trying to get off a second shot when the Hussars brought him to the ground in a scrum of bodies. With truncheons and jackboots, they administered their own rough justice, beating the would-be assassin to a pulp.

Someone helped me to my feet. Villagers laughed in relief, shouting about what I'd done.

Hero! they cried. *He's a hero! The boy who saved the King!*

21

REC

Antiseptic odors, wobbly gradations of light. Metal wheels scraping linoleum, polyphonic beeps in my ears.

Awake or dead? In the dark, in a sweat-stained hospital gown, I couldn't tell which. My head felt as though a bowling ball had been jammed up my nose. Some contraption attached to my penis impaled me to the bed. Only by remaining as still as a corpse could I hope to limp into the netherworld of sleep or death, whichever would bring an end to *all this*.

Fingertips gently pressed ice flakes on my lips. I looked up at a smiling, gray-haired nurse.

"Welcome back to the living."

Thick bandages encased my torso. Gauze was wrapped tightly around my leg, just above the knee. Sutures protruded like barbed wire from the back of my skull.

"More good news," the kindly nurse said. "Catheter comes out today. Big relief, huh?"

For hours I watched cloven-hoofed demons in white lab coats flit past my bed. Gradually, a real-life figure came into focus, an authentic-looking human being who delivered his prognosis in a deep, operatic baritone. Bruised ribs, moderately inflamed leg wound, second-degree burns on wrist and elbow, a nasty bump on the head. *Nothing too serious,* the rich-throated physician said, *a few days' rest and you'll be just fine.* Welcome to the world of empty promises.

Neither the gray-haired nurse nor the baritone physician explained how I got here, and life in Intensive Care was too chaotic for anyone else to stop and answer my questions. Finally, a nursing attendant named Leon took pity on me, sharing a copy of yesterday's *Daily News,* headlined RUN-AT-MOUTH DIPLOMAT CHEATS DEATH FROM CAR-BOMB.

Leon looked at the paper, then up at me. "You don't remember none of this? Maybe I shouldn't say ..."

Pushing a single word through my parched lips took all the effort I had. "Say ..."

"All right." He settled in the chair beside my bed, as if about to read a bedtime story. "Man, sure is *something.*"

At 8:36 a.m., the previous morning, a person or persons unknown had remotely detonated three pounds of plastic explosive secured to the Bentley's undercarriage. The force inside the blast radius shattered apartment windows, turned fire escapes into mangled steel, and rocked a delivery truck onto its side two blocks away. Multiple fatalities included Javier Cruz, 39, doorman at 345 E. 72nd Street, "a familiar face in this quietly affluent neighborhood," as well as one Emil Vaka, age unknown, a transplanted Keshnevite and "the intended victim's driver." Sofia Constantine, of the renowned Constantine shipping line, had been airlifted to a burn clinic upstate, while Ambassador Gabriel Ash escaped with only minor injuries—"Minor!" I feebly choked out—currently listed in stable condition at Mt. Sinai Hospital.

The crime-scene photos were horrific, bodies under bloodstained sheets, smoke and dust clouds, scenes of chaos more likely found in war-torn Lebanon than on the Upper East Side.

What had I said or done that compelled someone to try and set me ablaze? Maybe those crackpot exiles in Flatbush were behind the assassination attempt, or a rogue faction of Petrescu's secret police. The orders to kill me might have come from the Minister himself.

Who wanted me dead? Better to speculate on who *didn't*.

Day bled into night. I slept fitfully, woke to blistering pain in my leg. Nurses came and went, draining precious fluids.

I woke deep in the night, addled by pain and the drugs taken to mask it. The ICU was deathly quiet, beds around me bathed in purplish light. Someone sat on the window-ledge— Emil Vaka, in a blast-shredded uniform, his features blackened, smiling in that cracked way of his. *No hard feelings, Ambassador.* The weeping sounds I made woke a hit-and-run patient in the next bed over; he began moaning in sympathy, and soon other patients came alive, as it were, a chorus of the damned in the night-time ICU. When I looked again, the window-ledge was empty.

The attack on Keshnev's leading diplomat was a mystery as well to Lieutenant Nathan Shapiro, NYPD. He turned up my room in a cheap suit and ill-fitting toupee, peppering me with questions while I floated in a doped-up haze. *Who are your friends? Who are your enemies?* Though he kept a pencil stub poised over a notepad, Det. Shapiro recorded none of my disjointed responses. With a nod at a uniformed cop seated outside the ward—"Just a precaution"—he left, promising to check in later.

When I next opened my eyes, a bleary late-afternoon light suffused the ward. Standing at the foot of the bed was

Inspector Pieter Best of UN Security. I looked up from my horizontal vantage point at his well-tailored suit and a long pale scar under his chin—inflicted, no doubt, during some mercenary adventures in Rhodesia or Mozambique. How long he had stood there watching me shiver and groan in my sleep?

"On behalf of the United Nations community," the Inspector said, "I convey our deepest hopes and best wishes for your speedy recovery. Also, the Secretary-General sends his personal best regards."

"What's going on? Who killed Emil Vaka?" I struggled inelegantly, and with considerable discomfort, into an upright position. "Tell me what happened."

"No, no, no ..." He shook a manicured forefinger at me. "The incident is far too upsetting to discuss with a man in your condition. All I can say is, an investigation is underway ... but, since this deplorable act of violence took place on a city street, strictly speaking, it's in the hands of the NYPD. For UN Security to intervene on your behalf would be an unpardonable breach of jurisdiction."

"What the hell are you talking about? Someone tried to kill me!"

"Rest assured," Inspector Best said. "It's being looked into."

My attempt to rise indignantly only resulted in needlesharp pain in my joints. "Don't *look into it!* Don't check back later! Round up some of your soldiers of fortune and find the bastards who did this."

My little outburst echoed through the ICU. Only days ago, I'd spurned the Inspector's offer of bodyguard protection. Hardly surprising now if his concern for my well-being fell short of the mark. He studied the life-monitoring equipment set up by my bed, as if determining which button, when pressed, might shed the world of Gabriel Ash.

"Some in the UN say you brought this on yourself," he said.

"All the nonsense you spewed in the Council chamber! Who are *you* to scold the world for its misdeeds?" His gruff, man-of-the-veldt features darkened. "May I remind you, sir, the Boers whom you so casually belittled are *my* people. Painting them as mere victims is repugnant and defamatory."

I fell back in bed, wracked with pain. Inspector Best rose and walked to the door, offering a last, two-faced smile. "Once again, sir, our most strenuous wishes for your quick recovery. Have a nice day."

No one seemed to care very much about the crime perpetrated against me, or the urgency with which my assailants should be caught and punished. Mostly, people just wanted to be rid of me.

In the morning, I was transferred to a private room on the tenth floor—bed, desk, closet and bathroom, curtains kept closed on a floor-to-ceiling window. To my surprise, a bounty of flowers and sympathy cards filled the room. One get-well card depicted a tranquil beach sunset and inside, written in Francesca Cavour's come-hither scrawl, "Don't die before we can fuck again." A card from Hilda, my secretary, expressing typically overwrought emotions: "Awful, what they did to you! Awful, awful!" Even best wishes from Gunter Kleist, whom I'd publicly humiliated outside the Delegates Lounge; the delicate line drawing of nude young men at play on the front of the card suggested a wryness on Gunter's part that the Goethe quote inside did not: "If you start to think about your moral and physical condition, you usually find that you are sick."

Was this a genuine outpouring of sympathy, I wondered cynically, or a reflection of the secret fear share by all public officials of getting blown to bits in the cold light of day?

Nurses on the tenth floor smiled a lot, called me by name,

gushed over a giant bouquet of flowers sent by the Office of the Secretary-General. At the same time, these nurses treated me like any other patient, the injuries sustained in a terrorist car-bombing being in their eyes no more or less notable than casualties from a five-car pile-up in the Holland Tunnel. This matter-of-fact approach, as much as drugs and physical therapy, helped speed my eventual recovery.

But not yet. Late in the morning, I stumbled from bed and made for the bathroom. A therapist had left behind a walking cane, which proved invaluable for my short journey; still, my body felt as though someone had methodically smashed different parts of it here and there with a croquet mallet. Inside the bathroom, I accessed the toilet seat by awkwardly crouching and pivoting; after completing my business, I stood, tugged at the belt of my pajama bottoms, and waited for the whirling sensation to pass.

What a shock to open the bathroom door and find two strangers in my room!

The closed curtains kept my surroundings in a permanent dusk, so all I could make out at first was one figure seated on the bed and another occupying the chair. I hung back—frightened and confused, in altogether too much pain—in the bathroom doorway.

"Sir? We bring this to you."

My assistant Vadim held out a white terrycloth robe he'd taken from my apartment. He looked pale, unshaven, wearing a suit that looked lived-in for many generations. I snatched the robe away, threw it over my pajamas, and flicked on the desk lamp. Another surprise awaited me, and not a good one. The Consul sat in the chair, last seen in Central Park impersonating a mugging victim, transformed yet again with a shocking new ensemble. Blue gabardine pants, a Hawaiian shirt adorned with claw-snapping lobsters, and—please! no more surprises!—a checkered porkpie hat.

"How the hell did you get in here? I told the nurses, no visitors."

"We show our papers," the Consul said flatly. "We come in."

I turned my spite and indignation on Vadim. "Look at your appearance! Is this how you represent Keshnev in my absence?"

Vadim fought back a yawn. "Did you wish, sir, for a return to bed?"

Under no circumstances would I permit these men to see me prone and vulnerable. From the doorway I gazed down at the Consul's Tin Pan Alley attire, remembering how close he came to ensnaring me in his monstrous loyalty test. Whatever his true purpose for being in New York, my own personal welfare had nothing to do with it. I poked the tip of the cane in his shoulder blade and said, "Shoo." Sneering, he gave up the chair.

At my request, Vadim provided an update on the past few days, all while keeping an eye on his bizarrely clothed nemesis. On the day of the car-bombing, he reported, all UN plenary and deliberative sessions were cancelled. The following day saw some scattered delegate activity, nothing of note. Today, once it became clear Ambassador Ash's injuries weren't life-threatening, business in the General Assembly and Security Council went on pretty much as usual.

"But see!" The Consul waved a bony hand at the SG's floral extravaganza. "You are very much missed."

A statement had been issued by the Foreign Ministry, Vadim said. I winced as he repeated it verbatim: "The People's Democratic Republic condemns in great magnitude this act of coward-ness. We urge all nations to leap on the throat of imperialist hooligans and extinguish all life."

Vadim slumped against the headboard, depleted by his efforts. He pointed at a glossy magazine on the nightstand; on the cover was the latest blonde anorexic supermodel *du jour*.

"All they have in gift shop," he said, closing his eyes. He was asleep in minutes.

A cumbersome silence followed, the Consul and I daring the other to speak first. The porkpie hat—like the rest of his outfit, clearly of Salvation Army provenance—looked as if a truck had run over it. Watching him poked a finger inside bouquets and snicker at the get-well cards, I thought, What if this repugnant little changeling was my would-be assassin?

"Look at you in those fancy duds," I said. "Really getting into the swing of things in the Free World."

"Thank you." The Consul plucked a card at random, began reading aloud. "From Mol-lie Boy-ell, Dear Ambassador, please do not start—"

"Put that down, you idiot."

"—what you cannot finish." He let out an unnerving guffaw, made weirder still by the jaunty tilt of his porkpie hat. "You are some character."

Vadim twitched and moaned in his sleep, his hands thrashing about as if fighting off wolves. The Consul sat on the edge of the bed and addressed me in a whisper, presumably to thwart listening devices embedded in the hospital walls.

"New dispatch arrives from Foreign Ministry," he said. "Your return to Keshnev must be immediately."

I reminded the Consul that the two of us stood on American soil, and he lacked any authority here. The Consul reminded *me* that Minister Petrescu's authority was everywhere.

"How do you forget this?" he asked.

I looked at my slumbering second-in-command and pictured him in the clutches of SPU interrogators. They'd snap him like a twig, and Vadim knew it. That was why the Consul's presence sapped the life from him. But what the Consul said was true. In the world I inhabited—just days after averting death by immolation—the Minister's authority knew no bounds.

"In Keshnev, heads look up at you," the Consul grumbled. "There is pride for history you share with Gray Wolf, for role played in Great Struggle Against Fascism. But in America, some say you take advantages. Life has become too much comfortable. You live ... how do they say it? ... high in hog."

"On," I told him.

"What?"

"High *on* the hog. Or *off*. That's OK, too."

The Consul's cheeks reddened, suggesting for the first time a tenuous capacity for human emotion.

"Was it you?" I asked. "Were you the one who tried to have me killed?"

This took him a long moment to puzzle out—proof, I supposed, of his innocence. "Me? OK, *that* is joke."

"Right," I said. "You were too busy throwing together just the right ensemble."

The Consul shook his head, as if at the futility of it all. He leaned over and bellowed in my sleeping assistant's face.

"Hey! Come awake now!"

Vadim bolted upright, bug-eyed with terror. Seeing the Consul, recalling the circumstances that had landed him in his boss's hospital room, he seemed to age in seconds—his once-proud Communist spirit broken by fear of this man.

"No big problem!" the Consul said. "Car blows up in street, so what? For Ambassador, no big problem! This is treason talk, are you agreed?"

Vadim babbled a response, but not in words. I gripped the cane, raised it in the air with the frailty of a hundred-year-old man, and poked the Consul's foot.

"Get out. And take that ridiculous hat with you."

"Sure! OK! We will send dispatch, tell Ministry chief delegate disobeys orders." He seized Vadim's forearm, rendering him nearly dead from fright. "Go! Send now!"

The two men left, each unhappy in his own way. From the corridor came the soft skid of nursing shoes and the names of doctors announced over a squawking loudspeaker. I sat in semi-darkness admiring the cover girl in a string bikini, grateful for the soul-warping ways of the West.

22

REC

Later in the day, wearing my posh robe in this bleak hospital setting, I limped to the door of my room. I took a shaky step into the hallway and then I fell back, blinded by fluorescent ceiling tubes. Moments later I resumed the journey, tapping the cane in front of me like a sightless man. The vinyl floor under my slippers was slick and difficult to navigate. Split-second bouts of vertigo dogged my path and pain like some living thing burrowed deep inside my bones. Making this trek from hospital room to nurses' station became a test of my body and my traumatized will, a hurdle I must overcome. I reached a set of chairs at the end of the hall, as winded as a marathon runner.

At this busy intersection of corridors, doctors barked at nurses, orderlies scurried to empty bedpans, family members wandered around looking uniformly distraught. A wheelchair patient passed by, as did a somewhat more mobile patient trailing an IV on wheels. After two long days alone in antimicrobial darkness, this beehive of activity came as welcome relief.

"Sir? Sir?"

I sat with an elbow on the cane, my leg throbbing as if hot oil had pooled behind my kneecap. A moment passed before I realized the voice rising out of the chaos addressed me.

"Sir!"

A heavyset woman at the nurses' desk held a telephone receiver in her outstretched hand. I stared at it, at her, like a child at a puppet show.

"Your daughter, sir! On the line!"

"What?"

"Your daughter's calling!"

Tess? Confusion reigned. I tried coming to my feet. "OK, let me get to—"

"No, no, sir. Take it right here."

Before I knew it, a passing orderly raised me up in muscular arms and dropped me in a chair nearest to the nurses' desk. The nurse thrust the handset at me, amid clucks and giggles from others on the staff; even for these jaded medical professionals, a transatlantic call from the deck of a Royal Navy warship in the Falkland Islands didn't happen every day. I wondered what these warm-hearted souls would think if they'd heard my daughter's parting words to me in the Waldorf. *Fuck you, Father.*

"Hello?" Bursts of static filled the line, a fragile connection. "Tess? Are you there?"

"—first chance I've had ..." Her voice was barely audible over the roar of turbine engines. "—out to sea and ..."

"How are you?"

"—cold here, very cold, all the time ..."

"Tess, I can't hear—"

"—soldiers, you know? More like boys, really ..."

A crash-cart rumbled down the hall, nurses and internists in close pursuit. They readied equipment in front of a patient's room and swarmed inside. Meanwhile, my globetrotting daughter's voice fluttered in deep space.

"—something about a ... *bomb?* In a *car*—?"

"No, no, I'm fine. What about you?"

Static crackled over the line, then a patch of dead air, the stillness of the void. From out of the depths came her voice, frail as gossamer.

"—in the restaurant that day, awful things I said ..."

"Tess—"

"I'm not, I didn't mean it—"

"I know," I said, too softly to be heard.

"—*any* of it ..."

A last torrent of static, then unendurable silence. "Tess! Tess!" She was gone. I felt the same shuddering grief as last night in Emil's ghostly presence. Two men dead because of me, a daughter in harm's way, and what could I do about it?

Nurses returned to the station, happy and raucous about a life saved. "Nice chat?" one of them asked, gently taking the phone from my hand. I pushed out of the chair and began the voyage back to my room, the only shelter known to me in a world beset by misery and death.

The next day, over Vadim's objections, I convened a press conference in the hospital meeting room. Time for this "intended victim" to have his say.

Seated alone at a long table, I smiled as journalists and camera crews filed in, more than a few of them visibly licking their chops. My understated outfit—charcoal-gray blazer, white shirt, no tie, open at the collar—nicely complemented my early-morning haircut and manicure *en suite*. The plan was to strike just the right pose of unshakeable confidence, ship of state staying the course and so on, all while batting away reporters' inane questions and demonstrating via snappy off-the-cuff remarks the sangfroid and easy charm for which I was widely known.

What I didn't foresee were the narcotizing side-effects of pain medication taken a few hours earlier. Cameras flashed in my eyes. Everyone in the crowd seemed to be shouting at the same time. I dodged their pesky inquiries as best I could, firing off one incisive *bon mot* after another—at least I think I did—before finally calling it quits. Members of the Fourth Estate gave me funny looks on the way out, and I thought I knew why; I'd bamboozled the media at their own game and come away with my dignity intact.

I was sure of it. I just couldn't recall any specifics.

On that same day, the body of Emil Vaka, my dear friend and driver, was lowered into the earth. Vadim handled the logistics of transportation for me—a taxi with a single motorcycle-cop entourage from the hospital—and soon I stood, a bit shakily, in my alpaca coat in a cemetery in Queens. A handful of mourners were gathered by the graveside while a bearded Eastern Orthodox priest mumbled incantations into the wind. Some distance away, a ragtag band of Keshnevite émigrés huddled beneath a lofty elm.

I stayed upright more or less throughout the service, but the weather turned unseasonably cold and now I trembled inside my coat. As Vadim led me to the waiting taxi, one of the émigrés hobbled forth and took hold of my elbow with crooked stick-fingers, speaking in a rapid dialect I didn't comprehend. According to Vadim's translation, the old crank urged me to investigate "mysterious circumstances" behind the deaths of my parents, Robert and Julia Ash, some forty years ago. Others in the old man's crew advanced as a shuffling mass. *Learn the truth,* the émigré said. *See who are your real enemies.* Then the aged scarecrows in black suits whisked him away and Vadim hustled me into the waiting car.

Rumors again, hints of secrets buried in the past. I didn't understand what the old man was talking about, nor did I think the chance to learn the truth would come as soon as it did.

Of my injuries, the leg wound proved slowest to heal. A doctor making afternoon rounds noted my discomfort, injecting me with a dose of what he archly termed "strong medicine." I fell into a feverish dream-state, the kind from which you desperately want to escape but never can. Chasing my doomed little brother through the woods, sitting in a puddle while fleshy body parts rained down from the sky, cringing from Emil's embrace in the afterlife.

I woke in the morning to the smell of bay rum cologne blending miserably in my nose with the hospital's ammonia-stink. A figure stood over the bed, backlit by hallway fluorescence.

"Gotta say, pal—you've definitely looked better."

Mark Pearson flicked on the desk lamp and dragged the chair beside my bed. Yale bulldog tie, impressively hand-tailored suit. Sturdy jaw and rows of good teeth, that emperor's gaze through which all other mortals are found wanting. I recalled our cocky banter in the Delegates Lounge and shuddered at our curbside war of words in Harlem. This sinister presence lurking in the background, never asked-for but always there. How did I let the CIA into my life?

"Could you ...?" I pointed at a glass on the nightstand. Pearson deliberated a long time before handing it over.

The water restored my voice and what was left of my wits. "The offer we discussed last week, remember? Well, I've given it some thought and ... I accept."

He stared at me. "Not following."

"'Jump over,' you said. 'Come join the winning team.'"

Pearson's laugh sounded twigs scraped together for kindling. "Is that how we're gonna play it—me making a plea on your behalf? 'Uh, boss, you know that clown on the Security Council—yeah, the Keshnev guy who delivered that whacked-out speech? Gets his ass nearly blown up, comes running to us the next day, begging for asylum. Not *before* a car-bombing, when he might have been of some value, but *now*, when pretty much he's a global laughingstock. Sound good, boss? Ready to take a flyer on this fella?'"

A nurse poked her head in, scanned the softly beeping monitors and withdrew. My head throbbed from residual pain and a heavy sense of oppression in this man's presence. The room, awash in get-well bouquets, felt as damp and humid as a greenhouse. I fought to keep my eyes open. How could anyone *breathe* in here?

"Hey, Ambassador! Stay with me."

"I, I'm here ..."

Pearson leaned close. "Don't you get it? Things are different now. Any offer of asylum made before we fully understood what kind of bad guys you run with is strictly null and void."

Run with? "I don't—"

"Let's tally up, shall we? Three pounds of *plastique* detonate in broad daylight on the Upper East Side. Multiple casualties, one of your own men down. You yourself come *this close* to sitting in the gutter with your entrails in your hand. Tell me again, Ambassador Ash. Why should the USA give a flying fuck about what happens to you?"

I smiled, floating on a river of slumber and pain meds. Even in this drug-addled state, I knew any threat this CIA man might pose was but a grain of sand in the endless shoreline of agony Petrescu had waiting for me.

"Didn't you hear what I said?" This was long after Pearson left. "I *accept.*"

An eternity passed, or maybe half an hour. I lay in bed, badgered by pain, my spirits leaden after a day-long parade of liars, bunglers, and fire-breathing patriots. A night nurse, observing my distress, brought two yellow pills and a glass of water. "No need to be hurtin', sweetheart." The door she left open let in a sliver of light, but here in the darkness, horrors thrived—a child's hand scorched by fire, shards of flesh-piercing glass, severed body parts covered in soot and ash.

The pills kicked in and I slept. In a dream far more pleasant than any in a long time, six-year-old Tess led me by the hand to the mastodon exhibit in the Natural History Museum. I lifted her towards the creature's gaping maws and my beautiful daughter squealed with delight. I woke from the dream smiling—and when had *that* last happened?—hoping the worst of the nightmares was over.

Then the telephone rang.

I picked up the receiver and mumbled some sort of greeting from deep within my pharmaceutical stew. Static greeted my ear, the peculiar low-level buzz of intercontinental cables. My heart raced. Could it be Tess calling again?

"*Olsha, y licht Ambassadorskii!*"

I sat up straight, every vestige of soothing medication

expunged from my system. "Minister! What a—what a surprise! But isn't it very late where you are?"

"Where I am is not day or night," the familiar, nicotine-scarred voice said. "Here, lights burn at all—"

A roar of atmospheric electricity drowned out his words. *Now* was the moment to hang up, claiming a broken connection—happens all the time, no way for me to return the call—but I couldn't do it.

"—last set eyes on each other, how long ago?" Minister Petrescu said. "Five years, ten? If a madman had his way, we wouldn't be talking now."

"And yet," I said stupidly, "here we are."

"Well, then? How are you feeling?"

"I'm fine." I pictured him alone in his basement office in the Foreign Ministry, smoking his foul-smelling Sobranie cigarettes. "My driver was much less fortunate."

"—a terrible tragedy, yes, of course ..." Bursts of static rattled in my ear like hail striking a tin roof. "—police, what do they know? There must be suspects."

You mean, other than you? "Whatever they know, they're not sharing."

"What to make of all this, Comrade Ambassador? There is so much I don't understand."

"Nor I, Minister."

"Maybe if you come and explain to me, we can both understand better."

Confessing my sins to Minister Petrescu seemed like the worst of all possible strategies. "No need," I told him. "Things are different now. I'm turning over a new leaf, I see where it all went wrong—"

"*Turn? Leaf?*"

I had to keep talking or lose my grip entirely. "At the UN, Minister. I'll make a clean start there. Reassess my priorities, work harder on behalf of the People's Democratic Republic, and become, I hope, a better person."

Silence. No one was buying this, least of all me.

"What was it old King Josef used to say about you, after he settled into exile in Mayfair and took on British airs? *Gabriel Ash*, the King would say, *now there's a slippery fellow.*"

He laughed at the memory, the coarse sound of it carrying across thousands of miles of underseas cable. If I hung up now and he tried calling back, I simply wouldn't answer, likely would never again in my life pick up a ringing telephone. Slowly it dawned on me it wasn't laughter I heard coming from the bowels of the Foreign Ministry; in fact, Petrescu was shouting at the top of his corroded lungs.

"—ignorant, self-absorbed fool! Look at the damage you've caused, the shame you bring to our country!"

I cowered like prey trapped in the tall grass, awaiting its devourer. More colorful obscenities came flying at me, but a moment later it was over. Minister Petrescu was calm again, the voice of reason.

"Time to come home, old friend."

PAUSE

Weary as I am, sleep eludes me. At night when I close my eyes, bodies burn and cars erupt into flames.

Tonight, for some reason, Anca doesn't bring any dinner. Cold, hungry, robbed of sleep, I'm only dimly aware of the acrid odor stinging my nose. A guard shouts in the courtyard; soon others shout, too, spurring on the panicked cries of livestock. From my barred window, all I see are dark, placid trees. A thin vein of gray smoke seeps under the locked door, curling around my ankles.

"Help! Fire!" I cry. "Let me out!"

I pound on the door. Miraculously, it comes open.

It's Stefan, in a rumpled jacket, gesturing urgently at me. "*Lache!* Hurry!"

A bell is clanging, frenzied voices rising in pitch and volume. Stefan shoves me down the winding stairwell, dense with smoke, and I press a hand to the stone wall for balance, stumbling on the descent. When I reach the landing, the guard making his way up comes to a halt, looking surprised to find the prisoner two steps above him. I rear back and kick him squarely in the chest.

He tumbles backwards down the steps, still wearing a look of surprise, his head repeatedly striking stone. We hurry past his broken body and, reaching ground level, open the door and step into chaos.

Flames shoot out of the barn, sparks igniting the stables and guards' thatched houses. One desperate soul runs across the courtyard with both sleeves on fire. I squint through the smoke and see only a single water-hose in play, long and knotted, requiring the strength of several men pulling and tugging at it, all for a feeble spurt of water. Bells keep clanging. Ash falls from the sky. Stefan pushes me towards the east gate and a sloping road.

"This way!"

Stefan pushes me to where a castle gate stands unprotected. Heat scalds my face as I race through and onto a gentle slope in the ground. A battered green Peugeot idles nearby. A short, thickset man stands beside it, urgently beckoning us over. And now Anca emerges from the passenger side, the light of the blaze refracted in her smudged and joyous face.

"We go now, OK?"

PART TWO
PERSONA NON GRATA

23

Travel by day is impossible. The threat of capture lurks around every bend, behind every gnarled tree. We shelter in remote woodland, abandoned railway stations, often by the side of seldom-used roads. Luckily for us, the desolate countryside is full of places like that.

Four passengers sit cramped inside the Peugeot—Oleg, the hot-headed Estonian driver, Stefan who early on claimed the front passenger seat for his own, Anca and I seated in back. Oleg exudes a musty odor, like cheese left out too long in the sun; in his mid-fifties, I think, dark hair and large ears, hyper-vigilant by nature, not to say paranoid. At the first hint of trouble—a set of oncoming headlights, a distant car-horn—he swings the Peugeot off the road, hiding us in whatever secluded foliage is available. For some reason, Anca ascribes great wisdom to Oleg's navigational skills. Her husband up front seems less impressed, complaining about our frequent stops and starts.

Tonight, the Peugeot drives through arid backcountry, illu-minated by a wistful quarter-moon. If any escape plan exists—

beyond sparking a diversionary fire in the castle and then running like hell—no one's told me.

Oleg's big ears suddenly perk up. Without consulting anyone, he steers the Peugeot off the road into a cluster of trees.

"Something out there," he says.

Stefan rolls his eyes. "*Ne, ne,* we do not stay here. Too much open ground."

"But something—"

"*Ne,* not *always* something. Is bad for us to stay."

Our fate depends upon the leader of this little tribe, but since fleeing the castle there's no clear sign who that should be. Stefan and Oleg bicker constantly—*this* is better route, no, *that* is—while I sit and brood in back, dressed in someone else's discarded jacket and pants. Anca, I suspect, is the source of contention among the men; once, during a strident quarrel up-front, I leaned forward and asked, "Are you two brothers, is that it?" Anca's sharp elbow in my ribs reminded me it was none of my business.

Life on the run seems to suit her. In the castle she went about her work tight-lipped and stoical. Now, when the impulse strikes, she'll lean her head out the open window and laugh into the wind. If the drab clothes she wears haven't changed, something has in the way she inhabits them.

But what's the *plan*? Why does it seem we're driving in circles?

I doze, falling into a dream of horses on fire, Minister Petrescu rising out of the ashes in full military regalia.

"Hey, Comrade," a voice calls out. "Everybody back there A-OK?"

I open my eyes, blink several times. We're driving again.

"Hungry? Thirsty?" Stefan says, turned around in his seat. "Need take shit, maybe?"

Oleg, half-turned in the driver's seat, wears a sneer just like that of his front-seat companion. Anca beside me smiles in a vaguely unfriendly way. All three of them swerve between concern for my well-being and a mocking indifference.

"He is fine," she says, looking out the window.

Fine. We've slept in weed beds, traipsed through dog shit, stewed for days in our own juices. A smell of dried sweat and fear.

"Shhh!" Oleg says. "What is that?"

The Peugeot slows. I listen hard, hear nothing. Stefan groans, "Not again."

Within minutes, Oleg has us sequestered out of sight in a clump of pine trees. We can all feel it now—a growing rumble in the floorboards, the leaden thump of cheap tires on a blacktop road. Two jeeps pass by, then a lorry rolls along the road, grim-looking soldiers in back, a trussed-up and blindfolded prisoner at their feet.

None of us speak until the armored convoy is long gone. Stefan is first to let out his breath.

"Stay here, I think. Is better we keep hidden."

"*Ne,*" Oleg says. "Here is not safe. We keep going."

Stefan looks at him in disbelief. "What is wrong in your head? Do you not see for yourself? Army is everywhere!"

"Oleg is right," Anca says from the back-seat. "Too much danger here."

At which her husband's head snaps around. "This is up to *you* now?"

"Let's just think for a moment," I say, jumping into the frightened silence. "Think about what we should do."

"No think." Oleg starts the engine. "Keep going."

24

Our third day on the run and tempers are frayed. We're sandwiched inside the Peugeot barreling down the road, weary of each other's company and such close proximity to body funk. I'm not the only one desperate to escape these confines.

Dawn breaks. We sit awhile inside the parked car, transfixed by sun-tinged bands of green and yellow ascendant in the sky. Then, by unspoken agreement, we leave the Peugeot and start walking. It's time to locate shelter. The trees give way to a flat, dusty landscape, less-than-ideal terrain for fugitives like us. My joints ache, I'm cold and hungry. For days we've slept in tall weeds and roach-infested cellars. It's no way to live.

"What now?" Stefan nods irritably at his partner. "You make like you know, but I do not think so."

"Don't have a worry," Oleg says, his eyes straight ahead. "I know."

"You! Who gets lost inside phone booth!"

I interrupt, pointing at a hill on the horizon. "Might be some shelter there."

Stefan walks on, grumbling to himself. "*Skirdisch,* all of you *skirdisch.*" Loosely translated, *peasant fools.*

"He is my husband," Anca mutters, bringing up the rear. "You cannot have him."

The hill is steeper than it looks. Midway to the top, the ground flattens to a stone outcropping that overlooks a sparse forest below. Here we find a mineshaft, long abandoned, now little more than the mouth of a cave. Artifacts are scattered about—beer cans, cigarette butts, a wan-looking condom— but no sign of recent habitation.

Over the afternoon, feeling relatively safe, we engage in rare outdoor activities. Gather firewood, scoop water from a nearby stream, even kick around an old soccer ball found amid the debris. I watch from the sidelines as Anca playfully jousts with Oleg for control of the ball. She laughs and scampers, new color in her face and a freedom in her lithe body I haven't seen before.

Pearl-gray evening shadows daub the hillside. Stefan gets a fire going and soon we enjoy a watery stew of dry biscuits and pilfered tomatoes. Oleg consumes his meal with gusto and, wiping a shirtsleeve over his mouth, announces his intention to walk down the hill to the village.

"What village?" Stefan asks sharply.

"On road, over there. We pass before here."

"That is five, six maybe kilometers away. In dark!"

Oleg scowls. "So?"

"*So*? What you do is stupid."

"Shut up! *You* are stupid!"

"Not so much as you!"

Both men stand, fists balled. I've had enough of getting mixed-up in other peoples' problems to last a lifetime. A moment passes, then Stefan makes a rude brushing-away gesture.

"Go! OK, go! So what!"

Oleg trudges downhill, quickly swallowed up in darkness. Awkward silence hangs around the campfire, each of us uncertain as to our new roles—I'm no longer a prisoner, they're no longer my caretakers—and not knowing what to say. Stars twitch to life in the blue-black sky. Stefan rummages in a sack and comes out with a bottle of *slavka.* The fermented plum brandy lubricates our little *soirée,* and soon we're laughing about our troubles.

"Tell us," Stefan says to me.

"What?"

"Yes," Anca says drunkenly. "We feed you, take care of you, how long? Many months! We have right to know. Tell us!"

"Right to know *what?*"

"In America, you get offer from US for defection, is true?" Stefan asks. "This is what we hear."

Anca sways in the light of the fire. "You come home instead. Something happens here, you end up in castle. Almost killing of Gray Wolf!"

"Why?" Stefan asks. "What happens when you come back? What are things you do? Tell us."

Trying to describe events as they unfolded between returning to Keshnev and ending up in the castle seems like an impossible task. But think of all those tapes consumed in the fire, my lost testimony. Quiet moments arise in any life on the run, and I can help fill them if asked to contribute a small part of my life story. I knock back a healthy shot of *slavka* and begin.

Ten years had passed since I last visited Keshnev. On the eve of being recalled, I discovered how hard my adopted homeland had worked to put itself out of reach.

Airline connections between Keshnev and most European

cities were prohibited, flights from the US banned outright. Different routes had to be devised. As a result, travel time from the Free World to deep behind the Iron Curtain had become absurdly protracted —twelve hours aloft from La Guardia to Heathrow, then a six-hour hop to Athens, another flight into Bucharest yet to come.

At last, when I set foot on Old World *terra firma*, a full two days had passed since leaving Manhattan and only two weeks since my discharge from Mt. Sinai. A cab took me from the terminal to the Romanian National railway station, where I hobbled on a cane to the nearest ticket counter. A customs official looked at my identity papers and turned to a colleague in the next glass both over, loudly announcing my destination. Together, they shared a good laugh at my expense. With so many reasons to flee the People's Republic of Keshnev, who on earth ever wants to *enter*?

Once aboard the train, I learned that getting from Point A to Point B in Keshnev was erratic at best. The southbound train on which I was traveling should, by any reasonable standard, be headed south. Instead, its northerly, counter-clockwise arc skirted the Ploiești oil fields—industrial bile spewing from refinery smokestacks, passengers coughing and holding their noses—before the train changed course and finally headed the right way. My arrival at the border took place many hours behind schedule.

Making matters worse, some local delicacy I'd purchased hours ago in the train terminal was giving me grief. The day-old pork sandwich wrapped in grape leaves looked suspect from the start, but hunger and a rush to get back on the train overcame my doubts. Now my stomach made obscene sounds and I required several trips to the lavatory. By the time I stood in line at the customs desk, last step in re-entering my home-land, the worst of it had passed. The man in front of me was missing an arm, the woman behind him clutched a live chicken to her breast. The customs clerk waved them through, but chose to study my passport at length, squinting and grimacing at each page, as if finding a single typographical error might be grounds for my detention.

Oh Keshnev!

The clerk asked, "Your business here?"

"Official," I snapped, out of my depths in this endless travel. "Same as yours."

"You are who passport says you are?"

"Of course! Gabriel Ash, chief delegate to the—"

"But *here*, like *this*?" He made a show of leaning over his desk and looking around. "Why is no one come? Who at this end is waiting?"

"The Minister for State Security."

This caught the ear of the clerk's supervisor, a short man in a bulky suit with an almost violent way of asking how he might be of assistance. He scanned the passport photo and looked up at my real-world features. Frowning, he turned to the customs clerk and slapped him across the face.

"My apologies, Comrade Ambassador Ash! Please, by all means, sir. Welcome to Keshnev."

During the long journey from New York, I imagined what my first steps on native soil would feel like—a galvanizing moment, a chance for the whole whirligig mess of my life to snap into focus. But the countryside outside of the train station had no such healing powers, just a barren vista of pine trees and wooden huts, clouds overhead the sickly white hue of grub worms.

Once upon a time in a village not far from here, I played with other children in empty fields like this. Such sepia-tinted memories had no place in this unhopeful landscape.

Later, aboard the train headed for Olt—a creaky locomotive of the prewar era, stinking of coal dust and Turkish tobacco—we entered a tunnel where I was left alone in the dark with my thoughts for five excruciating minutes. I tried remembering examples of happy times spent in Petrescu's company, or, if not *happy*, moments between us that might pass as *normal* in human relationships. The train emerged from the tunnel, but I had yet to come up with anything.

In the railway station in Olt, passengers disembarking immediately felt the Gray Wolf's presence, years after his departure from public view. A giant mural of Our Great Leader —not the present-day ex-dictator living in seclusion, but a young, steel-jawed guerrilla fighter—hung from the rafters, and a similarly vast oil painting of Minister Petrescu, his chosen successor, adorned the wall above the exit. Under their punishing gaze, ordinary Keshnevites came and went, eyes down, keeping to themselves.

Outside, a murky brew of soot and fog shrouded *Strata Friedrich Engels*, the city's main thoroughfare. In my exhausted state I might have walked straight into the river Jaszy, but a cab screeched to a halt in front of me, the driver shouting, "Get in! Very cheap!" Inside the cab's overheated interior, I fell into a jagged half-sleep, the ride across town no more than blurred fragments of a dream.

The Hotel Metropole, a crumbling stone edifice on the fringe of Olt's commercial district, had withstood Nazi occupation and decades of Stalinist rule. The hotel lobby was spacious, with a huge wooden reception desk. The broad-shouldered woman seated behind it reached down and took my identity papers, shuffling through them like a pack of cards.

"*Tash kempf!*" she cried.

A bellhop appeared in a theater usher's red uniform two sizes too small for his middle-aged girth. I had no choice but to follow him up three flights of stairs, close behind droopy buttocks yearning to be free. In the room, the bellhop dropped my satchel on the bed, which let out a human-sounding groan. He seemed satisfied with a tip of 20 *klei* and soon he was gone. Taking a cursory look over my surroundings, I collapsed on the grunting bedsprings, asleep within minutes.

The next day, I waited hours for a welcoming telegram or a government flunky's knock on the door. None was forthcoming.

How would Petrescu greet me after all these years away? Would he be thrilled to see me or out for blood? Even in the distant corridors of the UN, his penchant for torture was well-known. Cigarettes burned into flesh, rubber truncheons beating the soles of a victim's feet while he dangled upside-down from a hook. If it came to that, how much could I withstand?

The Metropole had lost its prewar luster. The ceiling light in my room didn't work, the walls were painted a bilious green, and the toilet, when flushed, sounded like a crying child trapped in a well. Breakfast arrived via enfeebled room service, runny eggs, a cup of acidic sludge passing for coffee. Lunch was a choice between inky soup and rancid-smelling meat loaf. I dared not imagine dinner.

State-run television, with only two channels, offered little distraction. One channel featured a garish *opéra bouffe* set in an Arabian palace; on the other, newscasters lauded the nation's record-breaking wheat production, as well as the unsurpassed readiness of our armed forces. Foolishly, I thought my name might come up—wasn't I "news" of some kind?—but no mention was made of a disgraced diplomat slinking home with his capitalist tail between his legs. I paced the room, mentally commanding the phone to ring. Bad enough being recalled and my reputation besmirched—but to come all this way and be ignored! Outside the hotel window, daylight drained into dusk the color of pig iron.

The phone did ring once, late in the night—a click when I picked up, then a strange echo of voices, then silence. "Hello?" No answer. I switched on every light that worked and searched for microphones hidden under the bed or in a closet. When I encountered some gluey substance on my fingertips at the base of the toilet bowl, I called the search off.

In the end, a single listening device turned up, the size of a buffalo nickel, fastened to the underside of the desk. I wondered if it had been planted there in my honor or if the venerable Hotel Metropole was riddled with bugs.

The next morning, everything changed.

Footsteps crunch in the dark beyond our campfire. When the agreed-upon warning signal fails to materialize, I grab a hunk of wood and stand between Anca and whatever menace lurches our way. Oleg sprawls into view, his face smudged with dirt, twigs trapped in his hair, too agitated for any secret code. Only after plying him with *slavka* do we get a coherent report from him.

On the way to the village, he tells us, an old man crossed his path—"friendly, likes to talk"—and invited Oleg to the home of a village elder, where a group of old men were gathered around a black-and-white television set, debating world affairs.

"Then I see news about us! On TV!"

Puffing up his chest, Oleg does a fair impression of a stone-faced newscaster on state-run TV. "Evidence found at scene points at criminal elements on run, who try escape into Polish

People's Republic. First Secretary Gomulka of Poland is proud friend of Keshnev people. He says Polish forces will capture fugitives and return for justice."

This last statement set off gales of laughter among the village elders, Oleg reports. It's well-known First Secretary Gomulka would sooner eat insect larvae than befriend Keshnev.

I'm confused. "Polish forces chasing us? How is that a good thing?"

"Because of *note*," Oleg says impatiently. "Note we leave in castle. We go north for escape, it says. *Polizie* find note, call it evidence. They go north but we go another way for Kluj, on coast. *Polizie* are much hated there, no one will help them. *Now do you see?*"

The campfire sputters, a last gasp of heat and light. As we crawl to our respective corners and settle in, I notice Anca tugging her bedroll to the mouth of the cave, some distance from where her husband lies. A sign of marital strife? With these two, it's hard to tell.

But there's a plan, after all, and not a bad one.

25

Oleg, I'm told later, was once a shopkeeper in Olt's Jewish Quarter—a good provider, with a loving wife and child. One day, a customer feeling shamed by a long unpaid debt reported him to the police. Although a subsequent inquiry turned up nothing wrong, it was determined Oleg must pay restitution to the State for having to go to all the trouble of arresting him in the first place. Local officials withdrew permission for him to run his shop, relocated family members to other East Bloc countries, and bled dry his life savings. Overnight, the shopkeeper lost everything; no surprise he hates Communists of all shapes and sizes. I doubt he has any idea who I am or what I've done, but if my actions harm Petrescu's regime, that's good enough for him.

Oleg wants to hear more of my story. They all do. *We have right to know.*

Two days after my arrival in Keshnev, the bellhop delivered a printed invitation to a state dinner at the Foreign Ministry. A tailor conducted a personal fitting and, three hours later, a sleek, custom-made tuxedo appeared—this, in a country where it takes weeks to buy a loaf of bread. "That's more like it," I said, tipping the elated bellhop an extra 30 *klei*.

My euphoria lasted only until the limousine ride through the city. The notorious Planz Quarter was once the haunt of art smugglers and fallen European playboys; now I saw row after row of crumbling block towers. Old men gazed out of broken windows. Feral dogs clashed over the spoils of an overturned trash can. From my backseat window, I saw two men roughing up a third man in an alley. The assailants raised their tomb-stone faces as the limo passed, then resumed pummeling their victim.

Oh, Keshnev!

Nausea rose in my gut, stomach-wrenching revulsion at what had become of the old country. I hated Petrescu for ordering my return, hated the secret police eavesdropping on my hotel room, hated even the man under siege in the alley. The sooner I could plead my case and expedite passage home, the better.

Government buildings loomed up on every corner, each structure with its own hideous pillars and statuary. Klieg lights installed on the roof of the Foreign Ministry building—a bleak ten-story monolith—beamed down on arriving guests. I fell in with a crowd of cigar-puffing *apparatchiks* and their brawny wives, all of us moving down a herringbone-parquet hallway into a stately ballroom. The mincing waiter led me to a table in the rear, far from the podium and head table, around which the evening's festivities would revolve.

I sat alone, simmering. Too many ups and downs for my dignity. First my unheralded border crossing into Keshnev, then the surprise VIP treatment at the Metropole, and now at an elegant state dinner, this ridiculous seating arrangement.

Would I ever receive a proper welcome home, or had I become *persona non grata*? It seemed the powers that be couldn't make up their minds.

Eventually, two couples and a single woman—small-boned, with dusty blonde hair, in her mid-thirties—joined me at the table. Of the husbands and wives, I registered little beyond ample waistlines and boisterous high spirits. Vera, as the blonde woman introduced herself, held far more interest for me. She had an appealing smile, but something in her voice, the slight tilt of her head, and the way the chandelier light caught her face suggested some underlying sorrow. A self-described lowly morgue technician, Vera was only attending tonight's dinner because her sick boss couldn't make it. In a green, low-cut dress, she charmed us all with tales of berserk mourners and cadavers gone missing.

"Is true what they say?" One husband, a beefy gent with eyebrows like furry caterpillars, pumped his fist up and down in a universally obscene gesture. "Men come to morgue, make *yaki-yaki* with dead bodies?"

The wives roared with laughter; they'd come tonight to be entertained, and by God, this was entertaining. I watched Vera fiddle with a gold band on her finger.

Dinner was being served at other tables, notably those nearest the podium. As for the rest of us, the plates of scrawny chicken breasts drowning in turnip sauce would arrive on the waiters' timetable, not ours. In Manhattan, I would have loudly complained about this appalling lack of customer service. The others around the table seemed grateful just to be here.

And there was wine.

Upon discovering a diplomat in their midst, talk among the couples turned to conflict in the Falklands. The husband with squiggly eyebrows had strong feelings about the war, as did his drinking buddy, a middle-aged man so tightly cossetted into a rented tuxedo that his eyes bulged like a frog's. *Why?* these men and their wives wanted to know. Why did England go to war in the first place? Why not welcome the junta's willingness to take the colony off their hands?

"Two bald men," I replied.

They gawped at me, witless as cows.

"Someone far wiser than I am said, the war is like two bald men fighting over a comb."

Vera's laugh cued the others and briefly, hilarity reigned. Swept up in anti-Western fever, Eyebrows pounded his big Communist fist on the table. "Fuck England! Fuck Margret Thatcher!" His pal Frog Eyes agreed. "Fuck Iron Lady!"

The wives howled with laughter, nearly in tears. Vera sighed and turned her button-nose profile elsewhere.

"You tell Iron Lady, OK?" Frog Eyes said. "Tell her for us, *Fuck off.*"

"Sure," I said. "Anything else?"

"America, too!" he shouted. "Tell all of them, *Fuck off.*"

I took a sip of the disastrously inferior wine, sensing Vera's embarrassment on my behalf. "At the UN, I serve as the voice of the People," I told the couples. "Therefore, I serve as *your* voice."

Excited murmurs swept through the ballroom. Curtains opened, admitting a pair of white-haired commissars in shiny tuxedos slowly heading towards the podium. A third man followed, wearing a gray field uniform and black hobnail boots. All eyes fixed on him as he and the commissars settled at the main table. Even from this polar distance, I knew who I was looking at. Thicker and stockier than I remembered, and still sporting an implausibly full head of black hair.

Minister Petrescu, in the flesh.

The ballroom grew deathly silent, as quiet as Vera's

morgue, until someone remembered to applaud. This triggered an ovation sounding much more supplicatory than heartfelt. Across the ballroom, a trio of musicians in lederhosen and Tyrolean hats struck up a lively polka. The two couples at our table, resigned to dinner not coming anytime soon, headed for the dance-floor.

"These people, I apologize for," Vera said. "Probably they are drinking before they come here." She noticed my sickened gaze at Petrescu. "The Minister ... Do you know him?"

"From long ago."

"Old friends! But why are you so much away at the table?"

I smiled, unable to choose from among my countless infelicities. I touched her hand, the one with the gold wedding band. "May I have this dance?"

The Tyrolean band played a lilting Alpine melody, as guests in their once-a-year evening wear waltzed across the dance floor. Holding a woman for the first time in weeks felt revelatory—the clean smell of Vera's neck, her breasts in the cocktail dress pressed against me, the exquisite nestling of her hip and my loins, a sort of carnal joint-and-beam arrangement.

"Why didn't your husband join you this evening?"

Vera raised her head from my shoulder. "What? Oh—no husband. The ring is a ... convenience."

"Deceitful, too."

She laughed, did a quick twirl on the dance floor. "Sometimes I like to be with the living!"

A short man came to his feet at a table nearest the podium and began addressing the guests. His bowtie was askew, his tux wilted from sweat. In a booming voice, he introduced himself as mayor of Trevya, a factory town in the southern provinces. The mayor lifted his wine-glass and made a slurred toast to the people of Keshnev, combining praise for their national fortitude with a drunken, weepy account of misfortunes in his personal life. The commissars glared in silence, while Minister Petrescu's attention seemed locked in on a bowl of borscht set in front of him. A merciful waiter finally took the sniveling mayor by the arm and guided him away.

The music resumed, a jaunty Polonaise that got guests dancing again, though now with spirits considerably subdued. Vera and I drew closer, a newfound intimacy born out of this awful, shared experience.

"You do not talk much about what you do," she said. "For a man, this is strange."

"What would you like to know?"

"Why you are here in Olt, not at UN."

"I've been recalled."

"'Re-called'? What is that?"

From the dance floor I had a clear view of the Minister, still looking down and contemplating his borscht. Probably he had no idea I was even here.

"Some bad things happened in New York," I said. "You could say I've come back to atone for my sins."

Vera's face went white. "Atone to ... *him*?"

"Don't worry. It'll be no more than a scolding."

"No," she whispered, clutching my hand as we danced. "*Here* can be so much worse."

I smiled, feeling as stupidly sentimental about life as the mayor of Trevya. "Vera, are you concerned about me?"

She looked up—wounded blue eyes, an almost unwilling smile—as if the two of us shared the same thought. *Tonight didn't turn out so badly after all.* I leaned in and kissed her.

"*Ne valusca,*" I said. "No more sadness."

Moments later—after bidding farewell to the inebriated couples at our table—Vera and I stood outside on the steps of the Ministry building. The klieg lights on the roof had shut down, casting the ten-story structure into darkness. Only a few cars were visible on *Strata Leniniskii,* even fewer people. Vera drew her coat tight against the evening chill, her gaze on me eager and acquisitive—*Your place or mine?*—and we kissed again, more urgently than before.

Suddenly a hand clamped on my shoulder and spun me around. I faced a burly man in a trench coat and a black fedora. A second man, dressed like his partner minus the hat, took hold of Vera's elbow and led her towards a waiting car. Vera struggled. The hatless man slapped her hard across the face.

"Hey!" I cried.

I took a step forward but arms thick as cordwood enveloped my chest from behind, a python grip steadily cutting off my oxygen supply. Before I was about to pass out, I saw the hatless man shove Vera into the car and, as it sped away, her bruised, mascara-streaked face pressed to the window. The hatless man signaled his partner to release me.

"What—" I gulped air. "What the hell is going on?"

"This is to inform you," the man with the fedora said. "You are under arrest."

Over my protests, the two men bundled me back inside the Ministry building, down a hallway and into a metal-grille elevator cage. No one spoke during our interminable ascent, and I kept my trembling hands by my sides, certain they could hear every thump of my jackhammer heart. Who were these men? What did they want? The elevator opened on the top floor to an empty corridor reeking of urine and garbage. The hatless man unlocked a door at the end of the corridor and pushed me up steps to yet another door.

Then we were on the roof.

26

We drive through the night in remote backcountry, the Peugeot's bumpy motion rocking us into troubled sleep. Stefan dozes in the front seat, Anca asleep beside me in back. In my dream, a white-coated waiter serves Chilean sea bass in a miso ginger sauce. I wake to rain hammering the roof of the car, the taste of sea bass fresh in my mouth. Up front, Oleg is flopped against the steering wheel. Something snaps him awake, then his eyes close and he droops forward again.

I reach out to tug at his coat just as a loud, jarring *thwunk!* rocks the car. "What?" Oleg says, as if he's misheard a question.

Trapped in a tailspin, the Peugeot flings its occupants out of their dreams and into a pinwheel-hell of flailing limbs and screeching metal. My knee bangs a doorjamb. An elbow narrowly misses puncturing my ear-drum. There's a final violent, sideways roll—Anca tumbling into me, screaming, *Stop! Make it stop!*—and our joyride comes to an end in a muddy drainage ditch.

For a long time, no one moves or speaks, the only sound

the beleaguered tick of the Peugeot's engine. My knee throbs, I must have bit my lip on impact; otherwise, I'm unharmed. The two men in front are slumped backwards in their seats, heads rolling in tandem, as if at long last they're in agreement about something.

Anca looks glassy-eyed, a shocking blue bruise on her forehead.

"Are you alright?" I ask.

"Yes, I think, maybe ..."

Groggy or not, she's first to vacate the crash scene. I watch her slither through a cracked window in her torn jacket and jeans, and even now I'm entranced—such is my affliction—by her fetching, determined little backside. She claws her way up and out of the rain-soaked ditch. I intend to follow, but close my eyes instead; minutes later, I wake up and the Peugeot is empty.

It's simple enough to push open the side-door busted on its hinges. Slogging up the incline with rain pelting my face and mud sucking at my boots is much harder work. The others are gathered in a semi-circle on the empty road, their wet dripping faces askew in the slick glow of the headlights. All three stare down at something.

"What did you *do?*" Anca cries.

"Me?" Oleg kneads the back of his neck, looking uncertain of his surroundings. "Nothing! I do not see—"

"*Ne!* You do not see! You sleep, not drive!"

I know the car struck something big, but still I'm shocked by what confronts me on the road. A massive elk lies in a pool of blood and viscera. Lit up by the off-kilter headlights, it seems not of this world, a thing meant for some fantasy realm of wind-tossed trees and silvery moons. But the pungent marsh odors of fur and shit are real, as are the mangled antlers and crippled hind leg. The beast lifts its snout, eyes rolling in panic, unable to make sense of the two-legged predators clustered around it.

"Shhh ..." Anca kneels, her wet hair clinging to her shoulders, and strokes the elk's wounded flank.

"Is no good here," Stefan says. "No good to stay."

She looks up, tears and rain in her face. "It has pain, can you not see that? If we go, it will die."

"So do we if we stay!"

As if roused by her compassion, the elk raises its snout again, a last spark of neuron-driven clarity lighting its eyes. But the effort's too costly. The elk heaves a sigh and the antlers settle back on the ground.

Oleg in the meantime comes to a decision. Reaching in a coat pocket, he takes out a small black revolver and waves the barrel at Anca.

"Get out of way."

She looks up, startled. "What are you doing?"

"*Move.*"

I seize her arm and pull her away, just as Oleg, in the detached manner of a cowhand and his hobbled steer, fires twice into the fallen creature's brainpan. Wind and rain muffle the shots. Anca breaks free of my grip and runs to the car in tears.

The Peugeot is damaged beyond repair—tires blown, headlights cracked, huge dents in the bumper and hood—but serves as shelter until the rain lets up. We sit inside in gloomy silence, our clothes drenched, our bodies bruised and aching.

Anca points at my knee. "Is your pain bad?"

"I'm fine."

"Let me see."

She sidles over and peels away the torn, bloodstained fabric, her fingers alighting on my injured skin. "It's nothing," I tell her, though in fact her touch offers sorely needed comfort. Meanwhile, the bickering between the two men resumes.

"What happens now?"

Oleg rubs an angry-looking welt on his neck. "'Happens'?"

"For us!" Stefan snaps. "Now!"

"Plan is same. We go by plan."

"This is crazy! *You* are crazy!"

Anca sits close, dangerously close. I feel her breath on me as she plucks shards of glass from my hair. In darkness, unseen by the quarreling lovers, I bring her hand to my lips. The knuckles when I kiss them are coarse from hard labor—but they're *her* knuckles, *her* flesh—and she smiles, looking pleasantly surprised. Something inside me rolls over and shows its belly to the universe.

"Who can help us?" Stefan moans. "Where will we get—"

"*Shhhh.*"

Oleg's jerky marionette head-motion silences us all. He eases out of the car, urging us with hand-signals to do the same, *quickly*. We all huddle in the mud-covered lee of the drainage ditch. Although the rain's let up, a primeval wetness remains, the *drip-drip-drip* of foliage in the dark. A low-level hum builds in my ears—something inorganic, foreign to these parts.

"*Lache!*"

Oleg breaks a path through tangled spruce and elm, and we're right behind him. Fallen branches crackles underfoot, but the noise is lost in the growing drone of machinery somewhere nearby. From a small clearing hidden by trees, we look back at the road we've just abandoned. There's a glass-and-concrete hut, powered by a truck generator on the side of the structure. One soldier sits in the hut, looking bored. Another soldier slouches outside on a metal gate blocking progress down the road.

If not for the elk, we would have driven straight into this checkpoint. If not for the rain, the gunshots ending its life would have been clearly heard from here. We exchanged worried looks. How long before someone finds the wrecked Peugeot?

A banged-up lorry rumbles into view and stops at the gate. The lorry driver cuts the engine, I can just make out his friendly smile and youthful features. Probably he hopes a little aimless chatter will get him more quickly down the road. Instead, the soldier at the gate extends a hand to the open window. *Papers, please.* These he scans indifferently, before handing them over to his partner who, by contrast, seems to study the documents as if they were the Dead Sea scrolls. It's not that they suspect the lorry driver of any wrongdoing; this is a game, a break in the tedium of their lives. The driver doesn't find the game amusing, his complaints over the need-less delay growing more strident. The soldiers look offended that he's not playing along. They shout back, drawing their rifles. Gunfire could break out at any time.

Seizing the moment, we plunge deep into the trees.

27

From atop the Foreign Ministry building, government structures ranged all over the city skyline. There was the People's Hall of Justice, lit up like a Vegas casino, and, farther out, the darkened walls of Dobruja prison. Closer in, warehouses and tower blocks seemed to cower in the Foreign Ministry's shadow, if buildings could be said to cower.

And for good reason.

"Comrade Ash! How good to see you, old friend."

Minister for State Security Petrescu welcomed me, standing in the shadows of a chimney and air-ducts. He wore latex gloves and had a leather apron tied over his field uniform. Behind him, obscured by his rough-hewn frame, I saw a corner of tarpaulin spread out on the rooftop, flanked by a pair of railroad lanterns.

The men who had escorted me here retreated behind the chimney shaft, leaving me wildly vulnerable and alone. Somehow, I must recover my wits, respond to the Minister's warm greeting, *and* plot my next move, all in the space of milliseconds.

"They told me I'm under arrest."

Petrescu removed the gloves and chuckled, a sound like rolling thunder in his barrel chest. "My apologies—a poor attempt at a joke."

"And Vera, the woman I was with ...?"

"Safe and happy in her home, I am certain of it."

Seen from afar at the state dinner, Petrescu appeared robust as ever, a man in his seventies impervious to time. Up close, I saw how the years had aged him. He was thicker around the middle by a good fifteen pounds. Bags of flesh hung under his eyes, the dyed-black hair of which he was so proud grown thin across his scalp.

"Did you hear the news, Comrade Ash? Argentine Phantom jets struck a British convoy the other day and sank two vessels." He clapped his gloved hands together. "The junta is giving your precious Englishmen a real bloody nose!"

A man's foot poked out on the tarpaulin, and then another —one foot wearing a shoe, the other a grimy sock. I heard a faint mewling, like that of a newborn kitten.

"Mrs. Thatcher will see this is no game," Petrescu said. "It may be the last colonial war in our lifetime, but it is no game."

I reminded him I'd expressed the same sentiments in my Security Council speech.

A smile creased his face, tiny lines of skin fanning out like tributaries from a watery source. "As I understand it, in your speech you did not ... what do they say in America? *Kletch tu vatya.*"

"Follow the script."

The wind sweeping over the rooftops grew fierce. Shrapnel-sized bits of litter and debris flew through a forest of radio antennae stretching to the horizon.

"I told the truth," I said. "The truth doesn't follow a script."

Choked groans rose from the tarpaulin. I edged closer for a glimpse, but the Minister blocked my view.

"Nothing's changed, has it, Comrade Ash? All these years later, you are still the smartest man in the room."

The woeful moaning swelled. Petrescu tilted his head at the chimney shaft, and the two henchmen pitched forth like overzealous valets, tasked with specific chores. Wrestle the prone figure to a seated position. Pour a bucket of cold water over his head, stunning him into awareness. Prop him up on his haunches and retreat into darkness.

It was the mayor of Trevya—one eye blackened and squeezed shut, drops of blood splattered over his white shirt. In mute horror I saw Petrescu fumble inside his apron pocket and come out holding a pair of needle-nose pliers. The mayor swayed on the tarp, his legs splayed and twitching.

Pliers?

"You're busy," I said weakly. "I'll come back later."

He blinked like a baby waking from a nap. "Forgive me, I'm a terrible host."

Another oblique head-movement and the valets sprang into action. Set up a folding table near the ledge of the roof. Place upon it two shot-glasses and a bottle of *slavka*. Avoid eye contact and once again slip into the shadows.

I couldn't quite grasp what was happening. Beyond a poorly worded toast at dinner, what had the mayor done to deserve this treatment? And why was I summoned to watch? Through years of a troubled acquaintance, I'd never witnessed the Minister's legendary cruelty first-hand. I had no wish to do so now.

"Comrade Ash! Don't make me drink alone."

I smoothed my coat, took a deep breath, and walked over the gravelly surface to the ledge. A glass of *slavka* awaited me on the folding table, his own glass filled and raised in the air.

"To the return of our distinguished chief delegate."

The glass in my hand wobbled for all the world to see. "And to the People."

"Yes, of course—the People!"

I drank quickly, hoping an infusion of *slavka* would settle my nerves. Instead, the cloying, syrupy plum brandy brought on a spell of lightheadedness, unwelcome while poised on the roof of a ten-story building. Stalling for time, I inquired after the health of the Gray Wolf.

"This time of year, he hides in his dacha on the coast. For the sea air, I'm told." Petrescu frowned. "If you ask him how things are going in this county, he will tell you, it is *klisch*—a mess, broken in pieces ..."

"Fucked," I said.

"According to Our Great Leader, everything is *klisch*. The army, the government, the means of production—all fucked. But don't worry! says this ninety-year-old man. Things will be different once he regains power. But to look at him ..."

"Yes?"

"A fact of life, Comrade Ash. Heroes grow old and die, just the like rest of us."

The Minister took a step closer to the ledge and looked to the horizon, as if moved to reflect upon the city spread out before him—*his* city, for all intents and purposes.

"Come, enjoy the view."

With reluctance bordering on catatonia, I joined him at the outermost parapet. Far below, tiny limos circled the driveway and pin-prick doormen hailed cabs for departing guests. Petrescu's body musk wafted over me, a vile blend of clove-scented after-shave and the sweat of his recent endeavors. Behind me, the valets surreptitiously advanced—angling for a glass of *slavka* or wordlessly ordered to throw me off the roof? Panic-fueled tabloid headlines flashed in my head. COMMIE

FREEFALL SPELLS JUSTICE, KESHNEV-STYLE and DIPLO-
MAT'S SWAN DIVE SUICIDE ONE LESS PROBLEM FOR
MANKIND. I took an incremental step backward.

"They tell me you seek permission to travel."

I nodded, still reeling from visions of my imminent demise.
"Yes, I'd like to see Rogvald, in the south. The village where I
grew up."

Petrescu's shoulder twitched, nothing more; a valet
appeared and handed him a piece of paper, which he in turn
showed me. In the lantern's wavering light, I saw a neatly
typed document on government letterhead, AUTHORIZED
stamped across the top, Petrescu's oddly feminine signature at
the bottom.

"You are free to visit the village of your youth," he said.
"After that, come back and wait here in Olt. Do not travel
anywhere else."

My ears tingled, as if I'd stumbled upon someone talking
about me in the past tense. "Wait for what?"

"Until we decide what to do with you."

"How long will that take?" I asked. "Any chance we could
speed the process along?"

The Minister for State Security had ruled a nation of infor-
mants and police agents for decades. He'd survived numerous
bloody coup attempts because, in the end, no one was as ruth-
less as him. *This* was the man I was toying with.

"Listen to me," he said. "Go nowhere else."

The mayor's mournful sounds grew louder. Petrescu
ignored them, though you could see the effort required in his
vein-bulging forehead.

"In New York," he said, "you commit inexcusable acts
against the People's Republic. Fraudulent use of funds.
Disloyal talk in the running dog press. With your words alone,
a riot breaks out at the UN. All this, *and* a bomb explodes,

killing an innocent Keshnevite citizen." He paused, a little breathless from this litany. "Tell me, Comrade Ash, why shouldn't I have you arrested—for real this time—and tried for crimes against the State?"

Gusts of wind no longer masked the mayor's anguished noises. *Think*, I told myself. Answer the wrong way and find yourself plummeting ten stories to Mother Earth.

"Because it will make you look bad."

How others viewed the Minister was a perennial topic of interest. "Oh?"

"Have me recalled for a tongue-lashing, fine," I said. "Anything more, like a show trial or prison cell, only confirms how the rest of the world sees Keshnev. A backwards country, stuck in the Dark Ages."

Petrescu mulled over my point. During this ambiguous interval, I stood just a bit taller, flushed with *slavka* and renewed self-confidence, thinking I'd pulled it off—so his existential sucker-punch caught me off-guard.

"What happened to you, old friend? When did you embrace so-called free thinking and abandon the cause of the People?"

"It's nonsense," I said heatedly. "I never did."

"May I offer some advice? On the day you're called upon to speak for yourself, resist your instinct for duplicity. Be honest, if you can—no fancy moves, no evasion. Explain how living in the West corrupted your Marxist principles and then you couldn't find your way back. A man with your gift for words can surely make us understand and forgive you."

"Or die trying," I joked. Idiot! Why put that idea in his head!

Finally, the mayor's lamentations were too much to bear. Petrescu set down his glass and strode along the debris trail to the chimney shaft. Somehow it was understood that I, his craven flunky, should follow. But I was paralyzed by dread of whatever would happen next. Petrescu turned and looked at me across the length of the rooftop, across an unbridgeable chasm of life experiences. The Faustian bargain we'd struck so long ago had collapsed completely.

"Comrade Ash, do you require a personal invitation everywhere we go?"

Once again, the valets had the mayor of Trevya propped approximately upright—scarcely conscious, a mushy, swollen pumpkin for a face—and whose whimpering seemed to annoy Petrescu beyond measure. I felt deeply dismayed at the reappearance of the latex gloves and needle-nose pliers.

"The investigation," I said, desperately. "What's the status? Is it coming along?"

The Minister looked up, puzzled. "What investigation?"

"In New York! The attempt on my life! What have you uncovered so far?"

He indicated the wretch on the tarpaulin. "Perhaps that is what I am doing right now."

"Excuse me, Minister, but that's absurd. This man had nothing to do with the car-bombing."

Petrescu grinned. "From what we hear, there is no one in New York who *doesn't* want you dead." Turning to his captive, limp in the valets' grip. "Do you know who this man is in our presence?"

The mayor looked up at me, uncomprehending.

"This is my old friend Comrade Ambassador Gabriel Ash. A very important man who speaks for Keshnev at the table of nations."

A wave of nausea came over this very important man. "Minister ..."

"What is wrong with you?" Petrescu demanded of the mayor. "Do you always drink too much and forget your manners? Think first, *then* speak, Mayor Whoever-You-Are. Talking as you did at dinner embarrassed me in front of my old friend."

The mayor emitted a gagging, infantile sound.

"*What?*"

"... yes, Minister—"

"We are agreed? Nothing of this sort will happen again?"

"... no, Minister—"

Which should, I hoped, be an end to it. Petrescu sighed, unappeased. As the valets held on tight, he knelt painfully and closed on his prey, the pliers in his gloved hands clicking away. A brief, intense struggle ensued. The mayor's limbs contorted at angles I hadn't thought possible, and his muffled cries, the howl of some species other than man, rang in the night air. My knees buckled. I fought the urge to throw up what little food and drink my stomach contained.

Then it was over. The mayor lay passed out, bleeding from his nose and mouth. Minister Petrescu slowly came to his feet, no longer the spry young torturer he once was, and with the end of his smock, wipe the pliers clean of forcibly extracted bodily fluids.

"This is Keshnev," he reminded me. "There is no script here."

28

The train for Rogvald and points south wasn't departing until late in the day. Plenty of time to sit on a bench and admire the huge mural painted across the high domed ceiling—a legion of farmers, soldiers, and factory workers marching arm-in-arm into a glorious socialist future. All the windows in the railway station were kept inexplicably shut, trapping fetid odors of greasy food and grubby humanity. The future seemed not at all glorious to me.

Still, I had permission to visit Rogvald. With any luck, I might locate someone who had facts, not rumors, about what happened to my parents.

I felt eyes on me, but no one among the scraggly travelers in the railway station showed any interest at all. The penetrating gaze came from a MOST WANTED poster on the far wall. I got up and walked over. A man in his mid-forties— raffish black hair, a sociopath's smile—was pictured in profile and full-frontal. ISMAIL LIKA, wanted for gunrunning and armed robbery, other crimes so heinous several neighboring countries had joined in the man-hunt. Ismail Lika grinned at the camera, though you couldn't say the dark eyes were in on the same joke. It seemed the Albanian mobster wasn't taking this whole international law-enforcement effort seriously.

When had studying a photograph so upset my bowels? This one did.

But in fact I *was* being observed—over there by the news kiosk, a dumpy-looking man in a brown suit, not trying very hard to look inconspicuous. His paunch and neatly trimmed salt-and-pepper beard called to mind Sigmund Freud in mid-career. My very own watcher! But couldn't SPU do better with respect to undercover surveillance than this rumpled little man?

As the day dragged on, I devised a little game at his expense. Whenever a train pulled in, I'd step on-board alongside other passengers, wait inside the carriage, then at the last second step off the train. Each time, my disgruntled watcher was obliged to do the same.

The southbound train arrived an hour late, idling long enough to board a desultory clutch of travelers before chuffing off again. I ended up in a crowded second-class compartment with fleeting views out the window of the river Jaszy—once a thriving hub of east European commerce, now a sluggish, befouled waterway in the heart of the city. On through Olt's outer suburbs, past a long stretch of concrete honeycomb apartment blocks encased by barbed wire, rarely a soul in sight. The bland scenery lulled me to sleep. In one dream I pursued the Consul through a ziggurat of blind alleys; in another, Molly Boyle and Ms. Alvarez stood naked over my prone body, clasping hands like big-game hunters after a kill.

I woke startled by the morning light and changes in topography. Overnight, it seemed, we climbed from ground-level farmland into a mountain valley, framed by the snow-capped peaks of Keshnev's Lesser Alps. I left the compartment to freshen up, a decision almost immediately regretted. Snot-colored water issued from the tap. Puddles of unidentifiable origin stained the floor. What I saw in the cracked restroom mirror further appalled me—a man on the cusp of late middle-age, unshaven for days, graying hair jagged from sleep. A far cry from the *bon vivant* cock-of-the-walk of yesteryear. The mayor of Trevya's species-transcending howl rang in my ears. No doubt the Minister for State Security was hard at work in his basement office, the foray into savage dentistry long since forgotten.

Hours later, the train clattered to a halt in Rogvald. The tiny railway station was shuttered, no one standing around to answer questions, no sign of public transportation. A signpost pointed west: ROGVALD .6 KM. I set off on foot, travel-bag in hand. If the Freud lookalike followed, I didn't see him.

Late autumn in the Keshnev countryside. Clouds bullied the sun into hiding. The path into Rogvald led through open fields and shivery meadows, with potholes and other ankle-twisting obstacles cluttering the way. I wandered off into a patch of conifers, drawn by a sweet scent from childhood, and lost my bearings in the old growth forest. All the frightening superstitions of the region came swirling back—angry bats tangled in your hair, locusts beyond number smothering the sky—before I returned, a bit shaken, to the right path.

A small red-brick hotel stood on the outskirts of town. The proprietor, a friendly man with tufts of thick hair bursting from his undershirt, slapped a key in my hand and sent me upstairs. Last room on the left, with an iron-frame bed and a nightstand scarred by ten thousand cigarette burns. Lodgings fit for a 19th-century anarchist bent on gunning down the Kaiser, yet somehow perfect for me. I got in bed and fell into a dreamless sleep, waking the next morning refreshed and excited about the day ahead.

The real thing, when it happened, far outstripped my puny imagination.

In the morning, the proprietor's chubby, lascivious teenage daughter served a breakfast of weak tea and warmed-over stew. Her hip brushed against my shoulder, a breast became embedded in my neck, she even dabbed a napkin at imaginary food stains in my lap. With expressions of gratitude to her and her father—seated a few feet away reviewing ledgers—I hurried off into town.

Under a blue sky cleansed by yesterday's rain, the village of Rogvald seemed largely unchanged from my youth. A few more commercial structures, some ramshackle huts on a bleak, unpaved grid, little else different or improved. A villager passed by in a horse-drawn cart. A woman in a sackcloth dress argued with a street vendor over the price of his squealing piglet. For Rogvald to adhere so closely to childhood memories saddened me, but also stirred a flicker of hope. I'd come this far, hadn't I? Maybe today I'd cross paths with someone who had knowledge of my parents and their last few months of life. Rumors, half-forgotten folk tales—anything was better than what little I had.

Today I dressed more casually, plain dark shirt and trousers, intending to stand out less among Rogvalders. An older man came by on foot, holding the reins of a large, complacent-looking ox. The man's square head and ponderous brow resembled the ox's similarly configured skull. He listened to my story of American missionaries who lived and died in these parts many years ago. When he answered—slowly, at my request, being out of practice in the local dialect—it was to apologize for knowing nothing about them. The ox gazed at me over his shoulder, wearing the same contrite expression.

A woman seated on a bench looked promising, but my approach spooked her, and she ran off. The only other villager present was a young woman in a tattered dress with a baby in her arms swathed in blankets. I called out from a polite distance, requesting a moment of her time. She agreed to hear me out, so I told her my story as she rocked the dormant child in her arms. To my surprise, she smiled.

"My *bubbka* tells me once very long time ago, shows pictures of *missionarskii*."

What luck! "Your *bubbka*—can I meet her?"

"*Ne,*" she said. "Run over by tractor."

"I—I'm sorry ... and the pictures?"

The infant in her arms let out an ungodly howl, jealous of attention bestowed on anyone but him. The young woman wilted before my eyes, transformed into a bone-weary creature on the brink of collapse.

"*Ne, ne,*" she said, moving along. "I do not have."

All morning, my bad luck held. The schoolboys careening into trash cans were far too young to help. A grizzled, toothless villager stalked off before I could finish my story. The dark tavern I happened across at the end of the road seemed rich with possibilities, but the sullen codgers inside wouldn't talk to me, rightly suspicious of the outsider in their midst.

I found an outdoor café in the village square, where I sat drinking bitter black coffee. The day had become unseasonably warm. My mood was bad, the coffee was bad, the service—courtesy of a surly waiter—was bad. I watched a gaggle of pea hens bustle across the dirt and wanted to mow them down with an AK-47.

What had I hoped to find in Rogvald? What good would come from harassing strangers about long-dead foreigners they knew nothing about? This quest of mine was probably doomed from the start.

Across from the café where I sat was the butcher shop my mother took me to as a child, chickens hanging upside-down from hooks until their last squawk. Next door, the provincial post office, in my memory redolent of sawdust and envelope glue, and the feed store with a hairline crack in the display window from eons ago. The village square seemed smaller than I remembered—once it held a cheering crowd, King Josef on his horse and a would-be assassin, now little more than a weed-choked plot of commercial real estate.

Shuffling footsteps broke the midday silence. A group of villagers was approaching on foot—heads bowed, all wearing black suits and black ankle-length dresses. A horse-drawn cart followed close behind, led by a man in black robes intoning what I guessed were Eastern Orthodox chants. Inside the cart, an open coffin was propped up upon a bed of straw; a blonde girl wearing a Sunday dress rested inside, her eyes closed, hands draped over her heart. As they neared the square, the grief-stricken Rogvalders began—I don't know another word for it—*manhandling* the corpse. One mourner snatched the dead girl's hand and rubbed formaldehyde-stiffened fingers against his cheek. Another one pressed her mouth on lips in rigor mortis. By the time my delicate Western sensibility recovered from the shock, the funeral *cortège* was gone.

Coming to Rogvald was a bad idea. I should have stayed in Olt, preparing to plead my case before the authorities—doing so, on the Minister's advice, with all the sincerity I could muster. Whatever happens, I realized with sudden clarity, I must not die in Keshnev.

Time to cut this visit short.

The Greek hotelier, surprised by news of my abrupt departure, looked sadly at his daughter washing dishes in the sink; he seemed to think if events had gone differently, she might be leaving as my wife. I set out on the same road as yesterday, intending to steer clear of dark forests where bats and locusts swarmed. Gone was my misplaced nostalgia and childish need for information; all that mattered was getting out of here—out of Rogvald, out of Keshnev, out of Europe altogether—now and forevermore.

Up ahead, by an abandoned church, a scrawny young man and an old woman were engaged in a dispute of some kind. The woman—frail, sclerotic, adorned in black muslin head to toe—poked a cane at the jeering youth, who easily batted it away. I took a step across the road, planning to intercede. The young man fled, apparently not liking the odds.

"Are you all right?" I asked the old woman.

She looked shaken, but unharmed. A strong scent of mothballs rose off her black widow's weeds. As her milky yellow eyes sought me out, I understood she was blind.

"*Que parle?*" she asked in a weak, splintery voice. "*Qui va là?*"

Startled by this burst of French, I looked more closely at her, the crown of sparse white hair on her head and crevices in her face as old as Mesopotamia. I couldn't believe what I saw.

"Madame Yerkes—is that you?"

"*Qui parle?*" The old woman's head spun around, seeking my location. "Who speaks?"

"Madame, it's me. Gabriel Ash."

"Gabriel? Who is Gabriel? *Je ne comprends pas.*"

It *was* Madame Yerkes, the Sorbonne-educated Frenchwoman who gave up everything many years ago in her lovestruck pursuit of the Baron of Yaz. The debauched nobleman, famously cruel to women, consumed her body and soul, then tossed her aside and retreated to his castle. Madame Yerkes settled in Rogvald a short distance away, becoming over time a trusted governess to local families. Even in my childhood, she seemed like an old woman; since then she'd aged greatly, a lifelong spinster-in-exile waiting in vain for the Baron of Yaz to come to his senses.

I took her hand and guided her dry, brittle fingers to my face, all while humming what strains I remembered of Mozart's *Sonata in B Flat Major*, which Madame Y—as everyone knew her—played on the school piano a lifetime ago.

"Ah, Gabriel—*mon dieu!*"

A smile breathed new life into her features, and she covered my hand with an old woman's kisses. Tears sprang to my eyes.

"Who was that man quarreling with you?"

"Oh, that is my neighbor's nephew, always begging for money." Her wrist fluttered in a casual, off-with-their-heads gesture. "*C'est un idiot.*"

A vegetable truck roared down the road, honking furiously and belching exhaust fumes in its wake. Madame Y's energy flagged. I sat her down on a low-cut tree stump, its surface worn smooth by many generations of backsides.

"But why, *mon petit infante*? Why are you here?"

"Shhh, Madame. Just rest for a moment."

I dotted perspiration from her translucent brow. The country air cleared of truck-smog, replaced by the consoling scent of fresh-cut hay. A songbird's lilting falsetto carried on the breeze.

"I remember one day walking on this road *avec votre pere et mere*," Madame Y said. "We came upon a man beating a dog with a stick. Your mother steps forward with no regard for her own safety—a man who beats a dog will do anything, *n'est-ce pa?*—but your father held back, as if he sensed the outcome. Whatever she said to him, the man fell to the ground in tears. We left him ministering to the dog's wounds and begging its forgiveness, *un penitent homme.*"

It *did* sound like my mother and father, clasping to a faith so vast it could move mountains, but which fell far short of saving their consumptive boy's life. The heat of the day and the funeral possession had soured my purpose here. Death seemed everywhere in this tiny village.

"Too bad my folks couldn't persuade the Germans to spare them," I said. "Where was Jesus of Nazareth when the Panzer tanks rolled into town?"

These harsh words cast Madame Yerkes into turmoil, her sightless eyes blinking rapidly, lips pursed as if on the brink of some dire prophecy.

"*Quelque chose pour vous*," she said.

"What?"

"Something for you, something you should know." Impatiently, she tapped her cane on the ground. "Help me up, *s'il vous plait.*"

We set off on a bumpy trail, blind leading the blind. We passed a barn in disrepair and two dray horses tethered to a fence. The Lesser Alps towered overhead, mountain peaks said to protect the innocent citizens of Rogvald from the horrors of the larger world. I grasped Madame Y's bony elbow, wondering, *Horrors like me?*

Up ahead was a rickety cabin that looked held together by twine and cow dung. Madame Y struggled up a step and banged her cane on the door. A phlegm-thickened voice grunted within. The sky darkened. Ravens laughed in the trees. This scene played out in my mind's eye—a sightless woman and a disgraced statesman stand on the threshold of a stranger's door—like some gothic fable out of old *Mitteleuropa*. My hands tingled. I felt a keen, child-like anticipation.

Then the door opened, and the story of my life changed.

29

Listening to this tale, my little audience displays varying expressions of amazement. Anca seems engrossed, while Stefan and Oleg alternately sneer, roll their eyes and sigh. But whenever the story of my earlier troubles in Keshnev comes up —around a campfire, or while we're secluded for the day in an abandoned farmhouse—they all want to know what happens next.

So do I, and I've already lived it.

A man named Dragos lived inside the cabin—grizzled, slow-moving, a bearded recluse older even than Madame Yerkes. He owned one table, one chair, one knife and fork, one cracked porcelain plate. The walls smelled of rotting fruit, with a faint whiff of excrement. He gave up the chair to Madame Y and invited me to sit beside him on an upturned milk crate.

Dragos had a story to tell, but in a dialect well beyond my grasp. Tugging her shawl closer, Madame Y agreed to translate.

Early in the war, he explained, when the occupying Nazi

forces began rounding up anyone they didn't like, his brother sneaked into Rogvald, a family member Dragos hadn't seen in years. His brother claimed that he and another man with him belonged to the Resistance and were here to rescue the missionaries in hiding. The plan was to get them across the border into Macedonia and then into Greece, maybe one day reuniting them with their beloved son in England.

"We can save them, my brother says, but it must be now." He spewed an oyster-colored gob of mucous in a shadowy corner. "*Zviet et prinke.*"

"My brother ..." Madame Y hesitated. "My brother is ..."

"*Zviet et prinke!*"

"A pig in hell!"

None of this made sense or matched what I knew to be true. My mother and father never escaped the Nazis; they perished along with other Rogvalders in the first wave of the *Blitzkrieg*, beneath the thousand-pound steel treads of a Panzer tank. This was reported to me in 1940 as a newly orphaned student at Cambridge, and later confirmed by the Ministry of Health. These facts I'd known all my adult life.

Now, from out of nowhere, this angry recluse had a much different story—and told so vividly in Madame Y's translation, I could see the drama unspooling before my eyes. My parents warily come out of hiding in a church attic, their meager belongings in a single suitcase, and climb in the back of Dragos's brother's car. As the car drives off, Mother whispers, *I want to see him. I want to see my son again.* Father nods fervently. In their excitement, they fail to notice the exchange of glances between the two men up-front.

"Wait a minute," I interrupted. "Why is he telling me all this?"

Madame Yerkes turned her gaze and for a wild moment I thought she could see me, clear as day. "A promise, *mon cheri*. I made Dragos swear if you ever came back, he must tell you what his brother told him. And *voila!* Here you are."

Dragos resumed the story. Deep in the night, the car with my parents inside speeds across a bombed-out landscape, hunks of armored vehicles smoldering in the moonlight. The journey finally ends in a forest, near the banks of a fast-moving stream. The car is parked facing the water.

What is this? Father asks. *What is going on?*

No answer from up front, only a polite request to get out of the car.

Dragos paused and spat again in the corner.

"My worthless thug of a brother," Madame Y translated, "do you know what he says? A confession on his death bed! *Dragos, forgive me, not my fault,* he says. *Orders are orders.*"

How confused and frightened my parents must have been. Told to walk out on a ledge jutting over the stream, standing with their backs to shore as the men unveiled pistols from inside their coasts. Father gripped Mother's hand so tightly she almost cried out.

Forgive us, Father. We have failed you.

"Whose orders?" I asked him.

Madame Y sobs quietly, slow to translate.

"Tell me who ordered this."

A short time later, I stood in the hillside cemetery just outside Rogvald. I remembered the old man's sigh as I made my demand, as if given the chance, he would have taken the secret to his grave. Soon, I thought unkindly, Dragos will be interred here along with Madame Yerkes and other villagers. Now I looked down at an age-mottled headstone with two names engraved on the front:

Robert Ernest Ash   *Julia Gillespie Ash*
1890-1940   *1894-1940*

No good thing does He withhold from
those whose walk is blameless.
Psalm 84:11

It was like hearing of their violent deaths all over again, or, because *this* version sounded more like the truth, much worse. *Loss* is what I felt, the sheer inconsolable weight of it, loss for myself, for my twice-murdered mother and father. Alone on the hillside I made terrible sounds, weeping, gnashing my teeth; the next thing I knew I was kicking the headstone, the force of my boot adding to the countless scuffs and cracks it had suffered over the years. I felt the headstone starting to give. It was easy, and gratifying, to kick the whole thing in a heap on the ground.

But I *wasn't* alone.

My old pal Freud stood across the road in a field of thistles and weeds, from where he had a front-row view of me defiling my parents' empty grave. I wanted to rush him, get my hands around his throat, and squeeze until his eyeballs bulged and his psychoanalytic tongue flopped uselessly in his mouth. Instead, I turned away, shamed by what I'd allowed that pitiful servant of the State to witness.

Tell me who ordered this.

Gravya Wolfen.

30

In the days since the Peugeot collided with the elk, a slapdash network of underground sympathizers has helped us on our way. They grant sanctuary in their cellars and haylofts, risking their lives to aid and abet us. Fortunately, traveling as a foursome isn't considered odd in these remote parts. People are always on the move—some with children, some not—in search of food and shelter. Our misbegotten quartet raises no eyebrows.

We're pretty far inland, by my guess, and beyond the helpful reach of any subversive elements. Hungry, weary, sick of life on the run, we opt for a classic roadside subterfuge. The three men hide in a patch of tall grass and the attractive young woman stands by the side of the road, seeking to flag a ride.

Hours pass. A farmer in a horse-drawn wagon passes without missing a hoof-beat. A family in a covered wagon offers her a tight squeeze among children and farm animals in back. Anca declines. Late in the day, a beat-up Fiat rumbles over the hill and stops nearby. A man's hand extends from the open window, waving her over. I can't make out the driver in the grainy light, but Anca seems wary. She steps closer to the Fiat and then halts completely, alarmed by whatever she sees. In that instant, the driver strikes like a cobra, snatching her wrist in his big paw and preventing her escape. I feel a stab of rage behind my eyeballs.

Stefan and Oleg are crouched beside me. "Stay here," I tell them.

Standing from the tall grass, I make a big show of humming a wordless tune while zipping up my trousers—*My bladder's empty, all's well with the world*—only to be taken aback by the sight of the driver's hand restraining my wife/girl-friend/sister. Forced to turn at my approach, he loses hold of Anca; she huddles behind me, trembling. I lean in towards the open-passenger window, intending to politely defuse the situation and, if possible, get that ride. Like Anca, what I see stops me in my tracks.

"What is this? Who in fuck are you?"

There are grisly welts on his brow, a lumpy head, and violently asymmetrical eyes.

"A traveler," I reply, "who believes he can leave his wife alone while he takes a piss in the field. Darling ..." I look over my shoulder at Anca. "Are you all right?"

She's slow to answer, transfixed by the hairy pustules on the driver's face. "Just a ... confusion, I think."

His head falls back, teeth rattling in crow-like laughter. Just as quickly, his features darken; the twin black holes that serve as eyes glare out from the many ridges and declivities of his face.

"What is this?" he says. "You want ride, so she stands here like bait?"

"We're ordinary citizens," I tell him. "Looking for a generous Keshnevite to help us on our way."

The driver's subhuman expression suggests he'd rather

beat me to a bloody pulp and run off with my wife instead. He glances at Anca, a bubble of covetous saliva on his lips. This won't do. I stand back from the Fiat and signal to the tall grass. Stefan and Oleg emerge, blinking in the sun like bear cubs roused from hibernation.

This unforeseen event startles the driver all over again. "Fuck on this!" Tires screech on blacktop, gears are noisily stripped. The Fiat roars by Stefan and Oleg and disappears over the next hill. Anca is still trembling.

"Will he report us?"

Yes, the world's ugliest man might find a phone booth somewhere and alert the authorities about suspicious characters at large. Something in the driver's spectacular disfigurement tells me he wants nothing more to do with *polizie* than we do.

Suddenly, her balled-up fist smashes into my shoulder.

"Do not leave him out here like bait!" she cries.

"What? I wouldn't—"

"I mean this, Gabriel! Do you promise?"

It's the first time she's called me by name. I rotate my shoulder a bit theatrically, as if to alleviate the pain of her blow. "I promise."

We resume our trek across open terrain—easy to spot any challengers coming on foot, also easy for enemies to find us. But no threats appear. At the end of the day, we make a fire in the lee of a hill and partake of a dinner of purloined apples and dried jerky. A cold evening, all of us aching in our bones. Despite the dire circumstances, the others insist that I resume my story.

31

Many years ago, the International Court of Justice indicted the Gray Wolf for crimes against his own people. Our Great Leader never stepped foot outside Keshnev, thus remaining safely out of reach of the Hague. His eventual downfall came not from the long arc of justice, but at the hands of Minister Petrescu, who overthrew his regime and banished him to a dacha on the Black Sea coast.

No one could say how many countless dead Our Great Leader was responsible for, nor had anyone ever held him accountable for anything.

But he would answer to me.

Soon after desecrating a headstone in the village cemetery, I stood before the notice board in Rogvald's railway station and studied arrival and departure times like any other ordinary citizen. In fact, I was committing to memory the names of a half-dozen stops between here and the capital—my mandated destination—particularly those stops with connecting lines to the coast.

On board the train to Olt, I sat in a third-class compartment with a gang of field laborers. Flat countryside rolled by outside the window, long dark spaces dotted by moonlight, a perfect blank slate on which to see my mother and father falling from the ledge, their bullet-riddled bodies tumbling downstream.

Go nowhere else, Petrescu said. After what I'd learned from Dragos, how could I return to Olt and just wait? A new idea began taking shape in my head, a bit fuzzy around the edges.

Sometime after midnight, the train halted in Tiplik, a speck of a town in the hinterlands that served no purpose except offering an eastbound link to the Black Sea. "Our stay here is brief," the conductor said, poking his head in third-class. "Please remain where you are." The laborers around me slept on, indifferent to delays.

I looked out the window. The shuttered railway station had a look of deep-rooted neglect, as if centuries had passed since anyone last set foot here. A solitary lamp illuminated the empty platform.

Our stay here is brief. If I wanted to do something, it must be now.

I eased out of the compartment, travel-bag in hand, brushing aside a muslin curtain and quietly entering second-class. Four small compartments ranged along a narrow corridor. I scanned each upon until I came upon Freud, my watcher, curled up on a bunk and snoring as if no force on earth could rouse him. One end of a wallet poked out of his coat pocket. Sly reprobate that I am, I opened the door, reached inside, and took it.

Minutes later, standing outside on the coupling between carriages, I glanced up and down the empty tracks. No stray militiaman or uniformed *polizie* anywhere around. Engines thrummed, a steam-whistle blew, the ancient locomotive eager to be on the way.

There was still time to plead ignorance of train schedules or a problem with the language and then slink back to my seat in third-class. But when was the last time I marshaled the facts of a situation and came to a reasonable conclusion? A second whistle signaled the train's imminent departure. Steam and fog descended on the railway station. I took a deep breath and stepped off the coupling.

For a wild moment it seemed clear I'd made a huge mistake, *another* huge mistake. But the train started moving, and the sight of Freud's face in the window—eyes shut, cheeks flaccid, a slime-trail of saliva on the glass—revived my sense of purpose.

One a.m. Alone on the abandoned railway platform, the solitary lamppost at the far end swallowed up in fog. I sat on a bench and closed my eyes. A series of rapid-fire nightmares followed—landslides, muggings at gunpoint, a stampede of horses—and when I woke minutes later, the platform was blanketed in an otherworldly mist. I could taste the grit of it on my tongue.

I wasn't alone.

A rustling sound came from the nearby trees, then the faint stirrings of leaves. I listened intently, but heard no grunts or snorts, no other hostile-sounding noises. Just a soft, steady ... *panting*. I froze. Out of the fog a creature appeared, resembling a dog but much larger, with yellow eyes, sunken haunches, and a ridge of mud-streaked fur along its spine. My hand scrabbled over the bench in search of a weapon and finding none. I heard a *thwump* and saw fresh prey drop from its jaws onto the platform—a twitching rabbit, badly mauled. The wolf stood in the weak glow of gaslight, staring at me. *Run*, I told myself. The beast's feral gaze made clear it would leap the short distance and sink its fangs in my throat before I could get a scream out.

A long moment passed. The fog thickened, making the

night air even colder than before. Raindrops fell, a light drizzle that drew the apex predator's attention elsewhere. Retrieving the hare in its jaws, the wolf trotted across the platform, smothering me in its musk, and vanished in the trees.

To come so close to violent death was exhausting. I stretched out on the bench and slept until dawn.

In the morning, a surge of warm air burned away last night's ominous vapors. Birds gossiped in the trees from whence the wolf had come, but I felt encouraged by the new day and the blandishments of the sun. Every moment drew me closer to a reckoning with Our Great Leader.

Around noon, the eastbound train pulled in. I found a spot in the large third-class compartment amid peasant women and their squalling brood, whose neonatal uproar brought an end to my sense of contentment. Squeezed between mothers and their babies, I was conscious of how my clothes smelled and of pesky new back pain from a night spent sleeping rough. A middle-aged passenger seated across from me slept on despite the heat, his large square head lolling in motion with the train. He looked vaguely familiar, but I couldn't think straight over the infernal racket.

Damn these little shits and their caterwauling! What did they have to complain about? Petrescu's thugs weren't after *them*.

I reached in my coat and took out Freud's wallet. A laminated Communist Party card identified him as one Mirko Gerghic, tractor-parts salesman and founding member of the People's Southern Region Agricultural Collective. The blurred face in the photograph—youthful, almost handsome—bore scant resemblance to the Mirko Gerghic *I* knew. Only the young man's pitiless stare matched the present-day version.

I fished out a plump roll of *klei* from the wallet and tossed it out the window.

Upon emerging from a tunnel, the train lurched to a halt. The suddenness of going from steady motion to a dead stop woke the dozing mothers while inexplicably sedating their young. Out the window there were only long, flat acres of barren farmland.

This absence of clamor also woke the middle-aged man across from me. When his gaze found me, I felt my breath catch in my chest. There was the same crinkly hair and sinister grin, just as depicted in the MOST WANTED poster. Somehow it had come about that I happened to sit on *this* train and in *this* compartment, opposite one of the eastern Europe's most notorious criminals—and who, judging by the hard glint in his dark eyes, knew that *I* knew who he was.

Or a dead ringer?

The longer I stared, the less certain I was. What self-respecting Albanian mobster would board a train in broad daylight and risk capture by *polizie*? The locomotive's engines rumbled to life again, a furious clatter of steel and steam that woke the howling devil-children and lulled Ismail Lika back to sleep.

Later in the day, passengers disembarking in the port city of Sporba were obliged to sidestep several uniformed *polizie* kicking a tramp in the stomach. In the commotion, I lost track of Ismail Lika—if that was who he was—last seen exiting the terminal in a hurry, as eager as I was to avoid capture and arrest.

Sporba, once the haunt of deposed dictators and the aimless rich, looked far removed from the salad days of stately yachts and beach cabanas. I saw a storm-battered pier, a few dispirited fishing vessels in the harbor, a seawall cracked and ruptured beyond repair. A frothy sea bubbled over the garbage-strewn shore.

The promenade led into town under tungsten-gray clouds. Off to the south, cliffs rose high above the city. Somewhere up there, nestled among poplar groves, was the object of my journey.

In a second-hand shop off the boardwalk, I traded in my current wardrobe for a more indigenous look—flannel pants, a lichen-green pea coat, and marginally comfortable work boots. The salesclerk answered my questions about the area with professional indifference; for this courtesy, and for agreeing to dispose of my old clothes, I tipped him 75 *klei* of Mirko Gerghic's hard-earned money.

On the streets of Sporba, my quest nearly ended before it began.

Walking down a narrow street, I became aware of a slow-moving vehicle trailing behind me. Tires eased over cobble-stone, pedestrians ducking into shops and taverns. A quick glance over my shoulder confirmed why—two darkened faces in an unmarked car who could only be SPU. Tempted to double-back into an alley, virtually proclaiming myself a high-profile fugitive, I walked on, hands in pockets, cap on my head, just another guy on the street. A block more of this petty harassment and the cops lost interest, driving off.

Up ahead, a nicked-and-gouged Yugo careened to a halt. A hand reaching out the window beckoned me over. Taxi! I slid in back, thrust instantly into a Levantine maelstrom of the senses. Atonal clarinets blared from car-door speakers, the interior of the cab dense with the sinus-cleansing fumes of patchouli and goat cheese. The driver turned to face me, a friendly man with a bulbous nose named "Mahmoud," according to the identity card stapled to the back of his seat.

"Yes?" he shouted over the tambourine-heavy folk music. "Where to?"

I shouted back, "Can you turn that off?"

"What?"

I pointed at the tape-deck in the dashboard, almost vibrating with sound. "Oh, yes." Mahmoud turned it down but not off. I named a suburb the salesclerk had mentioned earlier, close to where I wanted to go, but nothing that would set off alarms.

"Yes! We go!"

He stepped on the gas and wrestled through gears, doing all that seemed possible to get the Yugo moving forward at more than a snail's pace. A captive of this *souk* on wheels, I forced my thoughts elsewhere, on memories of my parents in Rogvald, on the Gray Wolf and the terrible crimes he must be held accountable for. After what seemed an eternity of driving uphill along switchbacks and dead-end roads, the Yugo approached the top of the cliff.

I tapped Mahmoud's shoulder and announced my true destination. He slumped in the driver's seat, as though he'd just learned his dog had died.

"*Ne, ne,*" he said, shaking his head. "Cannot go there. Forbidden."

"Of course, you can. It's just up the road."

"*Ne!* Extremely forbidden."

"Mahmoud, there's a saying back where I come from, maybe you've heard it? *The customer is always right.*"

I held out for him the last of my misbegotten *klei*. Mahmoud deliberated for some time, then took the money. The Yugo chugged around one more bend, stopping at the base of a steep driveway.

"This is fine," I told Mahmoud. "I'll take it from here."

The Yugo stuttered off out of view, trailing sounds of Ottoman harem music.

Somewhere up this winding driveway was the Gray Wolf's dacha. A path doglegged past a warning sign *NE TRESPASSE E DOVNU* ("Trespassers Will Die") and into a green canopy of trees. Here was my first obstacle—a guardhouse built into a concrete wall surrounding the dacha. I drew closer, stamping my feet so as not to startle anyone. A guard woke up and jostled his partner; both leapt to their feet and shouted at me. When I stepped to the window and slapped a document carrying the Minister's signature against the glass, all efforts at intimidation ceased. Even at this distance from Olt, the dreaded name carried great weight.

Bells rang. A gate swung open. A gate swung open. I walked through, breathing rapidly, a line of sweat on my brow, the pounding in my head fueled by equal parts fear and bravado.

Next up was a hut manned by a lone sentry. He rubbed his eyes, yawning like a house-cat, but the document on Ministry letterhead snapped him wide-awake. After an urgent *tête-à-tête* via walkie-talkie, the guard waved me through.

Our Great Leader's residence was a modest two-story structure looking far more spartan than other villas in the grove of trees overlooking the sea. The nation's founding father lived here in seclusion, not seen in public for almost a decade. I paused on the front steps, reflecting on the wisdom or folly of my actions. I had good reason to escape surveillance and take advantage of what little freedom I had. *Someone* should track down the Gray Wolf and confront him for his crimes. Why not me?

I knocked on the mahogany door; it opened a moment later. Yuri Popov stood there, Our Great Leader's long-suffering bodyguard, in worn slippers and a scraggly, faded bathrobe.

"Gabriel Ash! Look at you in that outfit—like some crazy peasant!"

"*Mir e selouth*," I said, smiling. *A stranger in disguise may be your best friend.*

In the light of the foyer, I saw how badly Yuri had aged. Tufts of white hair dotted his skull like tumbleweed. His eyes had a clouded aspect. The jagged scar across his cheek—inflicted fifty years ago by a bayonet-wielding SS officer in the battle of Kursk—seemed even more deeply embedded in his flesh than I remembered. He asked what I was doing in Keshnev.

"Don't you read the newspaper, Yuri? I was recalled to the capital to atone for my sins."

He began shuffling down the long hallway. "*That* I can believe."

In the darkest days of the Revolution, when Dobruja's stone chambers overflowed with political prisoners, Yuri Popov had proved to be a gifted interrogator. His signature move—cracking the spines of his victims, guilty or not, leaving them alive and crippled forever—carried him into Our Great Leader's inner circle. For years he'd been the Gray Wolf's right-hand man.

"Gabriel, so good to see you!"

Yuri wrapped me in a bear hug that was, despite his advanced age and physical decline, impossible to escape. All while patting me down for weapons.

"Tea?"

"No, I—I'm fine."

His lodgings at the end of the hall smelled of cooked cabbage and boot-polish. On the kitchen table sat a plate of half-eaten mutton; Yuri seemed to regard it skeptically as if he'd caught the mutton in a lie. It occurred to me he himself might have been implicated in my family's tragedy. For all I knew, *he* could have been the one accompanying Dragos's brother in the car that took my parents away.

Tiny beads of sweat trickled down the back of my neck. "Spur of the moment thing," I said, "this idea to, uh, just drop by. I probably should have called first."

"We don't answer the telephone," Yuri said. "Who calls? Who comes to visit? People don't just appear ... except you."

"But most people aren't lifelong friends, are they? I knew the Gray Wolf in London. Our friendship is part of the People's history."

A flash of suspicion crossed the old man's face, a reminder that smooth talk wasn't the answer to *every* situation. If the worst happened, I hoped Yuri would kill me outright, not leave me broken for life like all the others.

I tilted my head upward. "So, is he ...?"

Yuri nodded. "Upstairs, yes. In The Great Room."

"Mind if I pop in and surprise him?"

A muscle twitched in the old torturer's face. "Nothing surprises him anymore," he said. "But you are welcome to try."

32

Late in the day we come to a tiny settlement in the hinterlands, its only saving grace a dock on the Alyuska canal that leads to the coast. Barges and small craft are said to navigate this waterway to the coast, but the turgid water and algae-stained pilings look distinctly unwelcoming. Why would any vessel willingly anchor here?

We pitch camp uphill from the canal and eat dinner—canned beans, dry biscuits—in silence. Nightfall brings relief from waterborne insets, but sleep is fitful. I toss and turn in my bedroll, unwashed, malnourished, miserable, and cold.

Gurgling, mechanical noises wake me at dawn. Squirming free of the bedroll, I walk downhill just as a tugboat comes steaming around the bend, her prow and crow's nest rising out of the morning mist. The others have joined me by now, the arrival of the tugboat prompting furious speculation.

"Are they bandits? *Polizie?*"

"Should we hide?"

"What do they want?"

The tug that docks at the pier looks ancient, broken-down

and patched-up again several times over. Black smudges on the hull—where the name *Minerva* is etched in corroded lettering—suggest she may once have come under hostile fire. A tall man in a khaki uniform stands on the foredeck, mist cloaking his features.

"Who are you? Identify yourselves, please."

All eyes turn to me, apparently group spokesman. "Travelers," I call out.

"To where?"

"Kluj, on the coast. We're in need of transportation."

"Can you pay?"

I look at my accomplices, all of them short on cash. "Not much."

Wrong answer, judging by the silence that follows. A second man appears on deck—shorter, more demonstrative—pointing at us and expressing loud noises of disapproval. The taller man seems amused by this. He steps out of the mist with a leathery smile on his handsome, sea-battered face.

"Welcome aboard."

Minerva, under the flag of the Danish Merchant Marine, is headed for the coast after guiding a coal barge to a construction site upriver. Her crew consists of Captain Riis, First Mate Pincher, and a second mate, no name given and rarely seen. Thanks to the captain's generosity, we've each had our first shower in days—not much more than a trickle of water from a hose in the lower-deck head, but for us, a godsend.

While the others are still cleaning up belowdecks, I walk the length of the tug, some twenty-five feet stem to stern, and ponder my longer journey from *then* to *now*. From a comfortable life in a pre-war brownstone to house arrest in a medieval castle, and passage under false pretenses aboard a down-at-the-heel merchant marine vessel pushing for the Black Sea. Viewed in this light, events of the recent past assume a strange sort of logic. Treasonous pillow-talk in a hotel bedroom leads to blood-splattered depravity on the roof of the Foreign Ministry. Affairs with women too smart and beautiful for me lead to a budding passion for the wife of my ex-caretaker. Revelations about the deaths of my mother and father lead to the Gray Wolf's dacha, and all the misery that followed.

"There you are!" Anca says. "What are you doing here?"

"Admiring the sunset."

Together we watch the sun drop off the edge of the world, the last colors of day bathing the parched hills and farmland. I'm conscious of Anca's slender, freshly showered body under jeans and a fisherman's coat borrowed from the crew; except for the long hair falling to her shoulders, she might be a stowaway in a Victorian novel. I'm stirred as well by memories of our enforced intimacy in the castle, on the road, the happy look on her face when I kissed her hand. Does she have yearnings like mine, or am I just "cargo" in her eyes?

"What happens when we get to Kluj?" I ask.

Anca shrugs. "With me, they do not share plans."

"Can you and Stefan get out, too?"

"Me and Stefan—go to America?" She laughs bleakly. "Is nightmare."

"But—"

"You go to New York's City. Make speech, spit in Petrescu's face. *This* is what we want."

Minerva steams past an embankment where two men in hip boots cast fishing lines in the waters of the Alyuska; their eyes narrow, cigarette butts are flicked in our direction. A reminder that for every underground ally we find, many others in Keshnev wish us dead.

"Anca, I'm sorry, but that's not going to happen."

"What?"

"Forget New York. Forget the UN. When I'm out, I'm *out*."

Her look of confusion tears at my heart. "It's the last anyone hears of Gabriel Ash."

A motorboat close to starboard sends waves rocking up against *Minerva*'s hull. Anca falters at the railing. I hold her and she clings to me, her face buried in my chest. Then we hear a heavy boot-heel scuff against planking somewhere nearby, and quickly break apart.

"Pleasant evening, tonight, don't you agree?"

First Mate Pincher—the one who so volubly protested our earlier arrival—offers an unconvincing smile. A small man in his mid-thirties, taut and compact in his starched naval uniform. I can sense Anca cringing beside me.

"Captain Riis extends an invitation to join us for dinner," he says. "Your friends, too. Do you accept?"

I smile with feigned goodwill. "Of course."

"Well, then ..." Anca eases away, murmuring, "See you then," and disappears down a hatch.

A clumsy silence ensues, during which First Mate Pincher fidgets at the rail and I simmer at the unwanted interruption. To be severed from her at that moment! I look more critically at the first mate, his oiled hair stuffed beneath a naval cap, the pencil-thin mustache flecked with gray. In a Victorian novel, he'd be the money-grubbing clerk. There's a forced, unnatural quality to his manner, even while making small talk about the Alyuska canal.

"... measures some two-hundred-and-forty-five kilometers from the interior to the coast, a manmade waterway that runs parallel to the Danube, but without all the heavy river traffic. Named for Keshnev's most famous astronaut."

"Our *only* astronaut," I add.

He stiffens. "Pardon?"

"Never mind."

A cry comes from the bow. *Minerva* is docking for the night on a quiet stretch of the canal. The second mate throws a rope out towards the landing, jumps after it and ties the rope tight around an iron cleat. Without warning, Pincher advances on me—a hostile gesture meant, I suppose, as a warning. Though I stand a half-inch taller than the first mate, I ignore his relative youth and strength at my peril.

"The captain invited you aboard against my advice," he says. "Forgive me, sir, but what do we know about you?"

I shudder, recalling the mayor of Trevya's deranged cries of pain. I'm in no position to alienate this man.

"We're looking for work," I reply. "We mean no harm to anyone."

"And this we must take at your word? Or should we, like all good citizens of Keshnev, report our suspicions to the proper authorities?"

As if on cue, a police boat comes speeding around the bend —siren howling, red lights flashing, a pair of grim-faced *polizie* at the helm—ignoring *Minerva* on the way to some dire maritime emergency. Pincher finds me hovering in the shadows.

"*Work*," he sneers.

A bell clangs. First Mate Pincher adjusts his cap, tightens the knot of his tie, and generally shakes himself free of my contaminating presence.

"This way, please."

Gummy masculine odors of sweat and grease permeate the air belowdecks. Mysterious stains are embedded in the mess-room walls—food, blood, other unknown substances—and a single porthole faces starboard.

"More wine, young lady?" the captain asks. "A modest bouquet, I'm afraid, but it's all we have."

"Oh, I ..." Anca looks flustered by the captain's charm and rugged good looks. "Well, OK."

A weather-beaten oak table takes up most of the available space in the mess-room. The table settings are a mishmash of exotic cups and plates pilfered from innumerable ports of call. I sit on one side beside Anca, her husband and Oleg across from us. Captain Riis occupies a chair at the head of the table, his starched-collar subordinate consigned to the far end.

Above the galley door hangs a quilt embroidery of a whaling ship on the high seas. Beneath the ship in faded, stitched lettering: THY WAY IS THE SEA, AND THY PATH IS GREAT WATERS AND THY FOOTSTEPS ARE NOT KNOWN. PSALM 77:19.

"Are you a religious man?" Captain Riis asks me.

I sip from a glass of vile red wine. "Only in foxholes."

Something about the captain isn't right. Gaunt, late forties, his rumpled uniform in stark contrast to the first mate's starched regulation dress. His longish hair is prematurely white—after a lifetime of harrowing adventures at sea?—and his pale blue eyes seem to take in everything around him with icy indifference. It's all one with the lethargic, unnautical way in which he ambled into the mess-room, and now sits among us nursing an air of amused detachment.

Can we really trust this man with our lives?

The second mate enters—a broad-shouldered youth serving as cook, deckhand, and able-bodied seaman—shakily holding a tray of plates and bowls in these tight quarters. First Mate Pincher scrutinizes his every move, from how well he sets the tray on the table to the proficiency with which he uncorks yet another bottle of the ship's odious red wine.

Not proficient enough, apparently. "Get out," Pincher hisses at the frightened deckhand.

Dinner is a shambles, from the filmy leek soup and withered scallions to a native fowl so incompetently roasted that large parts of it remain a violently undercooked pink.

I hang back, as does Anca, appalled by what's been set before us. Captain Riis seems to regard his plate like a man on death row disappointed by his last meal, while Stefan and Oleg consume their servings with slobbery pleasure.

First Mate Pincher slices the fowl on his plate with a bent fork and faux-Meissner dinner knife, arranging small portions like opposing armies on a tiny battlefield. He appears uneasy in the captain's presence, alternately reserved and agitated. Clearly this man itches for a ship of his own, constrained in the meantime by the laws of the sea to obey his superior's commands, however whimsical or perverse. Pincher consumes each battalion on the plate and wipes his mouth with a cloth napkin monogrammed VIKING CRUISES. Now he turns and addresses Oleg for the first time all evening.

"Comrade, if I may ask. What is your intended destination? Once we reach Kluj, I mean."

Oleg, busy helping himself to seconds, turns stupidly towards me. I gaze out the porthole. You're on your own, pal.

"We go to, to ... visit family," he says. "My uncle is sick. Very sick. Almost dead."

Pincher's face wrinkles, as if from a bad smell. "'Family'? Where is this?"

"... Odessa."

It's a noble effort on Oleg's part, but unsustainable and sharply at odds with what I've already told the first mate. Pincher stares at each of us in turn, a look of mock-surprise on his face.

"*All* of you are going to Odessa?"

"Yes," Stefan says. "Friends of family."

Anca nods, too frightened to speak.

"But where do you come from? What really is it that you

want?" His meddlesome gaze falls on me. "Why do you go begging for rides like Gypsies?"

At no point does Captain Riis intervene to halt the grilling. Slouched in the galley chair, arms lowered at his sides, he's focused on the dregs of red wine in his glass.

"We come from Rogvald," I finally answer. "A small village in the mountains."

Pincher's mustache is too thin, or he'd be twirling it. "Forgive me, Comrade, but you sound nothing like a mountain villager."

This can go several ways. I can tell the truth—awkward and complicated, probably better off left unsaid—or, if pressed, concoct an elaborate lie on the spot. But I won't be bullied by this man.

"We appreciate your hospitality," I tell him. "As for the rest of it? We'd rather not say."

Stefan and Oleg look aghast at my rudeness. Anca squeezes my hand under the table, either lending moral support or warning me I've gone too far. Pincher's neck flushes as pink as the undercooked fowl.

"Captain, may we have a word in private?"

His skipper stirs in the chair at the head of the table, waking from a trance. "No, we may not."

"But I—"

"*Enough.*"

Pincher is speechless, the rest of us mute as the grave. What kind of ship of fools have we stumbled upon? It seems the first mate is a raging martinet and the captain would likely sell his mother into slavery for the right price.

A voice suddenly hails from above.

"Ahoy!"

We—that is, the four of us on the run—freeze at the table.

Pincher looks upward, brow furrowed. Only Captain Riis seems unruffled, shaking his head and murmuring, "*Laszlo.*"

"Ahoy, *Minerva!* Prepare to be boarded!"

A burst of disembodied laughter echoes overhead, like hecklers in the peanut gallery of the gods. The captain comes to his feet, the first mate standing as well.

"No, no," Captain Riis tells him. "Stay here."

"Sir? My job is—"

"Your job, Mister Pincher, is attending to the comfort and safety of our passengers. Keep things quiet here, if you will." The captain turns and points at me. "You. Come along, please."

I step out into a narrow companionway leading from the mess-room to the main deck hatch. Captain Riis waits there, one hand on the steel ladder to the hatch.

"Can I be honest?" he says. "I left Mister Pincher behind because, well, he sometimes responds poorly in stressful situations. Bit of a hothead, maybe you've noticed? You, on the other hand, strike me as far more level-headed."

The companionway smells of tar and rotting fruit. I look up at the ceiling, wondering what the hell awaits us topside.

"You don't want me talking to the police."

"Police? Far from it." The captain seems more alert now, his spirits noticeably revived. "When we get up on deck, I'll do the talking. Just consider yourself a stage prop. Is that clear, Ambassador Ash?"

My name and title—spoken aloud for the first time in weeks—rings in my ears. I'm too stunned to do anything but follow him up the ladder.

The industrial zone is quiet at this late hour. Night vapors rise from the water, dulling the outlines of derricks and cranes. I'm struck again by the remoteness of my location, aboard a tugboat anchored in the boondocks of eastern Europe.

"Well, Ambassador? Remaining level-headed?"

"... sure."

A boat lies to port, roughly the same dimensions as *Minerva* but sleek and flashy, built for speed, not gruntwork. A deckhand aboard this pleasure craft—*Hermes* painted on the hull—tosses a line to us across a distance of eight or nine feet. The rope lands on deck and Captain Riis reflects a long time before picking it up and tying it to a cleat. Yes, there's a definite wakefulness to his actions, none of that earlier, moony-eyed bliss.

The deckhand aboard *Hermes* withdraws, replaced by a diminutive figure who lingers amidships, just beyond the glow of a kerosene lamp in the wheelhouse.

"Captain Riis."

"Laszlo."

A laconic greeting, but not, I think, the prelude to a knife-fight. *Minerva* gently rolls and pitches under my feet.

"Captain, you look much the same as last time I saw you—six months ago? A year?"

"Well, we can't see *you*," Captain Riis says. "Step forward, please."

Chuckling to himself, Laszlo steps into the light—a small man with dark, slicked-back hair, made smaller still by the bulky green anorak he's wearing. Compressed slits for eyes, a nose that looks like it's been serially broken and repaired, and —presumably for the captain's benefit—a sly barracuda smile.

"You're headed for Kluj, is that correct? I have something I'd like delivered there. A package, if you will."

"Any reason you can't deliver it yourself?"

Laszlo's grin widens. "Kluj isn't particularly welcoming at

the moment. So, when we came upon *Minerva* headed down-river, I thought to myself, why not stop and say hello?"

Captain Riis looks over at *Hermes*, calculating something or other. I know enough to keep quiet.

"What's in the package, Laszlo? Cocaine? Rhino horns? Shoulder-launched missiles?"

"No, no," the small man says, sounding genuinely offended. "Nothing like that."

Two figures appear on *Hermes'* bridge silhouetted in dark-ness, their jerky motions eerily akin to gripping and raising a rifle.

"The last time you asked for a favor, things didn't go so well."

Laszlo nods, with no lessening of his reptilian grin. "Beirut was chaos. No one likes when the authorities get involved. I assure you, it won't happen again."

Captain Riis shoots me a sidelong glance—*Don't believe a word of it*—and now I see he's got a slender, military-style baton in his hand, concealed from view beneath the gunwales. "That's an awfully big promise to make."

"All right, no promises," Laszlo says. "But I guarantee the package is no problem. Plus, of course, you'll be well-compen-sated for your troubles."

The unseen baton taps against the captain's leg. "You see, *that's* the problem, and why I must decline your request. I'm still owed for Beirut, not to mention profits lost from six months in dry-dock under PLO quarantine."

Somewhere upriver, a foghorn sounds. On *Hermes'* deck, Laszlo stamps his feet and plunges both hands inside the anorak, a little jig of frustration, as if doing anything else might invite havoc. The men silhouetted on the bridge snap to, alert for action; I hear muted voices, scuffling sounds, the unmistakable *click-click* of locked-and-loaded weaponry.

"Think of it not as a favor," he says, his smile only fractionally less than before, "more of an … accommodation. In exchange for which, in the unlikely event delivery doesn't go smoothly, you and your crew will face no undue penalties."

Captain Riis laughs. "Is that a threat?"

All that separates our vessels is a meager gap of air and water. Laszlo's armed buccaneers can vault that distance at any time and seize control of *Minerva*. Whatever grievances he shares with Captain Riis long predate my arrival, but because of the ragtag band of outlaws stowed away on board—because of *me*—something terrible could happen. If *Minerva* wasn't busy ferrying enemies of the state to freedom, the captain may have warmed to Laszlo's offer. Or, at any rate, bloodshed would be less likely to occur.

A surge in canal water bumps the hulls together. My instincts kick in, honed by a long career of spouting falsehoods. Up to now, Laszlo hasn't acknowledged my presence; I step forward, inserting myself in his line of vision.

"I'm afraid Captain Riis must decline on my behalf."

"Oh?" Laszlo looks me over, unimpressed. "And who the fuck are you?"

A light cautioning hand touches my shoulder; I shake it off. "A friend of a friend," I tell Laszlo. "Of many friends, in fact."

"What do I care?"

"*Minerva* was hired to transport me to the coast, unobstructed, so I can attend to urgent matters concerning these friends. One friend in particular, a man named Ismail Lika. Maybe you've heard of him?"

Inside the anorak, Laszlo goes very still, his immobile body language mirrored by the men on the bridge. ""Naturally, we were unaware of these arrangements," he says, as if the threat of piracy was a mere slip of the tongue. "May I ask what interests your friends in Kluj?"

I glance at the captain's hidden baton. "My friends would find that question to be ... how can I put this? None of your business."

A squall of emotions washes over Laszlo's narrow face—fear, shame, rage, other dark sentiments—and now I'm certain I've gone too far. Thanks to me, disaster will rain down on *Minerva*'s passengers and crew. Instead, both hands come flying out of the anorak and now Laszlo applauds us in the night air.

"Of course! I understand completely!" A nod for me, and for the captain, a smarmy bow. "My apologies, gentlemen. I won't disturb your evening a moment longer."

Captain Riis loosens the mooring rope and tosses it to the deckhand aboard *Hermes*. Soon her engines purr to life and the sleek pleasure craft pulls away, resuming her long journey upriver. Laszlo, standing in the foredeck, watches us watch him fade into darkness.

The industrial zone is quiet again, except for the drone of a warehouse generator. Inside my head, it's a murder of crows.

With Laszlo gone, we should rejoin the others. Captain Riis lingers on deck. I see by his taut shoulders and flickering gaze he feels the same charge as I do, adrenalin flooding our veins after a close brush with violence.

"How do you know who I am?"

"Funny, isn't it, Ambassador? Even out here in the asshole of Europe, we get news."

"*Old* news," I say in my own weak defense. "I doubt anyone cares."

"Other than those pursuing you? The ones Mister Pincher and I must answer to if we're caught harboring fugitives?"

Another foghorn blares upriver. The captain lets out a deep, cleansing breath.

"Just so we're clear, this business about Ismail Lika ..."

"Spun out of whole cloth."

"Ah, well ..." A glance fore and aft seems to satisfy him no one else is present. "Please understand, in no way do I judge or condemn you. How can I? I, too, am fallen."

He proceeds to unbutton the cuff of his left sleeve and roll the cloth up his arm, past his elbow. As the sleeve retreats, patches of disfigured skin appear, punctures and needle-marks etched in the dry flesh of the captain's inner arm. I'm no expert in such things, but the rust-colored scars look as if they were inflicted a long time ago. After enduring my childish scrutiny a moment longer, he rolls the sleeve down again.

"Of course, it's been ages since I touched the stuff."

Oddly enough, I believe him. The sight of his junkie stigmata inspires a measure of hope—insofar as Captain Riis stands here on deck before me, not lying face-down in a pool of vomit— hope for a new life of my own, a happier one, very far from here.

"You're right, Captain, I'm fallen just like you. But I don't want to stay that way."

"So, it's redemption you're after? And you said you're not a religious man."

I think of my mother and father's undying faith, even as their corporeal forms succumbed to multiple bullet wounds. AND THY FOOTSTEPS ARE NOT KNOWN. I turn away, not wishing to shed undignified tears.

"Best leave God out of this," I tell him.

The foghorn booms a last time, a siren call to Keshnev's maritime underworld.

Captain Riis sighs, runs a hand through his white hair. "It seems Laszlo is the demon sent to torment me, and God knows who's chasing *you*. What a fine pair we make."

"But, look how cleverly we just talked our way out of trouble."

"Yes," he says. "Lately that seems less and less like a good thing."

Little of what occurred topside carries over in the captain's account of events belowdecks. For guests and crew, he concocts a story of some befuddled old salt in a fishing boat searching for a wharf upriver. Pincher sits quietly throughout, arms-crossed and stone-faced, but others in our captive mess-room audience seem persuaded. I don't think the story's remotely plausible, but when called upon to confirm it I wholeheartedly agree.

The second mate enters from the galley, and I fear the arrival of some oleaginous dessert item. But his hands are empty, dessert evidently being a custom of landlubbers. Still, Captain Riis playfully chides the second mate for "neglecting our honored guests"—all in good fun, of course, and the second mate's pleased to be, however briefly, the center of attention. Pincher's baleful stare robs him even of this; soon he staggers off under the weight of the serving tray, leaving behind another bottle of *Minerva*'s dreadful wine. Captain Riis uncorks the bottle and refills my glass.

"Do you mind, Ambassador? I believe it's time we informed Mister Pincher of the situation."

I *do* mind, the word "Ambassador" in this setting about as unlikely a thing to say as "Bolshoi" or "jabberwocky." I flash a reassuring smile at my frightened cohorts, then nod down the table at Pincher. "Let's hope the First Mate's as broad-minded as you."

"Good point," the captain says, refilling his own glass. "When it comes to rules and regulations, he can be a bit of a stickler."

Pincher sputters a few useless syllables, flummoxed by this turn in the conversation. Across the table, Oleg nudges Stefan.

"Does this—I mean, is it they *know*?"

Stefan shrugs. "I do not know."

"Idiots," Anca hisses at them. "Yes, they know."

"Mister Pincher, do you recognize the gentleman seated to my left?"

"... a passenger, sir?"

"Oh, no ordinary passenger. This is Gabriel Ash, Keshnev's chief delegate at the United Nations."

Pincher's face turns a mottled red, the vindication of his proven suspicions clashing with an inability to grasp what exactly is going on here. The rest of us choose not to speak. Sensing Anca's distress, Captain Riis touches her wrist.

"Don't worry, young lady, we're not about to turn you in. Are we, Mister Pincher?"

Pincher, humiliated on his home turf, is slow to respond.

"*Well?*"

"No, sir."

With that, the captain abruptly loses interest in the proceedings. He settles back in his chair, wine-glass in hand, and resumes his languid, dope-fiend manner.

"Forgive us," he says. "We're unaccustomed to entertaining polite society aboard *Minerva*. But we're not barbarians. We'll escort your party to Kluj, as promised. After that is up to you."

"Understood."

"Oh, and there is one condition."

By now, I've experienced many facets of this man's character—courage, dignity, also a cruel streak fed either by the use of narcotics or the lack of them—but his motives are baffling.

"What really happened the night you went to the Gray Wolf's dacha?" he asks. "The regime has its own story, of course, but who believes them? Here's a chance to get the facts straight from the horse's mouth."

The faces of my partners-in-crime all light up with interest. I even detect curiosity behind First Mate Pincher's scowl.

"No," I reply. "I don't think so."

"Come on," Stefan says. "Tell us what happens in dacha."

Oleg nods. "Leave out no good parts."

I stand from the table, outraged by this demand, and poised for a stormy exit. A hand falls on my arm—*her* hand.

"Tell us," Anca says. "We will listen."

33

Walking up the narrow steps, I wondered what the Gray Wolf must look like now. No recent photographs existed, only the endless reproductions of a once-youthful countenance—the bearded demi-god in jungle fatigues—splashed on murals and posters across the country. When I last saw him years ago, Our Great Leader was in his late seventies—fleshy and rotund, yet still infused with that suffocating charisma and wild-as-stallions paranoia that ultimately took the lives of millions of citizens.

I paused on the landing, as breathless as if I'd just summited K2. Whatever dark impulses I harbored concerning justice and vengeance, this was *the Gray Wolf*, the legend instilled in us at an early age. I entered the Great Room, my senses in an uproar—fire crackling in the fireplace, the smell of pine trees and varnished hardwood, constellation lighting overhead and a blur of objects on the far wall. I fixed my attention on the far corner of the room with barstools and countertop such as you might find in any village tavern. A stooped figure was hard at work on something behind the bar.

"Comrade!" I called out. "Look who's here."

The figure hunched over behind the bar either didn't hear or chose to ignore me. Striding across the room, I debated the merits of skipping the small talk and plunging any sharp implement at hand—a penknife, a letter-opener—into the old Communist's heart.

"Comrade, look who—"

I pulled up short. Inside a stainless-steel sink was the partially skinned carcass of some large woodland creature, lying in a pink swamp of blood and fur. Goat? Wild dog? A sharp acidic stench filled the air.

"Comrade," I said, less emphatically than before. "It's me."

The Gray Wolf placed a serrated carving knife on the counter and turned to face me. Bags of flesh under his watery eyes, clumps of white hair sprouting like dandelions from his wrinkled skull. An ill-fitting khaki uniform hung off his frame, a bloodstained smock tied around his spindly waist. In all ways, a gaunt, shrunken version of his former self.

"Closer!" he barked. "Can't make you out."

I inched nearer to the scowling ex-dictator. "Comrade, it's me—Gabriel Ash."

"Who?"

"*Ambassador* Ash."

He sneered at my hand-me-down clothes. "Funny-looking ambassador ..." Then, as if triggered by some distant memory, he let out a crackle and told hold of my hands in his plastic gloves—a cold grip, slimy and unexpectedly strong.

"I remember now—the Missionary Boy!"

"That's right."

"Did Yuri send food up with you?"

"Just me," I said.

The Gray Wolf bellowed across the length of the Great Room, the timbre of his voice strikingly virile for a man of his age. No one who heard them could ever forget his powerful radio broadcasts just after the war, each from a secret location, where he badgered the right-wing government and exhorted *Workers of the world, unite!* All Keshnevite schoolchildren knew of his wartime exploits, how he singlehandedly destroyed a Nazi machine-gun nest, how partisans under his command staved off a Wehrmacht infantry assault. Many tales of glory and valor, more than should accrue in a single man's lifetime.

The dour, wintry man peeled off the gloves and washed his bony fingers under the tap. He didn't seem like much of a legend to me. *Heroes grow old and die*, Petrescu said that night on the rooftop, *just like the rest of us.*

Only now did I take in my surroundings—the recessed lighting, a row of trophy heads mounted on the wall, an ashtray on the coffee table carved from a boar's tusk. And at my feet, a repulsively lifelike bearskin rug.

"Ambassador, eh? I forget to where."

"The United Nations. In New York."

The Gray Wolf tugged at his scraggy white beard, as if neither rang a bell.

"I've been recalled," I told him. "Most likely at your orders."

"*My* orders?" He laughed, a sound like tiny bones cracking in his throat. "Who takes orders from me? That's a job for the Minister for State Security—when he's not busy killing off our citizens with his lunatic five-year plans. In my day, the people loved me not out of fear, but in spite of it. All they have today is the iron fist and a leader who cannot love them. Why? Because he has no heart."

The old man gripped the rim of the sink, winded by his bone-cracking rant. This was treasonous talk coming from anyone but a Hero of the Revolution.

"Ah! Refreshments."

Yuri Popov entered, still wearing a bathrobe and slippers, and set a tray on the counter. Two shot-glasses, a bottle of Żubrówka, a single plate of sickly-looking lemon cake. "What do you make of this, Yuri?" the old man said. "Our visitor claims he's been recalled to Keshnev but won't say why. Must be bad, don't you think? Should we call someone?"

"No need." Hurriedly I took out and flaunted the travel document with Petrescu's stink on it. "See? Fully authorized to travel."

They exchanged a look, the banished tyrant and his knot-muscled Praetorian Guard, between them a shared lifetime of a hunger for power, the rank suspicion of others, and plain old bloodlust. There was a taste in my mouth of cold metal, and I knew it was fear. What if news of my escape from surveillance had already reached the dacha and Yuri awaited a signal to break my spine in half? The old interrogator's smile inspired more dread than comfort.

"Gabriel can explain," he said as he took his leave of us. "Gabriel can always explain."

"Eat something," the Gray Wolf said, pointing at the lemon cake. "God knows I can't."

A sea wind rattled the dacha's old wooden frame. Shadows of the waning day crept over the wall tapestries and mounted animal heads, over the gruesome bearskin rug. Here I was, alone with Our Great Leader, free to bash his skull in with a fireplace poker and exact vengeance for my family, for *all* families. Or would a confession of guilt be enough?

I poured two glasses of vodka and raised mine in a toast. "*Le Polska!*"

"The People!"

The old man downed his drink well before I did. "So, Missionary Boy! Just back in Keshnev and already Petrescu's got his claws in you. I can't imagine the kind of trouble you're in."

"What if I said it wasn't entirely my fault?"

He waved a wrinkled claw of his own. "Details do not interest me." Now he was up and about, moving in a sideways, crab-like motion. "Come, I'll show you around."

First on the tour, the trophy wall, each animal head lovingly preserved *in extremis*—a black bear's quizzical stare, the rapacious gaze of a mountain lion, a wild boar's bulging eyes in the last terrifying seconds of life. All of them bagged by the man who ordered my parents shot and buried in a shallow grave. I watched him reach up and caress a Keshnevite bison's slick, whiskery snout.

All the senseless slaughter infuriated me. "Have you emptied the forest?"

The Gray Wolf's crusted lips bent upwards. "*Tel e mesch kavgo,*" he said. No one eats who gets eaten first.

Thanks to his stiff joints, the tour resumed at a glacial pace —darkened bedroom, serviceable kitchen—the old man pausing on the way to hawk up gobs of phlegm and expel them towards strategically placed spittoons.

"Here, look at these."

Photographs from Our Great Leader's eventful life crowded a wall at the end of the hallway. There was a pudgy-cheeked, twinkle-eyed baby, no hint of the psychopathology yet to come. A sepia-tinted portrait of his young bride—a fiery-eyed revolutionary every bit his equal—dead from a miscarriage at age nineteen. A blurred photograph of resistance fighters grinning at the camera, the young Gray Wolf among them, on a break from killing Nazis. In a photo taken many years later, he embraces a fellow despot, Marshal Tito of Yugoslavia; in another, he bows before—I looked twice to confirm it—Queen Elizabeth II.

"She had me in the servants' quarters," he said. "Did you know that?"

"Who?"

"*Who?* Her." A crooked finger pointed at the Queen. "1958, Windsor Palace. Took my trousers down, gave me the worst *plepki* of my life—and believe me, I've had some really bad—"

On the threshold of re-entering the Great Room, the old man snagged a heel on the bearskin rug. For a delicious split-second I pictured his slow-motion descent, the crack of a brittle wrist or cheekbone on impact with the hardwood floor —and while he was down, lending a swift kick in the ribs—but instead I caught his elbow, steadied him, and set him right. "Thank you!" he barked, pulling free of me.

My hands came away tingling from some furious life-force raging beneath the skin. Foolishly, I ignored it.

Using a pair of metal tongs, the Gray Wolf lifted the cleansed, hairless corpse onto a cutting board—lynx? bobcat? —and, with the carving knife, deftly eviscerated it. Bile and other gloomy fluids spilled down the drain in the sink. A quick rinse under the spigot, then back on the cutting board for a final inspection. Watching the process unfold, I felt with raw certainty the truth of Dragos's accusations. *Guilt* was there in the set of the old man's jaw, the slope of his predatory nose, the unnerving focus he had on the task at hand. He even *smelled* guilty, a curious odor, like damp cellar mold.

Gravya Wolfen.

He gave me a funny look, as if divining my thoughts. "Take that, will you? I'll lead the way."

I picked up the cutting board, dismayed by the weight of it in my hand, still plenty of meat on these bones. "Comrade, what *is* this thing?"

The Gray Wolf pushed open the French doors, grinning at me like a gargoyle. "Very tasty!"

A cold evening on the terrace, hinting at a hard winter to come. On this part of the dacha's wraparound terrace, we faced west, looking out on a dark, purple-tinged forest. There was insect chatter, a few trilling birds. I stood for a long time under the dome of stars, drunk on vodka, sweet-flowering jasmine, and the harsh brine of the sea.

A tug at my arm. The old man pointed a short distance away, where spotlights from the roof fell on a small clearing, cut out of the encroaching trees.

"This is where she comes and visits," he said. "If she likes what I bring her, all is good. If not, well ... she has very particular tastes." A nod towards the clearing in the light. "Go on, toss it."

"... toss?"

"Yes, Missionary Boy! Without delay!"

Dead as it was, the meat held a roseate glow and seemed to wriggle in my fingers. I hurled the wet, cold thing out to the clearing, where it landed with a *plop*. The forest, teeming with noise up to now, went suddenly quiet. The Gray Wolf stared at the open patch.

"So, Comrade, when will we—" "*Shhhh.*"

Rustling sounds came from the dark trees. I recognized the stirring of leaves, the low hungry growl, the *panting*. Fear rumbled in my gut, same as on the railway platform, fearing then and now that I'd soon be as dead as the meat made to lure her here. Even staring dead-on, I almost missed the blur of snout and jaw, the never-identified remains whisked from view.

Gravya Wolfen.

"Very good!" The old man clapped his hands, delighted by the results. "Very tasty!"

But this elation brought on a coughing fit. I stood by helplessly as he began hacking and wheezing, couldn't seem to draw breath. Would this monster keel over and die before I could get the truth out of him? Finally, after emptying a last dollop of spit over the rail, he ended the coughing jag.

"Are you all right, Comrade?" I asked.

"... never better. Come along."

I followed on the heels of his palsied shuffle. The terrace took a sharp turn, facing a wind-hollowed cliff rising high above the shoreline. Another hard turn and the Black Sea unfurled before us, water and sky seamlessly fused, shards of moonlight sprinkling the waves.

Gradually I became aware of the Gray Wolf's scrutiny, a pinched look on his haggard face, as if something distasteful had washed up on shore.

"Why did you come here, Missionary Boy? What is it you want?"

I looked over the rail to a tiled patio ten feet below. Gaslight played across the colored tiles. "Knowledge."

"Ha! Precious little of that here."

From the terrace, we saw Yuri in the Great Room, collecting glasses and the plate of lemon cake, never touched. Seeing the old man's affectionate gaze towards him, I envied the bond these two gangsters shared. No such companion existed in my life, not since poor dead Emil.

"Tell me about my mother and father," I said.

"Who?"

"The *missionaries*. Tell me about how they died."

The Gray Wolf gazed out on the sea. After so many years and so many people dead, how could I expect Our Great Leader to remember one murderous act?

But he did.

"It was wartime," he said. "The things you know for certain change from one day to the next. Friends become enemies, enemies become friends. When decisions had to be made, first we asked, *Is this good for Keshnev?* On that basis, we would decide."

"And my parents ...?"

"For missionaries from America to fall into German hands would be bad for them. Bad for us, bad for everyone."

A rat scurried across the tiled patio below. I felt giddy from vodka, sea air, and rapidly unspooling revelations.

"Why not smuggle them out of the country instead?"

"Too dangerous," the Gray Wolf said. "It was decided against."

I gripped the rail, feeling the metal cut into my skin. Better to murder my mother and father in cold blood and blame the Nazis for it—less hazardous than a rescue attempt, more useful for inciting world opinion.

"Propaganda," I said through my teeth. "That's all they were worth to you."

"In wartime, everyone makes sacrifices."

Lost in memories, the old man stared off, eyes clouding over, breathing labored—a doom-ridden character whom I couldn't help but pity. His totalitarian nostalgia made him an even greater monster—but *kill* him? How would that change anything? The Gray Wolf drew close, as if sensing my moral confusion, becoming in his limp and slither something vampiric, conjured up by the night to devour fools like me.

"Is that why you're here, Missionary Boy? Some busybody spills dark tales in your ear and now you want revenge?"

Something like that, I thought bitterly. His bloodless hand dropped on my arm, a weirdly paternal gesture.

"All of your life you give to us," he said. "You speak for our people in front of the world. You give our nation a human face. But you are not one of us. Your innocence of life has nothing of Keshnev in it. In this way, you are American to the core."

I smiled, trying to mask my distress. It seemed like the worst kind of rebuke. "With respect, I don't think—"

Another coughing fit came over him, chest-ripping sounds, gobs of spit flying everywhere, as convulsive and asphyxiating as if I'd thrown a plastic bag over his head. "Here," I said, reaching out to help, "let me—" A blur of motion flashed by in my peripheral vision, and then I felt something sharp pierce the skin of my arm. The sleeve of my coat was sliced open, a thin trickle of blood—*my* blood—seeping through the fabric. I looked up, stunned. The Gray Wolf stood a few feet away, trying to assess the damage caused by the carving knife in his upraised hand. Gone from his eyes was any sign of recognition or fondness for me; all that mattered was the death of his adversary, one more trophy for the Great Room wall.

Then pain set in, like the teeth of tiny carnivorous fish rending my flesh. I howled, startling him into a fresh assault. This time I was ready, sidestepping the blade aimed at my throat and slapping the weapon from his grip. We spun around on the narrow terrace, my back to the rail, my arms clamped around the old man's spindly chest, an awkward struggle beyond anyone's control. Now his gnarled face was inches from mine; I smelled his breath, the hot mustardy scent of a mass murderer. "One morning," the Gray Wolf whispered. "It took all of one morning to decide." If he said anything more, I never heard it over the thunder in my head. Taking hold of both shoulders, I raised him in the air, a papier-mâché bundle of flesh and bones, and with a godlike roar threw him over the rail. He seemed to float down towards the courtyard, staring up at me, a look of grave composure on his face up to the moment of impact.

·   ·   ·

Minerva steams on through empty fields and sparsely populated terrain. I stand on the main deck with Anca, who wears jeans and an old Norwegian sweater, clothes borrowed from the crew. She has trouble keeping her footing, as do I, both of us drunk on the bad red wine. Stars in their mindless plenitude crowd the night sky. The moon is a slice of low-hanging yellow fruit.

"Your story makes captain much amused," Anca says. "Not some others, I think."

"What about you? Did it make you much amused?"

She thinks for a moment, and shudders. "To be in same room as *him* ..." She drapes my arm over her shoulder and burrows in close to my chest—less a sign of affection, I think, more like clutching at a life rate. My story has left her sad. I hate myself for it. "In New York there are many women for you, I bet."

"A few. Not many."

"They like making fool of you, these women. Because of them, you get in trouble, do stupid things."

I laugh. Could there be a more concise summary of my life?

"Has to change sometime!"

A loud belch from a passing crewman sends us scurrying for cover. We find a hiding place in a pocket of darkness behind stacked pallets and netting on the aft deck. Tight quarters again, just like in the Peugeot. Giggling, Anca pulls me in for a kiss, sloppy and lustful—but I draw back, struck by an unforeseen pang of conscience. What did I just say to Captain Riis about seeking redemption? Having sex with another man's wife seems like a strange way to go about it.

"Who calls the shots?" I ask.

"'Calls'?" She laughs. "'Shots'?"

"Stefan or Oleg, who gives the orders?"

"Orders? *Ne, ne,* it does not work like that. Things between them are—"

Someone strikes a match nearby. Through a gap in the netting, I see First Mate Pincher out for an evening stroll, gazing out over the canal and smoking a foul-smelling cheroot. One idle glance in our direction would ruin everything. Anca's fear translates into nervous laughter; she covers her mouth with both hands, my hand over hers, both of us holding our breath. A long minute goes by. Pincher takes a last drag on the cheroot and wanders off.

But what Anca just said puzzles me. "Things between Stefan and Oleg are ... what?"

"Look at you," she says. "Big man of world, but you cannot see what is in front of your face."

I'm starting to.

"With me, Stefan has ... what do you call it? A marriage that is convenient. Nothing else."

So! Redemption is still possible. Inside our cave of darkness, we tumble into a celebratory embrace, Anca lithe and supple, me a great hulking oaf. Hands grope at clothing, zippers get tugged down—and now *she* pulls away, a happy smile on her face.

"This is trouble, I bet!"

PART THREE
SEVERED RELATIONS

34

"Beware the port of Kluj," cautions *A Stranger's Welcome to Keshnev*:

*For centuries Kluj is nest to thieves
and ladies from night. Babies for sale
in Third District. Cats and dogs
make yaki-yaki. Even women get
allowed physical pleasure.*

From what I've observed thus far out the window of a squalid apartment building on *Strata Republicii*, this description rings true. Outlaws and their wastrel offspring populate the neighborhood. Shouting matches, punctuated by hiccups of gunfire, erupt at all hours. Last night from our sixth-floor window, I saw an old woman in a tight, unflattering dress lure a citizen into the alley, whereupon her equally geriatric associate clubbed the poor soul and made off with his belongings. People here aren't much afraid of the authorities, known as "district constables." They seldom patrol the Third District, leery of its dark alcoves.

In Kluj, the guidebook warns us, *even air is evil.*

Last night, Oleg's underground contact, a thin fidgety man in a black suit, met *Minerva* at the docks and took us deep inside the Third District. He led the way up six flights of stairs, advancing first on one hobbled leg and then the other, until we came to a one-bedroom flat serving as our "safe house." No one asked if his affliction was hereditary, or the result of police interrogation.

Inside the safe house, the limping man kept an eye on the window. In Kluj, it seems, outright criminality is fine, but any whiff of subversive politics will draw the interest of SPU. And no one wants the secret police poking around the Third District.

"Two days," he says, handing the key to Oleg. "For safety of children, after that you leave."

The layout—a sitting room, bedroom, and half-kitchen— hastens the collapse of our fragile nuclear family. Stefan and Oleg claim the bedroom, since now that their secret's out, why not? Anca and I make do with a beat-up sofa and armchair in the sitting room. Since our arrival, I've slept each night on an old mattress on the floor. Anca, sleeping alone in the pull-out bed, says little, reverting to our cautious prison etiquette. I don't know why.

In the afternoon, I sit in the armchair while Anca in a winsome green dress stretches across the pull-out bed. I'm sunk in brooding admiration of her freshly brushed hair and the alluring curvature of her spine, when loud voices suddenly pierce the thin partition between rooms. There's a sickening *thump,* like the sound of a body slammed into drywall—then creepy, libidinous silence. Anca seems indifferent, but the noises send me cowering in a corner.

"Lovers' quarrel?" I ask her.

"Yes," she says. "And after that, sex."

By evening, we've all got cabin fever. Scorning the guidebook's advice—*Avoid Third District, where robbing and killing are free*—we leave the safe house and set out along meandering cobblestone streets. The air reeks of garlic and burning trash. Men in long coats strut about, openly armed to the teeth. Leather-skirted prostitutes—some of them shockingly young and innocent-looking—sneer as we pass by.

The Third District doesn't disappoint.

Soon we come upon a dimly lit tavern set on the waterfront. Our decision to enter separately and thus evade notice proves unnecessary; the tavern's polyglot clientele is intent upon its own pleasures. Longshoremen at the bar engage in high-spirited arm-wrestling, now and then pausing to sniff lines of white powder off the counter. A young man sits nearby, decked out in a strawberry-pink Chanel dress with matching pillbox hat, Jackie Kennedy, c. Dallas, 1963. Other men with the guileless stare of pedophiles drink in the queasy darkness.

Our little quartet looks bland by comparison, just as it should be.

For a while we drink *slavka* in a dark-paneled booth, soaking up talk around us of ships, cargo, and the rancorous sea. Stefan and Oleg's prior squabbles have dissolved into an unsettling post-coital glow; they even banter good-naturedly with Anca, who responds in kind while keeping her distance from me. Why? What changed after that night aboard *Minerva*?

As the others perk up, I feel my own spirits darkening. All those hours trapped inside the Peugeot, the miserable campgrounds, the elk bleeding to death in the road—if Anca withdraws from me, none of it has any purpose or meaning.

"What's the plan?" I snap at Oleg. "We got to Kluj, now what?"

He glances around, as if the tavern's inebriated buzz might not mask our talk of conspiracy. "Freighter comes soon, you get picked up. Then, Istanbul."

"How soon?"

"One day, two maybe."

"What happens in Istanbul?"

Oleg smirks at Stefan, making sure he heard my stupid question. "Is not my problem."

"Well—" I lean towards him over the table. "Here's a problem. Anca's coming with me."

Surprise plays out on their faces, none of the looks warm or congratulatory. Anca pales at the news.

"*Ne, ne*," Oleg says, shaking his head. "Is not plan."

"Plans change," I remind him.

Stefan appears outraged by this news, despite a loveless marriage and his own proclivities. He mutters and curses under his breath, over her protests.

"*Ne, ne*," Oleg says. "Not plan."

Gradually we notice the clamor of rough trade has receded around us. All heads turn to a black-and-white TV mounted above the bar, where an ashen-faced newscaster addresses the camera. A blurred photograph of the Gray Wolf in much younger days hovers over his shoulder.

"... following a vicious attack by agents of Western imperialism, Our Great Leader and Hero of the Revolution has succumbed to his wounds ..."

The tavern's soused regulars need a moment to puzzle this out. *Who* "succumbed"? The man we thought could never die? The longshoremen look dazed and sucker-punched. Jackie Kennedy weeps in his beer. Even in Kluj, the dead command respect; to my amazement, junkies and drag queens, dockworkers and child molesters, lift their glasses and toast the memory of Our Great Leader.

The Gray Wolf is dead. Long live the Gray Wolf.

Inside our booth, the mood is different. Stefan and Oleg jostle each other like snickering schoolboys, Anca barely conceals a smile. And me? Tracing a finger along the knife scar under my coat-sleeve, I remember the madman's last words, *took all of one morning to decide.* A smile creeps up on my face, too.

This suppressed hilarity gets caught in our throats when another blurry photograph appears on the TV screen—Gabriel Ash, a handsome man in a tailored suit, also pictured in more youthful times. I bear scant resemblance to the preening, bespoke narcissist on TV, a man I've come to despise. But why take chances? Any of the cash-strapped miscreants in this place would rat us out if a hefty reward is involved.

"Let's get out of here."

We holed up the next day inside the safe house, spooked by round-the-clock news of the Gray Wolf's death and funeral. Sadly, this does little to restore unity among our fractured crew. Once again, Anca declines to share the pull-out bed, and while no more copulatory noises come through the wall, the silence seems more troubling than the Greco-Roman sex ruckus of the day before.

Late afternoon. Sunlight flutters over the sitting room's meager décor. I sit in the armchair, enduring a headache and lower back pain from another night spent sleeping on the floor. Anca sits on the sofa, leafs through the ink-splotched pages of *Keshnev Daily Worker.* Her aloofness baffles and annoys me, as does the unsteady placement of the potted houseplant she's just left on the window-ledge. A strong breeze could topple it at any time, send it falling six floors to the earth.

I walk to the window, remove the plant from the ledge and set it on the kitchen table, out of harm's way. Anca looks up from the *Daily Worker*.

"Why do you do that? Put back."

"The ledge is too narrow," I tell her. "We don't want it plummeting six stories down on some unsuspecting citizen's head, do we?"

"I put there so plant can breathe. Plant must breathe."

"I think it's breathing fine right here."

She gets up from the sofa, retrieves the plant from the table and walks it back to the ledge. There she stands facing me, arms folded over her breasts.

"You cannot order where plant goes," she says.

"What? I didn't—"

"Orders my life is full of."

A voice from outside the window interrupts our little spat. Down on the street, Oleg is yelling at his underground contact. Whatever the problem—from our height, I hear only voices, not words—the limping man can't placate him. Oleg flaps his arms in disgust and enters the apartment building; a moment later, his contact hobbles away, one painful step at a time.

"What's *that* about?"

Anca frowns. "Oleg looks not happy."

In fact, the footsteps thumping up the stairwell violate the first rule of life on the run. *Don't draw attention to yourself.* Flinging open the safe-house door, Oleg stares at us as if we're distant in-laws who've long overstayed their welcome.

"Tonight," he growls, pushing past us towards the bedroom. "Happens tonight." And slams the bedroom door behind him. Brief silence, then a thundering crash rocks the bedroom walls and Oleg storms out, trying to put on a coat and getting his arms tangled in the sleeves.

"You are sure, tonight?" Stefan says, appearing behind him, tugging suspenders over his long johns. "Maybe we wait and—"

"*Ne!*" Oleg flings the coat to the floor. "Too much danger here. I do not wait. I go where *they* are."

The same angry footsteps echo down the stairwell. Stefan picks up the discarded coat, looks morosely down the empty hallway. Sighing, he turns and touches a hand to Anca's cheek.

"You were not this much work," he says.

Happens tonight.

After Stefan runs off in pursuit of his hard-headed lover, I'm all for hunkering down in the safe house. Anca feels otherwise; she brushes her hair, puts on a coat, and looks back at me from the doorway.

"Well? Do you go or not go?"

"I go."

Unlike last night, the mood on *Strata Republicii* is strangely free of menace. Shuttered windows, quiet alleys, a few bedraggled souls fliting through the darkness, no signs of pimps or rapists. Evidence of Third District debauchery is hard to find.

"Where did everyone go?"

"Invited to party, maybe," Anca says. "Not us."

We follow a maze of narrow streets leading to the town square, with benches, plane trees, and a view of carnival lights in the harbor below. An outdoor café is closed for the night, the cast-iron chairs empty but for one old man in a tattered army jacket. On the table beside him rests a shopworn accordion, at his feet a toothless rhesus monkey wearing diapers and a bellhop's red cap.

Anca approaches fearlessly, pointing to the harbor. "All those lights? What goes on down there?"

Thick curls of white hair sprawl down the back of the old man's neck. He answers her queries in a Romany dialect unknown to me, but which Anca translates with ease.

"Tusk Festival, it is called, one time of year people of Kluj give thanks for wild boar, all what boar gives to people of Keshnev. Big fun! Everyone is there!" She smiles at the Roma. "Why not you?"

He nods at his elderly companion slouched against a table-leg, yawning and scratching his genitals inside the diaper, his furry legs splayed out as if after a hard night of booze and women.

"Maximillian is unwell. He must have his rest."

Under our gaze, the monkey turns away, disdainful of human sympathy. With a sigh, the old man throws a strap over his shoulder and grapples the bulky accordion into place against his neck and chest.

"I will play for you," he says through Anca, "on this sad and beautiful night."

Stubby fingers pry open valves, pressing buttons and brass keys. From the battered squeezebox comes music of surprising purity and emotion, wistful refrains evoking the bittersweet autumn harvest, but also the cold windy solitude of the Russian steppes. Maximillian, shaking free of his torpor, begins dancing across the cobblestones, a feeble pirouette. Beside me, Anca is quietly weeping.

"What *is* it? Tell me what's wrong."

"You and me ..." She wipes fiercely at her tears. "It cannot happen, so why believe it can?"

"Anca, it can happen—it *will*."

"*Ne*, boats do not cross water for peasant girls like me."

The Roma plays on, his hairless partner re-enacting dance

steps from a lifetime on the stage, performed gracelessly now and with halfhearted execution.

I take hold of her arms, looking in her eyes. "Believe it. *I* do."

There's a last flourish of reeds and bellows, and the performance is over. At the snap of his master's fingers, Maximillian picks up an empty tin can and thrusts it at each of us in turn—rubbery gums bared, panting a bit from his exertions, unwilling to take no for an answer.

35

Do I believe it?

In this ominous port town, I feel rudderless, unsure of my motives, but also—as Anca runs for the steps leading to the harbor—swooning blissfully for my ex-caretaker's wife. She leads us down a stairwell, through a tunnel under a bridge, and onto Kluj's seaside promenade. We slip into a crowd of festival-goers, dodging pushcarts and drunken sailors, giving ourselves over to the ruckus of Slavic tongues and a distantly upbeat calliope. Bonfires cast shadows dancing on the sea-wall. In the night air, I smell petrol fumes and cotton candy.

Anca laughs. "Fun, yes? OK now for fun?"

Being out in the open like this is a huge risk, but I can't spoil her happiness. "You bet."

So, for a cheerful hour or so, we listen to fiddlers playing melodies under the stars, sample a host of festival-themed food—fried boar, boar kabob, pickled boar stew—and eaves-drop on turbaned fortune-tellers unveiling their customers' destinies, be they joyful or calamitous. It's no wonder residents of the Third District flock to this noisy, colorful event. Moral turpitude aside, everyone's just out for a good time.

Local artisans hawk their wares along the shorelines. There are buckles with engravings of boars and billfolds made from toughened boar hide. Anca lingers over a small cutlery set carved from a boar's tusk—a knife and fork with ivory handles that glint in the moonlight.

"My mother once has," she says wistfully.

I slap a lavish number of *klei* in the delighted artisan's hand and hold out the curio box containing the knife-and-fork set. Anca coos over her new possession, then with a grateful kiss returns it to me for safekeeping. A rare moment of lightness between us.

The good times extend to the pier, a wide wooden structure built high above the water. People at the base of the pier are merrily eating and drinking their woes away. A bit farther out, the crowd thins; Anca and I find ourselves in a spooky no-man's land—between the circus atmosphere we left on shore and, facing the sea, the shadows of men acting sneaky and craven in the bioluminescent darkness, as is our nature.

"This looks iffy," I tell her.

Anca laughs. "What is 'iffy'?"

We come upon a man seated on a milk-crate selling home-made pornography. Up ahead, workmen in mucked-up overalls queue in front of a plywood booth with a sign *SLIRGHI MEH!* (*Kiss me!*) on top. Inside the booth sits a young girl, red-cheeked and virginal, in a bare-shouldered peasant dress. A worker at the head of the queue is thrusting his pelvis against the front of the booth, the better to accommodate the peasant girl's frisky hand reaching through a hole at crotch-level. I hurry Anca along.

Oh Keshnev!

All this strangeness revives my gloom and paranoia. What are we doing? At any moment, all could be lost.

"You think we're almost there?"

"Yes, I see it, maybe."

At the end of the pier, the air smells cleaner, the half-moon shines brighter, the waves smashing against the pilings seem more intent upon destruction. Stefan and Oleg wait beneath a weakly glowing lamppost, joined by three new faces—a thuggish-looking man with red stubble on his jaw, a rat-faced woman wearing a motorcycle jacket, and a rangy man, also in leather and presumably her mate. As we approach, there's a charred odor of discord, and no one makes eye contact.

"You are come for freighter? Too bad," the biker-wife says. "Freighter does not come."

I turn to Oleg. "What's this?"

"Freighter comes," he says uneasily. "Soon."

"Or never," the biker-husband says.

"Shut up," Stefan tells him.

"Don't say shut up to him," the biker-wife says.

"You shut up, too."

On the verge of fisticuffs, they sense it, we all do—a charge in the air, the tingle on your skin caused by close proximity to law enforcement. Two district constables in black greatcoats stand beneath a nearby lamppost, smoking cigarettes and assessing our unlikely congregation a short distance away. You can tell what they're thinking—is arrest and custody worth all the trouble, just because we don't like the looks of them? As if in response, we each strike a pose meant to appear "natural" and "relaxed." Stefan and Oleg gaze meaningfully out to sea. Anca hangs on my arm, enraptured by my every word. The biker husband-and-wife, acting on their own mysterious instincts, join limbs in ways too gruesome to witness. This bit of light comedy plays on for several long minutes—the uniformed men with the powers of life and death under one lamppost, our motley band of ne'er-do-wells under another. A ship's horn moans in the harbor. One constable grinds a cigarette butt under his heel and tilts his head at his partner; together they're off to deal with smut peddlers and salacious kissing booths.

In the glow of our collective relief, a street urchin suddenly appears. The straw-haired boy—nine or ten years old, in shabby pants and scuffed-up sneakers—scans our group and fixes on Oleg. Rushing over, he whispers news of some kind in Oleg's ear. Oleg looks up at me.

"You," he says. "Come along."

I don't ask *why* or *where*, so strict is the command. Anca, confused, grips my hand as if to detain me. "It's all right," I tell her, unwilling to say more in front of these hard-bitten strangers. The street urchin leads us off the pier and onto the promenade, where a crew of laborers are busy hauling supplies off a flat-bed truck—aluminum tubes and makeshift control panels, heavy crates marked *pyrotechnii*—and dropping them in the sand.

Quietly we take our leave of the Tusk Festival.

Since coming to Kluj, I've slept poorly and consumed too much *slavka*. So, this after-hours trek through the Third District transpires for me in dream-time. Walking a few steps takes hours to complete, but I just walked three blocks in the blink of an eye. My feet feel like anvils and, alternately, puffs of smoke.

Turning a corner, the boy stops in front of a darkened storefront and raps on the window; a light goes on, shadows stir inside. The boy's little knuckles are poised to rap again.

"Wait," Oleg says. A minute later, a wispy young man in a threadbare kimono opens the door and hands a rusted key to the boy who gives it in turn to Oleg. "Good job," he says, then shoves the street urchin inside the shop with the ethereal youth. Over the boy's muffled protests, Oleg nods at me.

Get moving.

"What was that all about?"

"Where we go is *your* surprise," Oleg says. "Not his."

First, though, we must return to the safe house for some money he's left stashed there. Soon we're back in a part of Kluj I know, with familiar landmarks like the vintage Renault—stripped of its parts, sloppy hammer-and-sickle graffiti spray-painted on the hood—abandoned on *Strata Karl Marx*. Nearing the apartment building, Oleg abruptly stops.

"What—"

His hand flies up, silencing me.

Around the corner, police cars block the entrance to the building. Headlights come on just as two district constables emerge with a prisoner in tow. Limping Man is slumped in their arms, his clothes torn, his face bloodied. The older constable shouts at his younger partner, something about how useless their prisoner was, of no help in the effort to apprehend Keshnev's most-wanted criminal—*me*, that is. From our hidden vantage point, I see the older constable take a pistol out of his greatcoat and fire twice in the back of Limping Man's head. The body, already broken, crumples on the ground.

I let out an involuntary cry. Oleg stiff-arms me against the wall, his oily hand clamped over my mouth. I feel my stomach rising, a need to purge the deafening gunshot from memory, a blizzard of bone and brain tissue soiling the air.

"Not safe, I *tell* them!" Oleg says, walking briskly from the scene. "Why does no one listen?"

"We need to warn the others."

"*Ne.* This, first."

On into the Third District's sinister dreamworld, ending up again on the seaside promenade but this time, a kilometer south of the Tusk Festival. Drunken partygoers overtake us, a crowd into which Oleg folds effortlessly, glaring back at me, *Keep up.* But the bodies won't yield to my assault; I'm buffeted and bumped, pushed carelessly aside. In the heat of the moment, I barely register the sensation of fingers inside my coat, a pickpocket's fingers scurrying along my upper torso in search of a wallet or money-clip or, as it happens, the curio box I purchased earlier for Anca.

"Hey!"

Heads turn. The pickpocket breaks off contact and flees, the box tumbling to the ground and snapping open on contact. Crouched amid a storm of hobnail boots, I rescue the knife and fork from destruction.

"Hurry!" Oleg hisses from just off the boardwalk. "*Leche!*"

Across railroad tracks, past a salvage yard sheathed in concertina wire, coming to a boat-house at the end of the waterfront. This is where Oleg stops to address me.

"Two things," he says. "What motorcycle bitch says on pier? Not true."

"You mean, the freighter's here?"

"Very soon, yes."

I look to the north where the Tusk Festival plays on, a blur of lights and sounds, someone else's party.

"What's the second thing?"

Oleg unlocks the boathouse door with the rusted key and slips inside. I follow blindly into darkness, the stench of dead fish thick in the air. He pulls a cord and a light-bulb flares on overhead, stinging my eyes; at first it seems we're standing inside a huge airplane hangar with lofty walls and a high-beamed ceiling. As my vision clears, the dimensions appear much more modest—a wooden structure's murky interior, with three walls and, on the east-facing side, an opening to the Black Sea.

"This," he says.

36

On the landing sits a small craft's partly dismantled hull, up on blocks. Redbeard, the thug from the pier, rests his haunches on it while watching over a figure in a galley chair on the landing. I can't make it out, but there's something familiar in the slumped figure's military jacket and unnaturally black hair.

"Go on," Oleg says. "Do not be shy."

The slumped figure struggles to rise from the chair, but mooring ropes bind his wrists and keep him firmly in place. When I approach and Minister for State Security Petrescu lifts his battered face, I can't say which of us is more surprised.

"Our friends in Kluj," Oleg says. "They find him at big hotel checking in, snatch him up before everybody knows."

Bruises cover the prisoner's face, one eye swollen shut, bits of dirt and flesh caked in the dyed-black hair. I kneel in front of him, unable to keep the smirk from my face. What a going-away present!

"Hello, Minister Petrescu."

"—demand your immediate—" Petrescu coughs, spits up blood. "Surrender."

"This he says even when we are beating on him," Oleg says. "*He* gives orders to *us*."

To which the Minister responds by gulping air and shouting in our faces, "*Kly ech mamia!*" Your mother fucks goats. The age-old village curse appalls me, but Oleg laughs heartily. Then Redbeard steps between us and backhands Petrescu across the face, making him sway and teeter in the galley chair, close by the edge of the landing.

"All right, enough." Oleg pulls his thug off, directing him towards the exit. "Come with me. Things for us to do."

"What about *him*?"

"He says. End of questions."

Redbeard unleashes a gust of spit-flecked invective and storms out of the oathouse. A long moment passes; the Minister sits sunk-over and motionless.

"Well," Oleg says. "I leave him to you."

"And do what with?"

From inside his coat, he takes out the revolver used to put down the crippled elk and slaps it in my hand. "Do what it says in your heart."

Then he's gone, too.

The naked bulb spills light into nooks and crannies—toppled work shelves, a pile of old clothing, cast-off grappling hooks. Laughter and calliope music waft in through the open space on the east-facing side, distant lights clearly visible. The world's off having a good time while I babysit the kidnapped leader of our country. Worse yet, Petrescu has nodded off, demonstrating a lack of concern for his own physical safety that's frankly insulting. I tap the gun-barrel against his ear; he stirs, gazing up at me as if I'm Room Service and he's forgotten what he ordered.

"You're not supposed to be here," I tell him. "On TV, they said SPU went looking up north."

"The note you left ..." He coughs, licks at his dry lips. "... too crude and convenient. I decided on a whim to try Kluj."

"A whim that turns out to be a huge mistake."

"You mean, *this*?" He mimics a tussle with the ropes ensnaring his wrists. "Soon my men will be here. Then we'll have fun."

The weapon in my hand feels slick and clammy. *Fun?* A word never meant to leave this man's mouth.

"At that time," he says, "I will reach down your throat, tear out the little sack of your heart, and stomp it in the ground. You see? Fun."

The damp air, the heft of the gun in my hand, Petrescu's ugly smile poking out from under his contusions—it's too much, I can't think straight. I pace back and forth on the landing, down a ramp that eases into the open sea, then back again on the landing in the same agitated state.

"Look at you, waving that gun around like—which is it, Comrade Ash? Cowboy or diplomat?"

With each passing minute, Petrescu seems more revived from his wounds; the blood dried around his ears, his cheekbones no longer so darkly bruised. And he's right—my gun-toting inner turmoil owes more to Billy the Kid than Machiavelli.

"There's one thing I can do. I can use this thing to dispense some justice."

The Minister's baffled expression appears genuine. "Justice?"

"You must know what I mean. You're guilty of many sins."

"Am I?" He turns his head, straining to look over his shoulder as if the reason for my lurid accusations might be found on the open sea. I kick a leg of the galley chair, reclaiming his attention.

"There have been mistakes," he admits "Some overzealous blunders. All very regrettable."

"What about the Nazarenes?"

"Who?"

The gun trembles in my hand, begging to be fired. "My mother and father."

"A tragic misfortune of war, I'd say, much like those suffered by all our countrymen in the Great Struggle Against Fascism. And for which you've been well-compensated over the years."

"Are you talking about my life in New York?"

"Your *entire* life."

What I remember most about my entire life are those last few seconds before it nearly ended. The canopy on Seventy-second Street snapping in a spring breeze. Emil standing by the Bentley in his faux-Habsburg finery. A woman in furs walking a dog on a jeweled leash. Then the world explodes and nothing's the same again.

"I don't get it," I tell Petrescu. "First you give me my entire life, and then you try to take it away?"

He looks puzzled, or possibly bored.

"New York! The bomb planted under my car!" My voice echoes inside the boathouse walls. "Was it on the Gray Wolf's orders?"

"Untie me," he says in a stage-whisper. "All will be revealed."

"*Your* orders?"

The razor-bright glint in his eyes suggests reserves of strength and cunning far beyond those possessed by mortals like me.

"Don't look for enemies halfway across the world, Comrade Ash. Try closer to home."

Out the boat-opening, the wake of a passing barge sends

water spilling over the ledge and splashing at my feet. I stand there, bewildered.

"Your old friend and mentor," he says. "Deputy chief Litvinov."

Sergei? "Impossible."

The Minister laughs, wincing at some residual pain. "You're more certain of your delusions than you are of real life."

A sunny day on Fulton Street, songbirds and circus balloons in the sky. My old friend and mentor in his yachtsman's blazer listens to my tale of woe and promises in all sincerity, *I will look into it.* My stomach lurches up in my throat, as if I've been shoved out of a plane and spiraling in freefall at ten thousand feet. I land on my hands and knees, on the cold concrete of the landing, and retch over the side into black, churning waters.

"What a shame you won't untie me!" Petrescu says. "I could be comforting you right now."

I come to my feet, looking away from the sticky residue of food and *slavka* on the water's surface. A siren wails in the distance.

"It's true the idea may have crossed our minds to, well, you know ..." Petrescu fidgets in the chair, oddly squeamish on the subject of my violent death. "But an attempt on our own chief delegate's life? Even for us, that's too much. Keep in mind," he adds, "Mother Russia rarely consults us before taking action."

Tears cloud my eyes. I feel foolish and betrayed, beyond measure.

"Your conduct upset many people," he says. "Moscow was very embarrassed."

"Fuck Moscow. Moscow's too goddamn sensitive."

A great sigh issues from the man in the galley chair. "Comrade Ash, do you forget we are a *satellite* nation? Our fate is to spin around and around in the vast Union of Soviet Socialist Republics and draw no attention to ourselves."

"And this is acceptable?" I ask him. "A high-ranking member of your regime attacked on foreign soil?"

"In New York, we have someone to respond."

He means the Consul, of course—who, for all his threats and ploys, was never more than least of my worries.

"If you release me before my men arrive," he says, "you become a Hero of the State. Immediately. As such, we can't line you up against a wall and liquidate you like all the others."

I laugh out of sheer fright. Though I'm the one who's armed and he's shackled to a chair, power is clearly shifting between us. *Overzealous blunders!*

"Is that your promise, Minister? I let you go and no one gets hurt?"

"Well," he says, frowning. "Not no one."

I stand there in a fever of indecision, his force of will like poison in my veins.

"Quickly! Or we go back to stomping your heart in the ground."

The sirens are louder now, always louder, causing a dull ache behind my eyes. There's a sudden *thwump* coming from beyond the boat-opening, like the first salvo of artillery fire.

"Gabriel, this isn't like you." It's *Gabriel* now. "You're a talker, not a doer. A man in love with the sound of his own voice."

My gun-hand wobbles. "And every reason I can think of to shoot you dead."

"No," he says, shaking his head. "I'm not convinced."

I press the muzzle of the gun against his forehead. Why won't he beg for mercy, plead for his miserable life? The flat, cold eyes yield nothing.

"What would *you* do?" I ask him. "If you were in my place."

"Me? I would shoot you." He pauses thoughtfully. "The thing to remember is, I am not you."

"No." My finger closes around the trigger. "Never."

A deafening blast rocks the boathouse walls. I drop into a defensive crouch and Petrescu flinches in the chair, each of us straining to peer out the opening at—what? Cannon fire? Incoming mortars? A thousand multicolored lights burst overhead, then a second, even louder *thwump* rings in my ears like a crack in the firmament. Glittery flares shaped like spiders and palm trees pinwheel across the night sky, blasts of light and sound accompanied by an earthbound chorus of *ooohs* and *aaahs*. A comet erupts into smaller comets, trailing red-hot embers into the sea. The air reeks of sulfur and gunpowder.

Fireworks.

In the ear-splitting confusion, I fail to hear the door opening behind me. I turn to find Oleg's man, the red-bearded thug, entering with my lovely Anca.

"Freighter!" she cries out. "*Here*—"

A fresh barrage of pyrotechnics freezes us all in place—the startled newcomers by the door, Keshnev's former UN chief delegate on the landing dock with a gun on the prisoner, and presumably in charge. Across the open space of the boathouse Redbeard excoriates me for not finishing the job, his voice drowned out by the apocalyptic lightshow.

And even now, Petrescu demands my attention.

"It's time, Comrade Ash."

I turn on him, crazed by sensory overload. "Time for *what?*"

"Surrender."

Too late, I see Redbeard advance on my right. One sweep of his sinewy arm sends me crashing into a work-shelf, the gun twirling from my hand and lost to darkness. I clamber to my feet and see fear for the first time in the Minister's eyes—fear of Redbeard, a man he can't bully or intimidate, descending upon him like an angel of death. Redbeard kicks the galley chair off the landing dock and Petrescu tumbles backwards into the sea.

"We must leave!" Anca cries.

Over our heads, flame trails and comet bombs irradiate the sky, juddering blasts of sound that rock the concrete under my feet. Redbeard's gone, a faint ripple in the water where it was recently disturbed.

"Leave!" She tugs at my arm. "We must—"

Leave, yes, but a man is drowning. Seconds ago, I might have shot Petrescu and kicked his corpse over the edge myself —but I might *not* have, and since I'll never know, am I any better than him? Shaking free of Anca's grip, I tear off my shoes and dive in.

The water's bitterly cold, a shock to the heart. I quickly resurface, spitting out brackish water and gasping for air. Heat from the gaudy fireworks display scalds my face. Now a second descent into the inky depths—where's Petrescu in all this murk and mire?—the clothes I'm wearing unbearably heavy, a drag on my progress. A shaft of light from the man-made meteor shower pierces the darkness. There he is in the galley chair, snagged on the seabed amid rocks and weeds, Neptune on his upturned throne. One arm came free on impact and now the bloated figure drifts upwards, or attempts to, still roped to the chair by his other wrist. I grab at the rope and yank help-lessly at it, kicking and thrashing, caught up in warring currents, and then I remember—the knife! I retrieve it from my pocket and then, with dwindling strength and numbed fingers, hack at the rope until it finally gives way.

The Minister for State Security begins his otherworldly ascent.

I grab hold where I can—an elbow, a shoeless foot—dog-paddling skyward. Seaweed slithers over my face. My lungs burn. Blood pulses in my head. Something drifts by, bumping my shoulder—Emil afloat in his bomb-scorched uniform, then the Gray Wolf clutching a serrated knife, and Willy, my consumptive brother, his arms outstretched as if welcoming me home. The pudding-like texture of the sea closes around my nose and mouth, a soft voice cooing in my ear, dreamy and seductive. *You'll like it so much better here.*

I break the surface.

After fireworks, a kind of melancholy has settled on the water. I swim for the landing a short distance away, dead-weight Neptune in tow. Anca kneels at the bottom of the ramp and together we haul the sopping, inert form onto the concrete, out of reach of the sea. Petrescu's eyes are closed, he seems not to be breathing. Too late, I think, I couldn't get to him in—

A geyser of bilge water spurts from the drowned man's mouth. He's doubled-over with a chest-wracking cough, but *alive.* I help him sit up, feeling Anca's horrified gaze on me. *Why? Why did you save this monster?*

Sirens are closing in. Anca runs up the ramp to the pile of cast-off clothes, returning with a torn windbreaker and grease-stained jeans. I change quickly into the dry clothes.

"Please! We should go now!"

The Minister struggles to breathe, his face made skeletal by the underseas ordeal. Propped against the wall, he looks nothing like what he once was—a corporeal vessel of evil, a torturer *par excellence*—now only a drenched old man with rivulets of black hair-dye sluicing down his neck.

"... last chance ... surrender ..."

All I can do is laugh. "Is that how you thank a Hero of the State?"

Outside the boathouse, there's chaos of a different order. I guide Anca away before *polizie* converge on the scene, angry

LEE POLEVOI

men in uniform shouting commands at each other that no one obeys. On the promenade, we enter a slipstream of misfits and tattoo freaks offering a shelter of sorts. Police cars go raging by, district constables leaning out of windows and haranguing stragglers on the boardwalk. "Out of way! Out!" They've found Petrescu by now, I imagine, he's been treated for his wounds and likely heads the manhunt for his abductors.

Knowing this, but acting as ever against my own best interests, I stop Anca and look into her amber-flecked eyes. "You're coming with me."

This time, there's no objection.

North of the pier, the promenade gives way to barren sand and gravel. I follow her down a short incline and across a scrabble of rocks, into a cove flanked by tall trees and hidden from the road. Stefan and Oleg greet us there, minus the biker husband-and-wife team. Redbeard, dragging a motorized dinghy to the water's edge, sees us and loudly recounts the story of Minister Petrescu's watery demise—a version of events in which he plays the leading role, and which we don't dispute.

"Look out there." Oleg points out to sea, where a triangle of lights floats in the darkness. "That is freedom."

Time's short, so farewells must be brief. Stefan embraces Anca with surprising warmth, while I shake Oleg's hand and fumble for words of gratitude. "*Se eisch teste a ver,*" he says. Happiest are birds that fly.

Anca climbs in the dinghy and I join her amidships, sitting face to face on wooden slats. Redbeard, seated aft, mans an outboard motor clamped to the gunwales.

"We go?" he asks.

"Yes! Go!"

A tug at the pull-cord; the motor barks, sputters, noisily expires. Redbeard grips the tiller and tries again. This time the motor turns over, jerking the passengers back and accelerating the little boat at impressive speeds. Anca's huddled against my chest, but I happily face the wind and eye-blistering spray whipping off the bow. I shout at Redbeard over the sound of the motor.

"—don't know your name, but—thank you!"

The wind carves up his answer.

In the cove *polizie* arrive in force, spilling out of vehicles like heavily armed rodeo clowns. I fear for Stefan and Oleg, getting trapped in a hail of gunfire, but these men are schooled in a lifetime of evading the law and always a step ahead. From our rapidly receding dinghy, I see them emerge onto higher ground above the cove, racing for a getaway car on the side of the road.

The dinghy chugs past fishing boats at anchor and clears the harbor. Up ahead are the floating yellow lights we saw from shore. Redbeard lets out a jubilant cry. Joy—alongside the wind and sea-spray—brings tears to my eyes.

A sleek, low-slung vessel appears just offshore, idling while district constables wade through knee-deep water to board her. The police boat's motor roars to life, of incomparably greater horsepower than ours.

"Hurry!"

"Yes!" Redbeard shouts. "I am hurry!"

But the dinghy can't sustain her current speed, let alone go faster. The police boat quickly closes the distance, a long figure standing in the bow, cradling something in his hands and backlit by harbor lights. Anca points out sea.

"Look, there—"

A tramp freighter looms overhead, *Azura* painted on the barnacle-encrusted hull. Bearded deckhands in oilskin coats are gathered at the rail, waving and yelling at us, impossible to hear over the wind and *Azura*'s generators. From the quarter-deck, a floodlight plays across the water and finds us—a ray of hope, but also making the dinghy an easy target. A high-pitched whine zips by my ear; a second shot pierces the slats at my feet. I fall on Anca, shielding her with my larger, thicker frame. There's another high-pitched whine, and Redbeard clutches his throat, trying with both hands to stem the blood spouting from his neck. Waves strike the dinghy, and he topples overboard.

"Stay down!"

Scrambling aft, I grab the tiller, wrench the pull-cord, and open the throttle just as Redbeard did. My frantic efforts revive the motor and I steer the dinghy close by *Azura*'s port side. A last look back. The sniper has us in his sights—a clear kill-shot for me, then taking his time with Anca—but a second figure appears on deck, a man holding a walkie-talkie and, with his free hand, guiding the sniper's rifle aside.

Anca cries out again, pointing at the freighter. A rope-ladder unfurls from her main deck, soaring out over the sea and then slapping against the hull, beckoning us to heaven.

37

A lizard with a star-shaped patch on its spine has made this villa his home. All day long, the lizard sunbathes on the courtyard tiles or lies snug in the branches of a pomegranate tree. Limbs splayed, utterly motionless, a faint quiver of its miniscule ribcage the only sign of life. I sit poolside in a robe and swim trunks, admiring the reptile's complete indifference to forward movement. When the sun reaches its midday zenith, lizard scales and human flesh alike will bake in the Mediterranean heat.

My new bride swims in the pool, a luxury undreamed-of in her homeland, but one she's quickly taken to here. Soon she'll step out of the pool in a feathery bikini, her nut-brown arms and legs glistening in the sun. We'll make love and doze in the heat of the day, along with the star-patched lizard.

For our escape across the Black Sea and a new life on this anonymous island—for all this, Minister, I know I have you to thank. Pitiless tyrant you may be, but also a man of your word.

Church bells chime in the town square. Stirring from its

trance, the lizard fixes me with a monocular stare and for a long sweltering moment, our species makes contract. Then it scurries into the grass.

All is forgiven.

ACKNOWLEDGMENTS

Thanks and gratitude to those who offered valuable advice on craft: Jim Riffel, Tim Kane, Peggy Lang, Mark C. Jackson, Cary Lowe, Bonnie Bracken, Heidi Langbein-Allen, Jack Innis, and the late Chet Cunningham.

To first, enthusiastic readers: Bill Mittendorf, Fred Millard, Mike McDaniel, Doug Robert, Tom Heywood, Tom Larkin, John Bestoso, Pete Evans, Chip Hatch, Bill Benson, Howard Lyon, and the late Ted Heffernan.

To the expatriate writer's community of Cuenca, Ecuador.

To those who provided encouragement and support: Michael Pritchett, Laurie Renas, Karen Reeve, and Tara Taghizadeh.

To the great team at Running Wild Press: Lisa Kastner, Ben White, Abigail Efird, and many others.

With special gratitude to my wife, Maxine Fischer, and to my mother and father.

RIZE publishes great stories and great writing across genres written by People of Color and other underrepresented groups. Our team conssts of:

Lisa Diane Kastner, Founder and Executive Editor
Cody Sisco, Acquisitions Editor, RIZE
Benjamin White, Acquisition Editor, Running Wild
Peter A. Wright, Acquisition Editor, Running Wild
Resa Alboher, Editor
Angela Andrews, Editor
Sandra Bush, Editor
Ashley Crantas, Editor
Rebecca Dimyan, Editor
Abigail Efird, Editor
Aimee Hardy, Editor
Henry L. Herz, Editor
Cecilia Kennedy, Editor
Barbara Lockwood, Editor
Scott Schultz, Editor

Evangeline Estropia, Product Manager
Kimberly Ligutan, Product Manager
Lara Macaione, Marketing Director
Joelle Mitchell, Licensing and Strategy Lead
Pulp Art Studios, Cover Design
Standout Books, Interior Design
Polgarus Studios, Interior Design

Learn more about us and our stories at www.runningwild-press.com

Loved these stories and want more? Follow us at www.runningwildpress.com, www.facebook.com/runningwildpress, on Twitter @lisadkastner @RunWildBooks @RizeRwp

RIZE